CRIME BO$$

Playa Ray

Lock Down Publications and Ca$h
Presents
CRIME BO$$
A Novel by *Playa Ray*

Playa Ray

Lock Down Publications
Po Box 944
Stockbridge, Ga 30281

Visit our website @
www.lockdownpublications.com

Copyright 2022 by Playa Ray
Crime Bo$$

Lock Down Publications
Like our page on Facebook: Lock Down Publications @
www.facebook.com/lockdownpublications.ldp
Book interior design by: **Shawn Walker**
Edited by: **Sunny Giovanni**

Stay Connected with Us!

Text **LOCKDOWN** to 22828 to stay up-to-date with new releases, sneak peaks, contests and more…
Thank you.

Submission Guideline.

Submit the first three chapters of your completed manuscript to ldpsubmissions@gmail.com, subject line: Your book's title. The manuscript must be in a .doc file and sent as an attachment. Document should be in Times New Roman, double spaced and in size 12 font. Also, provide your synopsis and full contact information. If sending multiple submissions, they must each be in a separate email.

Have a story but no way to send it electronically? You can still submit to LDP/Ca$h Presents. Send in the first three chapters, written or typed, of your completed manuscript to:

LDP: Submissions Dept
Po Box 944
Stockbridge, Ga 30281

DO NOT send original manuscript. Must be a duplicate.

Provide your synopsis and a cover letter containing your full contact information.

Thanks for considering LDP and Ca$h Presents.

DEDICATIONS

This book is dedicated to the late LaShonda Johnson. Thanks for the fantastic editorial work you did on the *Kingz of the Game* series, and your advice on how to be a better author. You'll always be remembered.

To my longtime friend, Loquez Bell, and his wife Kimberley Davidson. To my brother Eric Perkinson and his wife DeYasmin. Also, to Osric Williams, Kimmia Webb, Lawrencia Dadzie, Abigail Dadzie, Suzan Dadzie, and Scott "Universal" Tobin.

AUTHOR'S NOTE

Welcome to a world where the public wears their masks, perdium. Yet, the judiciary system had its mask on since the inception. If it were up to the public, it would've be called "Halloween". Is it was up to the judiciary system, it would've been called "legal fiction". Now, it's left up to the reader to decide who should be prosecuted. ~ Cameron Wright

Prologue
October 23, 2004

Carlos West was seated in the driver's seat of his Chevy Malibu that was parked in the parking lot of his girlfriend's apartment. After taking another drink of Cognac from the bottle, he twisted the cap back on, and tossed it back on the passenger seat.

"She must think I'm stupid," Carlos muttered, looking at his watch that displayed 1:27AM. "I know she's in there with somebody."

As he swung the door open and got out, the black handgun that was in his lap crashed onto the pavement. Muttering, he slammed the car door, retrieved the gun, tucked it in the waistband of his pants, and tottered across the dark, dim-lit parking lot.

Reaching unit twenty-three, Carlos pounded hard and loud on its door, using his fist. Only waiting a few seconds, fighting the urge to yell out Tonya's name, though the alcohol was rooting for him to do so, he pounded again.

"Who is it?" Tonya's voice finally sounded from beyond the door.

"It's me!" Carlos forced, feeling the effect of the spirits. "Open the door!"

There came the sound of the locks being disengaged. Then, the door swung open to twenty-four-year-old Tonya, standing at 5'7", and clad in white spandex shorts, and black tank top. "Carlos!" She exclaimed.

"Who else you thought it was?" He asked, brushing past her.

"Nobody," Tonya answered, closing the door. "I just thought you were at home, asleep."

"Yeah, I just bet you did," he slurred, now facing her." Where is he?"

"Who?"

"Don't play with me, Tonya!" He raised his voice. "I'm not in the mood!"

"I'm not playing, Carlos," Tonya stated as calm as she could. "You're drunk. I hate it when you're like this."

"And I hate it when you tell fibs."

Tonya looked confused. "Fibs?"

"You know damn well what a fib is!" He raised his voice again. "Don't play dumb! I'm gonna ask you one more time: Where is he?"

"Carlos, I don't kn—"

"Okay," he cut her off, brandishing his gun. "When I find him, I'm gonna bury you both myself!"

"Carlos!"

Tonya followed him as he staggered toward her bedroom. Entering, he first checked under the bed. Then, opening the closet, he pushed her hanging clothes back and forth, causing some to fall to the floor. Satisfied that no one was there, he turned and brushed past Tonya, heading for the second room of the two-bedroom apartment, but as he made it to the door that was closed, Tonya grabbed his arm, stopping him in his tracks.

"Carlos, come and sit down!" She tried to reason.

Carlos yanked his arm from her grasp. "I'll sit down when I know it's safe."

With that, he pushed the door open. The room resembled a small office, with a small desk that held a computer, drive, and printer. There was a small file cabinet in one corner, and some boxes stacked in another.

Tonya followed Carlos inside as he went straight for the closet. With not a second of hesitation, he flung the door open. What he saw caused him to gasp and stumble backward a few feet with his eyes wide. There was another man standing there in his boxer shorts and holding the rest of his clothes and shoes in his hands.

It took a few seconds for Carlos to gather his wits before turning on Tonya. "I knew you were cheating on me," he hissed through clenched teeth. "I knew it!"

"Carlos, please!"

"Don't 'Carlos, please' me!" He spat. "I'm gonna kill the both of you!"

Before Carlos could revert his attention to the stranger, the man swung, striking him in the face, knocking him to the floor. Tonya let out a shriek as her part-time lover darted past her and out the door.

Carlos struggled to his feet, retrieving his gun. He looked toward the door, but his assailant was long gone. Therefore, he turned on Tonya, who began panicking and backing into a corner.

"Baby, I'm sorry!" She pleaded. "I swear!"

"Yeah, I know," he said, approaching her.

With an extremely high level of alcohol in his system and a new-found hatred in his heart for the woman he'd been with since high school and loved dearly, all Carlos could think about was retribution. Letting the alcohol and his emotions take over, he struck Tonya in the face with the butt of the gun. She screamed, using her hands to shield herself from other on-coming blows. The second blow forced her to the floor. She pleaded for her life as Carlos beat her repeatedly.

Playa Ray

Chapter 1

Tyrone Davis was thirty-seven years old and had been with the Linkton County Attorney's Office for over eight years, after spending three years as a public defender, and two years in private practice. It was during his first year as a public defender when he realized that he didn't have the passion for defending "criminals". He knew that he was on the wrong side.

Now, in a gray two-piece suit, he was sitting behind the desk of his office, looking through a folder when someone knocked on the door. "Come in!" he answered, leaning back in his chair.

Assistant District Attorney Danny Blake entered, carrying a manila folder in which he dropped on top of the folder Tyrone was looking through.

"What's this?" Tyrone asked regarding the folder as if it was contagious.

"Aggravated assault," Danny answered.

"I don't want that!" Tyrone now regarded Danny with furrowed eyebrows. "I want murder. Armed robbery. Money laundering; stuff like that. Why can't *you* take it?"

Danny answered, "I'm loaded. Hell, we all are."

"And I'm not?"

"Not like the rest of us." Danny shifted his weight. "Besides, you handle your cases quicker."

Tyrone hesitated a few seconds before leaning forward and opening the folder. "I know you've already read it. Fill me in."

Danny recited: "Guy shows up at his girlfriend's apartment at one in the morning, drunk. Encounters her secret lover. Has some sort of altercation with the secret lover. Secret—"

"Damn!" Tyrone let out, sifting through photos of a battered and bruised Tonya Smith. "Weapon?"

"Handgun."

"How old is this?"

"Six months."

Tyrone closed the folder and sat back. "Preliminary hearing?"

"He waived it," answered Danny.

"Defense?"

"Public defender."

"And he's currently being held at Linkton?"

"Yeah."

***

At the Linkton County Detention Center, Carlos and his cell-mate, Philly, were sitting on the bottom bunk in their cell, playing a game of casino, where Carlos had five wins to Philly's two.

"I'll be glad when they set me a court date," Carlos said, scooping up the two of clubs with his two of spades.

"I'll be glad when they go ahead and transfer me to prison," Philly replied, being that he had already been sentenced to twenty years for armed robbery. "My first store call, I'm gonna buy a radio and ten packs of cigarettes."

"Ten!"

"Hell yeah!" Philly said, scooping up a six of diamonds. "I'm gonna kick back and smoke like a chimney, son!"

"I hear you," Carlos told him. He and Philly had become close friends since Carlos' arrival at the county jail. It was just sad that Philly had to serve twenty years. "I'm not even trying to see prison," he admitted.

"If your girl sticks to the script, you won't," Philly assured.

"She should," replied Carlos. "I mean, she shouldn't, after what I did to her. But, she knew I was drunk. She cheated. I did what I did. We forgave each other. Now, we just wanna put it all behind us."

"That's good!" Philly asserted, nodding. "You don't find too many women out there like that, yo."

"I know."

At that time, they heard a female officer enter the dormitory, announcing a mail call. After the third name, Carlos heard his name called.

"That's my baby!" Carlos smiled. He placed his cards face-down on the bed and rushed out of the cell.

Philly picked up Carlos' cards, looked through them, then put them back. Moments later, Carlos returned, pulling a folded piece of paper from a white envelope.

"That's her?" Philly inquired.

"Yeah," he answered, scanning the letter from Tonya. "I think she sent me some money, too." Before he could get into the contents of the missive, his name was called over the P.A. system for an attorney visit. "Right on time, Philly!"

Entering the visitation area, Carlos entered the small visiting booth that only consisted of a steel stool that was bolted into the floor, and a large Plexiglas window. On the other side of that window sat a Caucasian female with dark, shoulder-length hair, and wearing a red blouse, which was all Carlos could see being that she was seated.

"Carlos West?" she inquired.

"Yeah," Carlos answered, taking a seat on the stool.

"I'm Sara Jennings," she told him, "from the Public Defender's Office. I was just handed your case today, so I haven't had a chance to go over it yet. I was here seeing another client and thought I'd see you while I'm here. So, how are you?"

"Homesick," he offered.

Sara nodded. "I can believe that."

"Do I have a court date?" He wanted to know.

"Not yet," she answered. "Would you be interested in taking a plea?"

"Nope," he answered curtly.

"It would probably be best if you took a plea."

"Why is that?"

"Are you familiar with Assistant District Attorney Tyrone Davis?" She asked.

"I'm not familiar with any prosecutor," Carlos told her. "This is my first offense."

"Well, this prosecutor has never lost a trial," the court-appointed attorney apprised.

"But we're not going to trial."

"If you don't take a plea, we will have to."

"What if the victim doesn't show up?"

"I guess there won't be a trial," she answered, then shot him an inquisitive look. "Is there a reason why the victim won't show?"

"She doesn't want to testify against me," he answered.

Sara maintained her inquisitive visage. "Are you in contact with the victim?"

"She's my girlfriend."

Chapter 2

"We would like to make you an offer."

For a moment, Tyrone studied Attorney Greg Bush, an older white male with long, gray hair that was pulled back into a ponytail. At the age of fifty-three, to all district attorney offices in Georgia, Greg Bush was considered a force to be reckoned with for his extremely long track record, and his miraculous consecutive wins. However, Tyrone wasn't worried. He had never gotten the *pleasure* of battling it out with the doyen defense attorney in the courtroom. Every time that chance came about, Greg would always call and set up a meeting to see if they could come to some kind of agreement, which is why they were now seated across from each other in the cafeteria of the courthouse.

"Bribery?" Tyrone now asked with a raised eyebrow.

"Well—" Greg started.

Tyrone cut him off. "I can see the headlines now: '*High-profile Attorney, Greg Bush, Arrested for Trying to Bribe High-profile Assistant District Attorney, Tyrone Davis, into Freeing a High-profile Drug Dealer.*' That wouldn't look too good on you, Mr. Bush."

Greg was nodding. "I see."

"Look," Tyrone said, enjoying this, "the best thing you can do is get your case moved to another courtroom. You don't lose cases. I don't lose cases. This would be a showdown. Somebody would have to lose, and it won't be me."

"Are you sure about that?" Greg challenged.

"I'm positive!" Tyrone took umbrage. "That's *my* courtroom! *Nobody* beats me in my courtroom! *God* can't beat me in my courtroom!"

"So, you won't take the offer?" Greg wanted to know.

"Nope," Tyrone answered as he stood to leave. "I'll see you and your client in court."

With that, he made for the entrance, smiling to himself. He already knew how he was going to play his cards, and, this time, Greg was going to have to play by his rules.

Or suffer the consequences!

***

After finishing up with a mountain of paperwork, Tyrone ended up leaving his office a little later than usual. He knew he should head on home to his wife, Lisa, and his eleven-year-old daughter, Ebony, but ever since the meeting with Greg Bush earlier, all he could think about was how he was going to make the attorney and his client dance to his tune, which entailed a trip to the Linkton County Jail.

Now, Tyrone was seated in the plastic chair of the visitation booth, when a tall, swarthy male with shoulder-length dreadlocks entered on the opposite side, clad in an orange, jail-issued jumpsuit. "Wayne Griffin?" Tyrone asked.

"Yeah," he answered, revealing a mouthful of gold teeth.

"I'm Assistant District Attorney Tyrone Davis," he informed. "I'm sure you've heard of me."

"I have," Wayne admitted, taking a seat.

"I've spoken with Mr. Bush today," Tyrone told him. "He tried to bribe me. Have you talked to him?"

"Yesterday."

"Well, he was arrested."

"What!" Griffin looked like he was about to jump through the glass.

"Bribery is a felony," Tyrone said, keeping a straight face.

"You had my lawyer arrested?"

"Nope," Tyrone answered, ready to play his hand. "But I turned down your offer."

"Yeah?"

Tyrone leaned forward, resting his elbows on the protruding slab of concrete. "Yeah. Now, here's *my* offer: I get the case placed on the dead docket; you sell for me."

"Hell no!" Wayne exclaimed. "I don't sell for *nobody*!"

"So, you'd rather serve a life sentence?"

"A life sentence!"

"This is your third drug charge, Mr. Griffin," Tyrone reminds him. "You can have ten paid attorneys. Neither one of them could save you from a life sentence, and don't even think about a bond."

"Why not?"

"Flight risk."

"And who decides that?"

"I do," Tyrone answered. "Deal, or no deal?"

Wayne looked as though he was ruminating this. Then, he asked, "How long will this take?"

"You'll be notified."

***

It was already dark when Tyrone finally pulled his black 2003 Mercedes-Benz into the driveway of his house and parked beside the gray Mercedes belonging to his wife. Upon entering the house, he punched in the alarm code, then made for the living room, where his daughter was watching television.

"Hi, Daddy!" Ebony lunged from the sofa and approached him with open arms.

"Hi, baby!" He embraced his only child. "How are you?"

"Fine."

"Where's your mom?"

"In the kitchen, cooking," she answered. "How was your day?"

"Great!"

"Did you put away any bad guys?"

"Of course, I did."

"I thought you got lost," asserted Lisa, who had emerged from the kitchen, carrying a large cooking spoon.

"I stopped by the jail on my way home," he explained.

"Are you hungry?" She asked.

"Sure."

Chapter 3

It's been three days since Tyrone met with Greg Bush in the cafeteria. Today would be the day that they came to some kind of agreement, because he plans on giving Greg a ring around lunchtime.

Now, in the courtroom, Tyrone was seated at the state's table, with assistant district attorney Michelle Johnson. At the defense table was Ellen Martinez, a Latino woman from the public defender's office, who was seated with two Caucasian women in their late-twenties, and clad in jail-issued uniforms.

"All rise!" the bailiff finally announced. The Honorable Judge Lathan presides."

They all rose as Judge Dennis Lathan approached the bench. He instructed them to be seated before taking his seat and regarding the documents in front of him.

"This case is the State versus Stacey Wells and Tiffany Sherman," he began. "Both defendants are charged with shoplifting. Defendants are represented by Ms. Ellen Martinez of the public defenders office. Would the defendants and defense counsel please stand.

Ellen and the women stood.

"Are the defendants aware of the charges that have been been brought against them?"

"Yes, Your Honor," Ellen replied.

"Does the defendants plea guilty or not guilty?"

"Guilty," she answered.

"Okay." The judge looked to the State's table. "And, for the State is Assistant District Attorneys Mr. Tyrone Davis and Michelle Johnson. Would the state please stand?" Once they were on their feet, he continued. "The defense is asking for probation. What is the State's recommendation?"

"Ten years," Tyrone responded.

"Probation?" asked Judge Lathan.

"No."

Ellen stepped in. "Your Honor, ten years is too steep. My clients are not terrorists. They have loving children at home."

"Apparently, Your Honor," Tyrone intervened, "the defendants weren't thinking about their loving children when they were out stealing. And might I add that this is not the defendants' first shop-lifting charge. This is not the defendants' first offense. In fact, Ms. Wells is currently out on bond for cruelty to children. Therefore, it's not safe to say she cares anything for her *loving* children."

"Your Honor," Ellen came back, "would you please ask the prosecutor to refrain from mentioning my client's prior offense, which has not yet been handled?"

Judge Lathan fixed Tyrone with a stern look over the top of his small eyeglasses. "Mr. Davis, please refrain from mentioning prior offenses. Does your recommendation still stand?"

"Yes, it does."

"Okay." Lathan regarded the beautiful Latino attorney. "Ms. Martinez, I'm going to deny your clients' request for probation. Would they like to withdraw their pleas?"

"I'm not taking ten years!" Wells insisted.

"Yeah," Sherman chimed. "I'd rather go to trial."

The lawyer shook her head. "Ladies, this is not a guy you would take to trial."

"Why not?" asked Sherman.

"Because he'll win. He always does."

"I'm not taking ten years!" Sherman huffed, folding her arms over her chest.

"Neither am I," said her co-defendant.

"Alright," Martinez regarded the judge. "Yes, Your Honor. My clients would like to withdraw their guilty pleas. Right now, my clients are asking the court to set a reasonable bond."

The judge shifted his gaze. "Any objections from the State?"

"Always," Tyrone answered.

"Under what grounds?" Lathan wanted to know.

"Flight risk."

"Could you elaborate on that, Mr. Davis?"

Tyrone recited, "Ms. Sherman is from Colorado, where she skipped out on bail after bonding out on a simple battery charge."

"And Ms. Wells?"

22

"In the police report," Tyrone began, "it stated that after defendants were confronted by mall security, Ms. Wells attempted to elude."

"Is she charged with attempting to elude?" asked the judge.

"No, Your Honor, but the report indicates that she would elude authority. If I'm not mistaken, we *are* authority."

"Is that all from the State?"

"For now."

"Okay," Lathan said. "At this time, I'm going to deny the defendants' request for bond. Defendants will remain at the Linkton County jail, awaiting trial." He banged his gavel. "Next case!"

***

"Have a seat, my friend!" Tyrone told Greg Bush, when the attorney approached the table. Tyrone had been anticipating this moment, which is why, after the courtroom recess for lunch, he immediately phoned Bush and asked him to meet with him at a mid-day bar and grill outside the city limits instead of the cafeteria, which he knew would be too crowded.

"I'm on a tight schedule, Mr. Davis," Bush informed, as he took a seat across from Tyrone.

"We both are," Tyrone replied. "However, I have a proposition for you."

Bush raised an eyebrow. "Bribery?"

"If that's what you wanna call it," Tyrone answered, disregarding the mirror effect that the attorney tried to use on him.

"Let me hear it."

"I won't dismiss the case," Tyrone started, "but I'll get it placed on the dead docket."

"How much?"

"Fifteen."

"Fifteen!" Bush exclaimed. "Are you serious?"

"Deal, or no deal?"

"You're killing me!"

"I'm saving you from humiliation," Tyrone offered, taking a sip of his bottled water.

"Maybe," Bush answered, "but with a price like that, I just might take my chances. Besides, I'm not the one who's going to prison."

"Now, don't act like you *can't* go to prison."

Bush caught on to the furtive threat. "And what's that supposed to mean?"

"Deal, or no deal?"

***

After his meeting with attorney Greg Bush, Tyrone was feeling quite exuberant though hungry, being that he didn't get a chance to eat for having to rush back to the courthouse. Now, he'd just made it to his office as Danny Blake was approaching from the opposite direction of the corridor.

"Tyrone!" Blake called out. "You got a minute?"

"I guess so," he answered, not really in the mood to chat.

"Good news!" Blake said, approaching. "Avery Stewart just announced his retirement."

"When?"

"Today."

"When is he retiring?"

"He didn't say when," the assistant district attorney answered. "It could be a year from now. All I know is that I'm taking his place."

Tyrone eyed the rotund man. "Says who?"

"Come on, Tyrone," he replied. "I've been pushing for this for nine years. Who do you know that's more suitable for the position than I am?"

"Me," Tyrone offered, with no hint of acidity.

Blake laughed.

"You find that funny, fat boy!" Tyrone took umbrage.

"I'm not laughing at you," Blake admitted, trying to contain his mirth.

"You don't think a black man can be head D.A.?" Tyrone persisted.

"It's not that," he purported. "I just didn't think that you would be interested in the position."

"Well, I am."

"I hope you know that it's not how many trials you win," Blake explained, "but *what* kind of trials you win."

Tyrone nodded. "I know that."

Danny went on. "This trial, next week, could put me over the top."

"What trial?"

"The Bruce Martin case."

"The guy that murdered his next-door neighbor?"

"Yeah," Blake answered, smiling. "He's toast! There's no way he can win."

"That'll be on the news, huh?"

"Sure will."

Tyrone pulled his cell phone from his pocket as if it had vibrated and looked at the blank screen. "I have to take this call," he told Blake.

"Okay," Blake replied. "I'll catch you later."

Entering his office, Tyrone closed the door, took a seat behind his desk, and placed his phone atop the desk. Closing his eyes, he replayed the conversation with Danny about the retiring of the head district attorney, and Blake's highly anticipated trial next week.

Perhaps Blake was right about this trial putting him over the top, making him a prime candidate for the position that Tyrone had been fighting so hard to obtain. The same position he felt belonged to him. The same position that he—if he could help it— will not allow to be passed down to anybody but himself.

"I can't let this happen," he mumbled, reaching for his cell-phone.

***

Making it to Danny Blake's office, Tyrone checked his watch before lightly tapping on the door.

"It's open!" Blake called out.

Tyrone entered. Blake was seated behind his desk with his lap-top open in front of him. Although he had a stationary computer, the smaller one was used for its internet connection.

"Working hard?" Tyrone asked, closing the door and taking a seat in a chair across from Blake.

"I'm always working hard," he replied.

"What'cha got there?" Tyrone nodded at the computer. "Big Booty dot com?"

Blake made a face. "Nooo!"

"You don't like big-booty black women?"

"Of course, I do," he answered, a sheepish grin spreading across his face. "But that's not what I'm looking at." He turned the computer around to Tyrone. On the screen was a picture of a boat.

"A boat!" Tyrone asked, seeing a mental picture of the boat capsizing under Blake's weight.

"Not just *any* boat," Blake replied, turning the computer back to himself. "A *dream* boat!"

"You fish?"

Before Blake could answer, his desk phone rang. "Danny Blake," he answered. "Excuse me…? I'm on my way." Hanging up, he stood.

"What's wrong?" Tyrone asked.

"Somebody hit my car," he answered, rounding the desk. "I gotta go to the parking garage." Blake was out the door.

After waiting a beat, Tyrone got up, locked the door, and crossed over to the file cabinet. Opening the second drawer, he searched until he found Bruce Martin's file. Opening the folder on top of the others, he pulled out his small notepad and pen.

***

Walking through the parking garage, Blake came upon the "crime scene." There was a Caucasian male police officer talking to a black female who looked to be in her early twenties. The rear of her green Ford Explorer was a couple of feet away from the rear of his blue Lexus.

"Mr. Blake?" the officer inquired.

"Yes," Blake answered, regarding the female, who had a worried look on her face.

The officer explained, "This young lady called and informed us that she'd damaged your car."

"Where?" he asked, not seeing the damage that the officer was speaking on.

"I barely tapped it," the female said.

Blake studied his car again. It took only a few seconds before realization kicked in. "That dent was already there."

***

Later that day, Tyrone took a trip down to the basement of the courtroom and approached a hole-in-the-wall booth, where the sign above read EVIDENCE.

"What's up, Tyrone!" the young, male sergeant greeted.

"Nothing much," he answered. "How's the family?"

"Everybody's fine. I appreciate that, too."

"No doubt," Tyrone replied. "Look, I need to get into the evidence room."

"No problem," the officer said, sliding the logbook over to Tyrone who slid it back. "Come on, Tyrone. You know you have to sign in."

"Not today," Tyrone told him.

"Why not today?"

"Because it's Friday."

The sergeant furrowed his eyebrows. "Meaning?"

Tyrone leaned forward so that their faces were just inches away from each other's. "Meaning: let me in, or you won't have a job *next* Friday."

The sergeant blinked. Apparently, Tyrone's words had hit home. Anybody that knew the prosecutor pretty much knew that he would make good on his word. The sergeant sighed. "Alright. I'll do it this time."

"And you'll do it the next time." Tyrone spoke with malice. "Now, buzz me in!"

Without waiting for a reply, Tyrone approached the steel door beside the booth. The sergeant buzzed him in, and within seconds, he was moving past rows of shelves that contained all kinds of evidence such as guns, knives, and blood-stained clothing. Tyrone found a silver handgun that was sealed in a plastic zip-loc bag and tagged with Bruce Martin's appellation. He studied it for a few seconds before slipping it inside his coat and making for the exit.

"You haven't seen me, right?" Tyrone said to the sergeant upon approaching the booth.

"Not today," he responded. "I mean, who comes down here on a Friday?"

Tyrone smiled. "My man!" he asserted, then made it for the elevators.

Chapter 4

"It's just a plea and arraignment," attorney Sara Jennings told Carlos West. "They will offer you a deal, which is twenty years, by the way."

"Twenty years!" Carlos exclaimed, regarding his attorney through the thick glass of the visitation booth.

"That's just an offer," she assured. "You should have gotten your notice in the mail."

"They haven't passed out mail, yet."

"Well, like I said, if you don't take the offer, we'll have to prepare for trial."

"My girlfriend is not coming," Carlos reminded her.

"I don't know," she said, shaking her head. "This prosecutor has a way of making victims show up in cases like this."

***

Later that day, Tyrone pulled up in front of a white house, parking behind a black Chevy Suburban. Getting out, he absurdly tugged at the collar of his trench coat to parry some of the spring breeze that immediately assailed him, which was atypically too cold for the month of April.

He had never dropped in on Charles on a Saturday, but there were things that needed to be done, and the clock was winding down. Besides, it's not like his visit would raise suspicion in Charles' mother, being that he stopped by periodically. Plus, she didn't know that the district attorney's office wasn't responsible for checking up on citizens that are placed on house arrest.

"Who is it?" Ms. Harvey answered the knock.

"Mr. Davis," he answered.

Ms. Harvey opened the door, with a broad smile on her face. "Hello, Mr. Davis!"

Tyrone nodded to the forty-four-year-old woman who was clad in blue jeans and a gray sweater, with her hair pulled into a bun. "How are you, Ms. Harvey?"

"I'm fine," she replied. "Come on in!"

"I'd rather not," he told her. "Could you call Charles for me?"

"Charles!" she called out. "You have company!" To Tyrone, she said, "He'd just gotten over the flu a few days ago."

"I've heard," he replied as Charles approached.

"What's up?" Charles asked.

"Pants leg," Tyrone said, for the sake of Ms. Harvey, who was still present, and perhaps worried that her twenty-six-year-old son may be hauled off to jail.

Charles lifted his left pants leg, revealing the house arrest monitor that was strapped to his ankle.

"Grab your coat!" Tyrone told him.

"Alright," Charles replied, retreating.

"He'll be okay, Ms. Harvey," Tyrone told her, now seeing the worried expression on her face.

"He's been doing good," she offered.

"I know," he said, as Charles returned. "That was quick."

"I had it in the living room," Charles said, stepping out on the porch, donning a black leather coat.

"You take care, Ms. Harvey," Tyrone said as he and Charles descended the steps.

"You too, Mr. Davis!"

"What'cha got for me?" Charles asked, once they neared Tyrone's car.

Saying nothing, Tyrone leaned against the fender of his car, pulled out his small notepad, and handed it to Charles, who took a moment to peruse its content. While he read, Tyrone studied the brown-complexioned man who stood at 5'11" and 165 pounds, thinking about how good of a servant he'd been, ever since Tyrone had delivered him from the life sentence he was facing, and immediately put him to work. Perhaps, he would keep the younger man on, longer than he intended to.

"You want this done, tonight?" he finally asked.

"Can your men handle that?"

"Of course," Charles answered offensively. "Do you have a picture?"

Tyrone pulled a folded piece of paper from his coat pocket and handed it to him.

Charles opened it to see a head shot of a black female, generated by computer. "That'll work," Charles asserted, folding the picture. "Warehouse?"

"Yeah."

Charles was silent for a moment before speaking. "What's up with my early release?"

"Early release?"

"Are you gonna get me off house arrest?"

"Did I put you on house arrest?"

"You requested it," Charles reminded him.

"I did, huh?" Tyrone replied, rubbing his chin. "I'll see what I can do. You just handle that." He circled around to the driver side of his Mercedes and, before getting in, pointed a finger at Charles. "If anything goes wrong—"

"It won't," Charles assured.

***

It was dark when April Copeland returned home from dropping her son off at his father's house. Parking in front of her own home, she took a moment to think about next week's court proceeding where she's scheduled to depone against the guy that murdered her brother in front of her three years ago.

Maintaining her composure, she wiped her eyes, killed the engine, and grabbed her purse. Just as she opened the driver's door, a black van pulled up and came to a screeching halt alongside her car. Before she could make sense of what was going on, the side door slid open, and two men in black clothing, ski masks, and armed with handguns jumped out. One of them grabbed her by the hair, pulling her out of the car. April screamed and put up a struggle, but, within seconds, she was heaved into the cargo area of the van.

***

Walking through the dim-lit warehouse building, Tyrone entered a room that was lit by one light. Under that light sat April, who was tied to a chair with rope, with her hands behind her back, and a black bandana over her eyes. Surrounding her were the three men that Charles had chosen for the mission. One of the goons handed Tyrone a ski mask, and, before he donned it, he motioned for them to put theirs back on. Once everyone's faces were concealed, he motioned for the same guy to take April's blindfold off. He could tell that she'd been crying, as she regarded him attentively.

"Ms. Copeland," Tyrone spoke, disguising his voice. "Nobody's going to harm you. All I need is your cooperation. Understood?"

She nodded.

Tyrone went on, "I'll make this brief so that we can get you home. You wanna go home, right?"

She nodded again.

"I thought so," he said. "What do you know about Bruce Martin?"

Her eyes widened with apprehension. "He killed my brother."

"And he has a trial coming up next week."

She nodded.

"You're supposed to testify?"

"I have to," she answered. "I saw him kill my brother.

"Well, I'm asking you *not* to testify," he told her.

"I have to testify," she protested. "I can't let him off the hook."

"Sure, you can," Tyrone offered. "He'll get what's coming to him."

"He deserves to rot in prison!"

"Or hell," he replied. Then, after taking a deep breath, he said, "Look, if you're gonna testify, testify. But I'm asking you to testify falsely."

"I'm sorry!" She was shaking her head. "I can't. He killed my brother."

"Why lose more family members?"

She blinked. "Huh?"

"Let me make it more clear for you," Tyrone said, pulling out a picture of a six-year-old boy, and holding it close to her face. "Who is this?"

Tears streamed down her face.

"Who is this?" he reiterated.

"My son," she managed, her voice cracking.

"Do you love him?"

32

"Yes, I love my baby," April answered, her teary eyes affixed to the photo.

"Then, act like it!" Tyrone said, placing the picture back into his pocket before heading toward the entrance. Getting to the entrance, he stopped and turned around. "Scratch my back, I'll scratch yours," he told her. "I promise."

Playa Ray

Chapter 5

It was Monday, and Danny Blake was ready to start jury selection for Bruce Martin's trail. Well, that was until he made his trip down to the evidence room and found that the gun used in the case was missing. This addled him because he'd went down and checked on all of his evidence two weeks ago, and he visibly remembered seeing the chrome .380 in the zip-loc bag that connected Martin to the murder of Cederic Copeland.

Now, inside the courtroom, he was seated at the State's table with assistant district attorney Alvin Newman. Attorney Betty Sadler, a white female, was seated at the defense table with Bruce Martin, a black male, who was clad in a gray dress suit. Also, Judge Connie Edwards, a black female in her early-forties, was already on her bench.

"So, what's the problem, Mr. Blake?" Judge Edwards was inquiring.

Blake got to his feet. "We have evidence missing, Your Honor,"

"Which is?"

"The gun that Mr. Martin used to commit murder against –"

"Objection, Your Honor!" Attorney Sadler interjected, springing to her feet.

"Under what grounds?" asked the judge.

"Under the grounds that it hasn't been proven that my client has committed any crime at this time," replied the 5' 6" attorney.

"Sustained," the judge concluded.

"Your Honor," Sadler went on. "I would like to move for a motion for mistrial at this time."

"Well," the judge started, "considering that we haven't started the trial yet, I'm going to deny your motion."

"Yes, Your Honor." Sadler re-took her seat.

Judge Edwards turned to the prosecutor. "Mr. Blake, what are you requesting?

"Well—"

"Missing evidence doesn't stop a trial," she cut in. "You do know that, right?"

"Yes, Your Honor."

"Any idea on what happened to the evidence?"

"No, Your Honor."

The judge looked at her watch. "Well, we need to go ahead and start jury selection. Are the witnesses here?"

Blake nodded. "Yes, Your Honor."

"Your Honor," Sadler spoke up, "I will like to move for a motion for limine."

"What are you trying to exclude?" Asked Edwards.

"The testimony of the State's expert witness. All the witness will do is testify about where the bullets entered and exited, and how gruesome the body was when they found it. I don't think that's relevant to this case."

"Why not?"

"I mean, we're not here to prove to the jury that a crime was committed— they know that a crime was committed. We're here to prove whether or not my client committed the crime."

"Your Honor," Blake spoke up, "the witness is already outside."

"What will she testify to?" Edwards asked.

"She's a crime scene investigator," Blake said matter-of-factly. "She'll testify about the crime scene."

"I appreciate her for coming," said the judge, "but her testimony would be time-consuming and frivolous at this time. Therefore, I'm going to grant the defendant's motion for limine."

"Thank you, Your Honor!" said Sadler.

***

In Judge Lathan's courtroom, Tyrone Davis was seated at the State's table. At the defense table was attorney Ellen Martinez from the Linkton County public defender's office, who was seated with her client, a white male in a jail-issued uniform.

"Your Honor," Tyrone was saying," the defendant was the driver of the stolen car. The steering column was damaged in order to start the vehicle. There was a handgun under the driver's seat in which the defendant claims to have no knowledge of. The State is offering five years for possession of a firearm, and three years for theft by receiving stolen auto."

"To run concurrently?" Judge Lathan inquired.

"Consecutive."

"Your Honor," Martinez spoke up, "my client understands and accepts the offer."

"Very well," Lathan replied, striking his gavel. "Next case?"

"That would be Wayne Griffin," Tyrone offered, without referring to the documents in front of him. "Possession of cocaine."

The judge turned to his court officer. "Bailiff, bring in Wayne Griffin."

When the bailiff escorted the defendant out of the courtroom, Tyrone leaned back in his chair and tried his best not to stare at Ellen Martinez as she gathered her things. He wasn't nuts about the thirty-four-year-old woman who stood about 5' 5" with long, dark hair, but it was hard not to relive the last moment he'd been with her, which was quite some time ago.

What broke Tyrone from his abstract musing was movement to the left of him, which was attorney Greg Bush who'd been seated on the first bench behind him. With his briefcase in tow, the older man made it to the defense table just as Martinez had gathered her things and took a seat on the first bench to await her next case.

"Good morning, Mr. Bush!" Judge Lathan greeted the attorney as he took a seat, placing his briefcase at his feet.

Bush nodded. "Good morning!"

"I haven't seen you in a while, Mr. Big-Time trial lawyer."

"I do my best."

At that time, the bailiff escorted in the tall, dark-complexioned man with dreadlocks, who was also clad in the orange, jail-issued uniform that seemed to be a couple of sizes too small. Nearing the defense table, he shook attorney Bush's hand before taking a seat beside him. The bailiff returned to his post, which was right beside the judge's bench.

"Are we ready to begin?" Judge Lathan asked no one in particular.

"Yes, Your Honor," Bush took the initiative.

Lathan looked over at the State's table. "Mr. Davis?"

"Ready."

The judge picked up a document in front of him. "In the State versus Wayne Griffin, defendant is charged with possession of cocaine. Is there an offer from the State?"

"Not at this time," Tyrone answered. "I'm requesting that the case be placed on the dead docket."

"Any objections from the defense?" Lathan inquired.

"None, Your Honor," answered the defense attorney.

"Okay." Judge Lathan jotted something down on the document. "This case will be placed on the dead docket until further notice."

***

Jury selection for Bruce Martin's trial had taken almost three hours. After a lunch recess, Judge Connie Edwards insisted that everyone be back in the courtroom at 1:30PM, and ready to proceed. Now, attorney Betty Sadler was seated at the defense table with Bruce Martin; the twelve selected jurors were seated in the box; and Danny Blake was standing in the center of the courtroom, conducting direct examination on officer McMurray, a white male.

"So, when you got there," the prosecutor was saying, "you observed Ms. Copeland?"

"Yes," the officer replied with a nod.

"And, what was Ms. Copeland doing at that time?"

McMurray looked as if he was trying to retain. "I remember her in the front yard, cradling the injured victim in her arms."

"Was he dead at the time?" Danny asked, shifting his weight.

"No."

"Did Ms. Copeland inform you that her next-door neighbor was the shooter?"

Attorney Sadler lunged from her seat. "Objection, Your Honor! Misleading the witness."

"Sustained," Judged Edwards replied, and the attorney re-took her seat.

"Were you able to question Ms. Copeland?" Blake posed, knowing he had to try a different tact.

"At that time," the officer began, "she was yelling, 'He shot my brother! He shot my brother!'

"Okay," Blake said slowly. "She was yelling, 'He shot my brother!' Did she, at any time, say *who* shot her brother?"

"Yes."

"She gave a name?" Blake was feeling elated now.

"Yes."

"And, what name was that?"

"Bruce Martin," the officer confirmed.

"Thank you, officer!" Danny Blake did all he could to keep a straight face, though he wanted to jump through the roof with the joy he was feeling at the moment. "No further questions, Your Honor."

"Cross-examination?" Judge Edwards asked, as the prosecutor returned to his table.

"Yes, Your Honor," attorney Sadler answered, getting to her feet, and crossing over to the center of the room. "Officer McMurray," she regarded the witness, "I am attorney Betty Sadler, counsel for the defendant, Bruce Martin. I only have a few questions for you. Now, after you were apprised that my client was the suspect, what actions did you take?"

"Well," the officer started, "I and several other officers went over to the house of the suspect, which was next door. Some officers went to the back door, just in case the suspect was there, and decided to make a run for it."

"Was the suspect there?" Sadler took advantage of the pause.

"No," McMurray answered. "I think it was his aunt who answered, and told us that he wasn't there. The next day, we obtained a search warrant, and entered the residence, looking for the suspect, and a possible weapon. Suspect wasn't there."

"Let me fast-forward a little." The attorney was pacing a little, now. "Suspect was apprehended the following night of the incident, correct?"

The officer nodded. "Yes."

"Was there any weapon, such as the firearm that was used in this case, found on the suspect?"

"No."

"No further questions," Sadler said, before making a B-line to her table.

"Re-direct?" the judge posed.

Blake stood, but remained at his table. "Officer McMurray, was the weapon used in this case, ever found?"

"Yes, it was," he answered.

"Do you remember where?"

"In a wooded area, not too far from the crime scene."

"Not too far from the crime scene," Blake went on, "is also not too far from the victim's house. Am I right?"

"You're right," McMurray confirmed.

"Which is also not too far from the suspect's house. Am I right, again?"

"You're right, again."

"To your knowledge," Blake resumed, "do you know if there were any prints taken, or found on the weapon?"

"Our investigator informed us that she recovered the finger-prints of Bruce Martin from the weapon."

"Thank you!" Blake sat down, feeling like he'd hit another home run.

Judge Edwards shifted her gaze to the defense table. "Re-cross?"

"No, Your Honor," replied Sadler.

"May this witness be excused?"

"Yes, Your Honor," Blake answered.

"State, call your next witness," the judge commanded.

Blake got to his feet. "The State calls April Copeland, the sister of the victim."

While the officer was being escorted out by the bailiff, Greg Bush, who was seated at the rear of the courtroom, amongst the camera crews from the two local news stations, pulled out his cellular and began dialing numbers.

***

Tyrone was in the middle of browsing his court schedule for the month when the call had come through from attorney Greg Bush, which is what he'd been anticipating. Therefore, he didn't waste time shutting off his computer, donning his blazer, and making for the elevators.

Usually, whenever a trial is taking place in a courtroom, the doors are locked and only unlocked by a bailiff upon the presiding judge's direction, but the doors to judge Connie Edwards' courtroom were not. Tyrone kind of tip-toed into the room, casting a glance at the two news crews before taking a seat beside Greg Bush. After locking eyes with Edwards for a brief moment, he shifted his eyes over to the witness stand where April Copeland was seated with a worried expression on her face, as she regarded Danny Blake, who was standing several feet away from her.

"So, when you returned home from work," Blake was saying, "what happened?"

"When I got out of my car," Copeland explained, "I saw my brother coming out of the house with his shirt off. His lip was bleeding and his right eye was kind of swollen. I asked him what happened, and he said that he'd just gotten into a fight."

Blake asked, "Did he say with whom he'd been fighting?"

There was a moment's hesitation before she asserted, "I don't think so."

"You don't remember if he told you?"

"He never did."

"Are you sure?" At that moment, Blake was under the impression that something was wrong, considering what she'd said in the initial police report.

Betty Sadler was on her feet. "Objection, Your Honor!"

"Under what grounds?" Judge Edwards inquired.

"He's badgering the witness," Sadler explained.

"Sustained," Edwards announced. "Mr. Blake, please move on to the next question."

"Yes, Your Honor." Blake nodded, then went back to work on Copeland. "Ms. Copeland, what happened after you found out that your brother had been involved in an altercation?"

"Out of nowhere," she answered, "some guy walked up with a gun, and shot my brother four times."

"Let me stop you there," Blake said, holding a hand up for emphasis. "You say 'some guy' walked up with a gun. Do you know who that guy was?"

Right then, April Copeland's thoughts went back to the night she was abducted, and one of the men making furtive threats while showing her a picture of her son. She wasn't a fool to believe that the masked man had went to all that trouble just to bluff her into freeing Bruce Martin.

"Ms. Copeland?" Blake pulled her from her reverie. "Do you know who that guy is that murdered your brother?"

"No," she finally answered, wiping tears from her eyes.

Blake stood there, staring at the woman for a moment before crossing over to his table where he sifted through some of his documents. Finding the one piece he was looking for, he returned to the center of the courtroom with it in hand. "Ms. Copeland," he began, "are you unfamiliar with the defendant, Bruce Martin?"

"Yes," she answered.

"And, how are you familiar with him?"

"He was my next-door neighbor."

"What kind of terms were you on?" Danny Blake inquired.

The woman shrugged. "He and my brother used to hang out."

"Have you ever had any kind of involvement with the defendant?"

"I don't know what you mean," Copeland replied, a confused look on her face.

The prosecutor knew that he was skating on thin ice, but he still gave it a try. "Have you ever had relations with the defendant?"

Betty Sadler was already on her feet. "Objection, Your Honor! That question is personal and doesn't pertain to the case."

"Sustained," the judge ruled.

"Your Honor, may I approach the witness?" asked Blake.

"You may," Edwards granted.

The prosecutor approached, and placed the piece of paper down in front of April Copeland, but Sadler was back on her feet.

"Your Honor, may I?" the attorney insisted.

"I'm sorry!" Blake offered. Retrieving the document, he took it over to the defense table, and handed it to the lawyer who gave it a once-over before handing it back and re-taking her seat. After replacing the piece of paper in front of the witness, Blake took up his same position in the center of the courtroom. "Now, Ms. Copeland," Blake proceeded, "what I've placed in front of you has been marked as State's exhibit one. Can you tell the court what that is?"

"A police report," she answered, after regarding it with a mere glance.

"Now, on that report, does it say anything about you telling the reporting officer who the gunman was?"

"Yes."

"And, what name does it say that you gave?"

"Bruce Martin," she said, matter-of-factly.

"But, today, you're testifying that you don't know who the shooter is?"

"I don't," Copeland gave with another shrug.

"No further questions," Blake said, retrieving the police report, then heading back to his table.

Judge Edwards looked over at the defense table. "Cross?"

"Yes, Your Honor," Betty Sandler answered, standing.

***

"I can't believe this!" Danny Blake exclaimed. "I had this case in the palm of my hand."

After April Copeland was excused from the stand, Judged Edwards bidded everyone a thirty-minute recess. Tyrone would have returned to his own affairs, but he was highly curious about Blake's thoughts on the missing weapon, and the victim's change of heart for the man who'd murdered her brother, so he offered to accompany Blake to the cafeteria, where they now sat across from each other.

"And you still do," Tyrone now replied. "It's not over. You still have closing argument."

"But, I don't have any evidence," Blake replied, shaking his head slowly. "I don't know what happened to the witness. I believe he had somebody to threaten her, but I can't prove it."

"What's with you and the judge?" Tyrone chose to change the subject.

"What do you mean?"

"Not only did Sadler object to everything you did," Tyrone went on to explain, "but the judge went along with it."

"I was out of line," he admitted, taking a sip of his bottled water.

"It doesn't matter!" Tyrone told him. "That's your courtroom."

Blake scoffed. "That's *her* courtroom."

"That's what the roster says," Tyrone begged to differ. "Do you think Judge Lathan runs my courtroom? Hell no! I wish he would get out of line. I'll send *his* ass to prison!"

"Judge Edwards and I don't have that kind of relationship, yet."

"Well, you better hurry up and bond," Tyrone told him. "Time is ticking."

"You can't win cases with no bond. If you can't win cases, you don't have a chance at making head D.A."

"I need that position!" Blake spoke with determination.

"Then, act like it!"

***

Everyone was back in the courtroom with the exception of the jurors. Seated at his table, Danny was still trying to figure out how Bruce Martin's murder weapon had just cabalistically disappeared, and how, all of a sudden, April Copeland has lost interest in seeing her brother's killer sent to prison for the rest of his life. This had 'sabotage' written all over it, but who would want to…

"Ms. Sadler," Judge Edwards spoke, interrupting Blake's thoughts, "will the defendant be taking the stand?"

"No, Your Honor," answered the attorney.

"Will we be doing closing arguments today, or tomorrow?"

Blake gandered at his watch. "We should have enough time," he answered the judge's question.

"We'll do closing arguments today, and give the jurors tomorrow to deliberate."

"That'll work," Blake agreed.

Edwards regarded the attorney. "Defense?"

"We're here," Sadler replied.

"Bring in the jurors!" the judge finally told her officer.

The bailiff left the room, only to return moments later with the jury members. While they were filing in and taking their seats, Blake cast a glance over at Bruce Martin who was also watching the jurors. Things just weren't adding up here. Sure, Martin could've had one of his gang banging buddies to scare the daylights out of Copeland, but there's no way on God's green earth that he could've had someone to break into the courthouse building and steal the murder weapon from the highly secured evidence room without the breach going unnoticed. It was just too bad that there were no cameras in that part of the building.

"Ladies and gentlemen of the jury," Judge Edwards addressed the group, "this part of the trial is what we call 'closing arguments'. The State and the defense will come up, one at a time, and argue their case to you. It may get a little intense, but not out of hand. I ask you all to pay close attention. After closing arguments, I will give you all further instructions. Then, you will be left to deliberate, but deliberations will be tomorrow morning. Now, you'll hear from the State."

The judge directed her attention to Blake who was already on his feet and moving towards the jury box. Stopping about five feet away from the jurors, he placed his hands behind his back and studied each of their faces before speaking.

"Ladies and gentlemen," he began, "I'm going to make this brief because you will hear from me again. Ms. Sadler will come up and give you all kinds of reasons why her client, Bruce Martin, should not be found guilty for taking an innocent man's life. You have to remember that her job is to defend criminals whether they're guilty or not. Well, that criminal sitting beside her, today, is guilty!"

"Defense?" the judge said, as Blake headed back to his table.

The attorney raised from her seat and crossed the room. Before taking his seat, Blake spotted Tyrone Davis sitting in the back, three rows behind April Copeland and her mother. Tyrone nodded his acknowledgement.

The interest that the other prosecutor was showing for this particular case was noteworthy, but Blake shrugged it off, took his seat, and focused on attorney Betty Sadler who was now addressing the jury members.

"Ladies and gentlemen," she spoke. "This is not a hard case to decide. Let's go to the testimony of the victim's sister. She testified under oath that my client, Bruce Martin, was not the shooter. This was her next-door neighbor— someone she's very familiar with. How could she not know if he shot her brother who, at the time, was one of Mr. Martin's friends? You've heard from the horse's mouth. Now, let's go to the evidence. I'm sorry! What evidence? There isn't any! The officer claimed that a gun was found. Well, where is it? I didn't see one. Did you? Hearsay!

"You've heard what my job is, but you have to remember that the prosecutor's job is to convict people, whether they're guilty or not and, believe me, they've sent innocent people to prison. Let's make sure that this innocent person doesn't end up in a place he doesn't belong. Thank you!"

Blake had to keep himself from smirking as he got up and traded places with the lawyer, who sauntered back to her table with her head held high, like she'd already claimed victory over the case. "Let's go back to the testimony of the victim's sister," he said, now pacing in front of the jury box. "Of course, she testified, today, that Martin is not the shooter. Did she assert that three years ago? No! At that time, she was absolutely, positively sure that he was the one. Why, all of a sudden, is he not the shooter? Who knows? Did you see the look in her eyes when she was up here? She was scared! Terrified! Why was she scared? Could she have been threatened? I don't see any other reason why she would let her brother's killer off the hook. Well, we won't let him off the hook. There's no way this killer should be released back into society. For what? So he can kill again? Who's next? One of you?"

"Objection, Your Honor!" Attorney Sadler intervened, standing. "That statement was totally inappropriate."

"Sustained," Judge Edwards replied, then regarded the jury members. "Ladies and gentlemen of the jury, I want you to disregard the Statement made by prosecutor, which was, indeed, inappropriate. Is defense requesting a motion?"

"No, Your Honor," Sadler answered, re-taking her seat.

"Why didn't you move for a motion for mistrial?" Bruce Martin whispered to his attorney.

"That's what he wants," she told him.

"You may continue, Mr. Blake," said the judge.

"Jury members," the prosecutor resumed, "it's time to do justice! It's in your hands. This guy is a murderer! He has no place in society. So, let's make sure he doesn't end up in a place he doesn't belong. All you have to do is find him guilty. Then, we can all rest. Thank you!"

***

"You did good!" Tyrone told Blake as they made for the elevators later that day.

The big man sighed. "Yeah, I guess I did."

"What was the offer?" Tyrone wanted to know.

"Life."

"And, if he loses?"

"Life without parole."

"That should've been the offer," Tyrone insisted. "He should get the death penalty if he loses. You're too soft on criminals."

"That's too harsh!" Blake protested, ringing for the elevator.

"You sound like a public defender," Tyrone said as the elevator arrived. "Goodnight!"

"You're not coming?"

"I have to catch up on some paperwork," he answered. "Get some rest."

"All right," Blake responded, stepping onto the shaft.

Once the doors closed, Tyrone spun on his heels and retreated in the opposite direction, thinking about what he'd done to sabotage Danny Blake's trial, which is something he'd never even entertained the thought of doing. However, being that the head prosecutor's position was now at stake, Tyrone knew that there would be other drastic measures taken in order to properly secure his position as a prospective title holder.

Making it to the chambers of Judge Connie Edwards, Tyrone checked his watch before rapping lightly on the door with his knuckles.

"Who is it?" her voice sounded from beyond the door.

"Davis," Tyrone answered.

Moments later, he heard the sound of the lock being disengaged before the door opened up to Connie Edwards, who was clad in an orange sweater and a pair of blue jeans. Saying nothing, Tyrone entered and took a seat in the chair before the judge's desk.

After closing and locking the door back, Edwards chose to perch up on the edge of her desk, directly in front of her visitor. "Can I help you with something?" she asked.

Tyrone looked up into her brown eyes. "I don't know. Can you?"

"How long has it been?"

"You tell me."

"Too long!" she retorted. "Can I get lucky tonight?"

"I guess you deserve it."

"My place?"

"Of course."

"What time?"

"I have to make a few stops," he told her. "Once I'm done, I'll be right over."

"And, how long will that take?"

"Connie!"

"Okay," she gave in. "I'll see you when you get there."

***

Charles was standing in the front yard of his home, constantly checking his watch. He knew that Tyrone was on his way. He just wished that Tasha would hurry back with what he sent her to get.

For the past two weeks, he'd noticed that his drug sales had been decreasing. Then, stumbling upon the two drug dealers, earlier, gave him confirmations that he was being rivaled. But, knowing about them wasn't enough. He was inquisitive about their product, which is why he'd sent Tasha, one of his customers, to purchase a sack of cocaine from them.

"Damn, Tasha!" Charles said, when Tasha finally approached. "What took you so long?"

"I had to wait in line," she answered, handing him a small plastic bag containing a hit of cocaine. "They're booming over there!"

"Is this a dime?" he asked, surveying the drug.

"It's fat, huh?"

"Yeah. It is."

"Can I smoke it?"

"No," he answered, handing her one of his, which was smaller.

"Why can't I smoke that one?" she whined. "It's fatter."

"I need it for something," he said, just as Tyrone pulled up in front of the house. "Get lost, Tasha!"

Tasha made off as Charles approached and climbed into the front passenger seat of the Mercedes. He handed Tyrone a wad of bills and waited in silence as he counted them.

"Is this all you did?" Tyrone asked once he was done.

"Yeah," Charles answered. "We got a problem."

"What kind of problem?"

"Some new guys moved in on Woodbine," he said, handing Tyrone the product. "This is what they're selling."

"Twenty?" Tyrone asked, eyeing the drug.

"Dime."

"Damn!" Tyrone exclaimed. "That *is* a problem."

"Major problem."

"I'll handle that," Tyrone said, handing him the drug back. "You just keep doing what you do. And don't think because you're off house arrest that you're off the hook. You'll just be more hands-on."

"How long will this be?"

"Until I say it's over," Tyrone answered, giving him a look that defied him to say otherwise. "Now, get out! I've got a date."

***

"I start next Monday," said Tonya, who was surfing the internet when the collect call came in from Carlos.

"That's good!" he replied. "How's your mom doing?"

"We haven't talked in two days."

"Why not?"

"I guess she doesn't want to talk," Tonya replied, though she and Carlos both knew why. "She hasn't called."

"Is my car still in good shape?" Carlos asked, clearly changing subjects.

"It's still holding up," she answered. "If they keep raising gas prices, I'll have to sell it and use the money to catch the bus."

"If that's what you have to do, do it."

"I was joking, baby," she said, getting up from her computer and leaving the room, headed for the kitchen. "We need to get you out of there."

"I wish I had a paid attorney," said Carlos. "I don't trust this public defender."

"You just gotta hold on, baby," she told him. "We'll pull through. I promise."

Chapter 6

Pulling into the driveway of a white and blue house, Tyrone parked behind a gray Jaguar, got out, and approached the front door where he rang the doorbell. Moments later, without answering, Connie opened the door, clad in a white lingerie set with lace straps on the sides. As he stood there getting an eyeful, Tyrone couldn't deny that at the age of forty-three and a yoga enthusiast, Connie Edwards was one fine woman!

"What's all this, Whitney Houston?" he asked, regarding her getup.

"It's called Victoria's Secret, Bobby Brown," she shot back, smiling.

"I know you didn't."

Connie laughed. "You should've seen that one coming."

"I should have," he admitted.

"Would you come on in!" she gestured. "It's not summertime!"

Tyrone raised an eyebrow. "Maybe. You should've thought about that before you came to the door all half-naked."

She thrust her hands upon her hips as if catching an attitude. After making her wait a few seconds more, Tyrone stepped inside, closing the door behind him. Connie threw her arms about his neck and kissed him passionately as he wrapped his arms around her waist.

***

It was approximately 11:27PM when Tyrone entered the front door of his home. He didn't plan on staying out so late, he had actually fallen asleep after his sexual romp with Connie. In fact, she was the one who'd awakened him, informing him that it was well after ten o'clock.

However, Tyrone wasn't worried because this wasn't the first time he'd arrived home at an odd hour. Plus, Lisa had never questioned his arrivals or departures, no matter what time of day it was.

Re-activating the alarm, Tyrone decided to get a drink of water before heading for the bedroom to dress down. Upon entering the kitchen, he was surprised to see Lisa sitting at the table, drinking from a red, plastic cup. Infront of her was a bottle of Patron, a pack of cigarettes, a lighter, and an ashtray with a lit cigarette hanging from the edge of it. Setting the cup down, she picked up the lit cigarette and took a drag on it.

"So, you smoke now?" Tyrone asked, taken aback by the display.

She didn't respond.

"What's wrong?" he tried again.

After exhaling smoke, Lisa said, "I want out."

"Out of what?"

"This so-called marriage," she answered, taking another sip of her drink.

"Have you found somebody else?" he asked, preparing himself for the inevitable.

"Apparently, *you* have," she retorted.

"Why would you say that?"

"Tyrone, it's twelve o' clock!" his wife pointed out.

"Eleven-thirty," he offered.

"What's the difference?" she raised her voice. "You probably have another family somewhere!"

"Don't wake Ebony!" he told her, keeping his voice leveled.

"I want out!" she repeated in a more composed tone.

"Okay," Tyrone gave in. "Do I have to sleep on the couch, tonight?"

"*I'll* sleep on the couch tonight!"

***

"Brian Cook?"

Carlos and his cellmate, Philly, were roused from their sleep at the sound of Philly's government name being called. Standing in the doorway of their cell was a male detention officer with some paperwork in his hand.

"What's up?" Philly answered.

"Pack it up!" the officer told him. "You're being transferred."

"It's about time!" Philly lunged from his bunk as the officer left.

Carlos sat up on his bunk. "They finally got tired of looking at you."

"Ten packs of cigarettes and a CD player, yo!" Philly said, as he moved about the cell, gathering his things.

"Don't go down there and catch cancer!"

"You just get out there and treat that girl right!" Philly now regarded Carlos. "She cheated on you, but like you said, you had women on the side, too. Not one of those women sent you one penny, yo. It's hard to find a woman like that. You're blessed, kid!"

***

The following morning...

"Just find out, and find out fast!" Tyrone voiced through his cellular before ending the call and placing it atop his desk.

Then, leaning back in his chair, he stared at the picture on his desk that contained Lisa, Ebony, and himself. The bright smile on Lisa's caramel-complexion face is what captivated him when they were only just high schoolers. He still found it strange that after all these years she wants to call it quits. Clearly, she had forgotten that they made a vow to love and cherish each other until death.

***

Danny Blake was on pins and needles as he watched the jury members file into the courtroom and take their seats in the jury box. He didn't need a rocket scientist to tell him that he'd lost the trial before it started. He just hoped that he said something that was persuasive enough to sway, at least, one of the jurors in his favor, which would definitely cause a hung jury, putting them at a mistrial.

That would give him enough time to redeem himself, and to investigate the missing evidence, and find out what induced April Copeland to change her mind about Bruce Martin.

"Would the foreman, please, stand?" Judge Connie Edwards implored once the jurors were all settled in. An older white man with gray hair stood, holding a piece of paper. "I understand that the jury has reached a verdict."

"We have," he answered.

"Could you, please, tell the court what that verdict is?"

The foreman held the piece of paper up to read, "We, the jury, find the defendant, Bruce Martin, on one count of murder, not guilty."

April Copeland, who was seated at the rear of the courtroom, got up and ran out, crying. Martin shook his attorney's hand, and all Danny Blake could do was shake his head in disappointment.

***

"That'll never happen again!" Ellen Martinez said to Tyrone, who was seated across from her in the cafeteria. "And that was a mistake!"

Tyrone raised an eyebrow. "A mistake?"

"The worst mistake I've ever made in my life!"

Tyrone simpered. "So, you're telling me that you just tripped up and somehow landed on top of me?"

"Don't play, Tyrone!"

"Can I come over tonight?" he asked, seeing through the facade that she was putting up.

"In your dreams!" she replied.

"Ellen!" he said, smiling at the attorney that always put him in the mind of the actress Eva Mendez. "They don't pay you enough to turn me down."

"I'm not a prostitute!" She took umbrage.

"Well, can I have my money back?"

"I've never asked you to give me money or buy me gifts."

"And, not once, have you ever declined, either," he pointed out.

They sat there, staring at each other for a moment.

"Can't you be serious for once?" she broke the ice

"I'm always serious."

"Well, can you listen, please?"

"I'm listening," Tyrone said, sipping his sweet tea.

"Robert Brooks," the public defender asserted.

"I'm done listening."

"Tyrone!"

"You know how I am about rape cases," he told her. "They're guilty until proven guilty."

"Not this guy," Ellen contended. "I mean, there's no evidence. There was no semen found."

"He used a condom," Tyrone offered with a shrug.

"There was also no sign of forced entry."

"He has a small penis."

"Tyrone!"

"Ellen!" he shot back. "The man is guilty! Life without parole!"

"This man is innocent, Tyrone," she begged to differ. "Don't send an innocent man to prison like that."

It wouldn't be the first time, he thought, but asked, "Are you asking me to let you win this case?"

"Maybe," she answered, taking a sip of her Pepsi.

"And, what's in it for me?"

"You know," she started, locking eyes with him, "I've never won a case against you."

"I've noticed that," he said. "Hell, who has?"

Ellen Martinez sighed. "You make me look as though I went to school for nothing."

"Don't feel bad." There was a grin on his face. "I make a lot of 'em look like that. Especially public defenders."

"Can you do this for me, please?"

"That case comes up next month, right?"

"Yes."

"We have enough time to talk about that," said Tyrone. "What's up with this rendezvous?"

"You can forget about that!" she retorted.

"See?" he simpered. "That's probably how Brooks caught his rape charge."

"That's not funny!" she spat.

"I'm not laughing."

***

All of Tyrone's cases for the day had been rescheduled. So, being that he didn't have much to do, upon leaving the cafeteria, he decided to drop in on Danny Blake and give him a few words of encouragement, knowing that he was in a stupor from the results of the Bruce Martin trials.

It was the least he could do, being that he was the reason for Blake's current desolate state. Besides, Tyrone didn't want him to become suspicious of his ulterior motives.

"You okay?" Tyrone asked when Blake opened his office door, looking the way Tyrone expected him to look.

"Yeah," Blake answered, voice parallel to his appearance. "Come on in!"

Tyrone entered and immediately noted that the office was unusually slipshod. However, he retained his comments as he took a seat in one of the two chairs in front of the desk.

After shutting the door, Blake rounded the desk before flopping down into his chair. Neither one of them spoke for a while.

"I can't believe I lost, Tyrone!" Blake finally asserted, shaking his head.

"You act like it's the end of the world," Tyrone replied. "You tried. That's all that counts. You still have a chance to make head D.A."

"What's with the pep talk?" Blake asked with a skeptical look on his face.

"Pep talk?" Tyrone feigned innocent.

"You're pushing for the same position," Blake pointed out. "Why are you trying to cheer me up?"

"That's what friends do, right?" Tyrone asked, forcing a smile. "They pick each other up."

The big guy sighed. "Yeah. You're right."

"I'm not worried about the competition," Tyrone insisted. "May the best man win." He pulled his vibrating cell phone from the inside pocket of his blazer. "Hello?"

"The park," a familiar voice said.

"When?"

"As soon as you clock out."

Tyrone concluded the call and looked over at Blake. "Gotta run, my friend."

***

Entering the park, Tyrone spotted Charles' Chevy Suburban. Parking beside it, he got out and climbed in beside Charles who handed him a large manila envelope, in which he extracted four, large black and white photos from.

The first one showed his wife, Lisa, hugging some white man in the parking lot of a restaurant. The second one showed them going inside. The third photo captured them exiting the restaurant, holding hands and laughing. The final one was of the two standing by Lisa's car, engaged in a passionate kiss.

"I know she didn't!" Tyrone spoke through clenched teeth. "A white man?"

"What's up?" Charles wanted to know.

"You know what's up," Tyrone replied, sifting through the photos once more.

"Dead, or alive?"

"Alive," he answered. "Meet me right here at seven."

"You're going?"

"Of course, I am!"

***

Tyrone pulled his Mercedes to the front of a white house and blew the horn. Moments later, Wayne Griffin, who was clad in black overalls with his dreadlocks pulled into a ponytail exited, donning his coat. When he climbed into the front passenger seat, Tyrone pulled off.

"Where are we going?" Wayne asked.

"Nowhere," Tyrone answered mechanically, his mind still on what Charles had revealed to him about his wife.

Making a right turn on the next street, Tyrone pulled to the side of the curb where a Caucasian man was standing alone on the sidewalk, looking extremely out of place, clad in a trench coat and round-brimmed hat. He approached the car as Tryone let the window down on Wayne's side.

"Be still!" Tyrone told Wayne.

"What!" Wayne had a look of apprehension on his face.

"Be still!" Tyrone repeated.

From the interior of his trench coat, the man produced a device that favored a large calculator and scanned Wayne's upper body, down to this crotch, then back up. "He's clean," the man confirmed.

"Thank you!" Tyrone said, rolling the window back up and pulling off. "You got that package, right?"

"Yeah," Wayne answered, pulling out a wad of bills and handing them to him.

"What's this?"

"The money."

Tyrone shot him a curious look. "When did you get the package?"

"This morning."

"You haven't sold it that fast."

Wayne smiled. "Of course not."

"You think you're slick, huh?"

"I'm Bat Man!" Wayne boasted. "Welcome to Wayne's Enterprise! As a matter of fact, whatever packages you got lined up for me, bring 'em all at one time. We can get this deal over with in one whop!"

"We'll discuss that later," Tyrone said, pulling up in front of Wayne's home. "Right now, I'm in a rush."

"Just let me know."

"I will."

Once Wayne dismounted, Tyrone pulled off. Attorney Greg Bush didn't know that after making a verbal agreement with him to get Griffin's case placed on the dead docket's list, Tyrone had actually driven out to the county jail and made a separate deal with the client, pretty much letting him know that the only way he would not see prison is if he agreed to do miscellaneous street jobs for the prosecutor. So, Tyrone ended up getting fifteen thousand dollars and a temporary servant out of the whole deal.

***

It was a few minutes before 7PM when Tyrone made it back to the park, now clad in black fatigues and boots. He didn't see any sign of Charles, so he parked, switched off the lights, but left the engine running for the sake of the heat.

While Tyrone was in his thoughts and surveying the area, a black Ford Explorer pulled alongside him. The big guy that was in the front passenger seat got out, also dressed in the same fashion as Tyrone, and climbed into the backseat of the truck. Shutting off his car, Tyrone grabbed his black gloves and handgun off the seat beside him, then dismounted, climbing into the front passenger seat of the truck.

"Fourth man in position?" he asked Charles who was behind the wheel.

"He should be by the time we get there," Charles answered.

***

John Carpenter was in his kitchen cooking and humming the tune to his favorite Brooks and Dunn song when he heard a loud crash. Wiping his hands on the dish rag and turning off the stove, he moved quickly to the living room.

Upon entering the living room, he was surprised and terrified to see that his front door had been kicked in by three men in ski masks carrying handguns. The biggest of the guys was putting the ruined door back into place. The other two approached with their guns aimed at him.

"What's up John?" Tyrone slurred, disguising his voice.

"N-Nothing," John stammered, automatically putting his hands up. "WWhat's going on?"

"Is anybody else here?" Tyrone asked.

"It's just me."

"Have a seat."

John pointed to the recliner. "Right here?"

"That's fine," Tyrone answered. "Relax."

Once the Caucasian man was seated, Tyrone and Charles lowered their weapons. Block, the third guy, was stationed by the window, peering out.

"John Carpenter, A.K.A. Romeo!" Tyrone asserted, looking down at the man who looked to be in his early forties. "How are you?"

"Fine, I guess," he answered, some of the apprehension gone from his visages.

"That's good!" Tyrone replied. "Let me cut to the chase. Do you know a Lisa Davis?"

"Um," John looked as though he was trying to retain. "I don't think so. No."

"No?"

"I can't recall anyone by that name."

"Let me show you a picture." Tyrone pulled a folded picture from his pants' side pocket and handed it to him. "Maybe this will help you out."

Tyrone sat on the edge of the coffee table in front of John, as he unfolded the picture that was of he and Lisa, exiting the restaurant, holding hands. Seeing this, John swallowed hard as he reluctantly raised his eyes to meet Tyrone's.

"You lied to me, John," Tyrone spoke, tapping John's knee with the barrel of his gun as he did. "I hate liars. What do you have to say for yourself?"

"I'm-I'm sorry!" he mustered.

"I agree," Tyrone said, holding a gloved hand out. "Can I have my picture back?" After folding it and placing it back into his pocket, he asked, "So how long have you two been dating?"

"A little over a month," John answered.

"Sex?"

"Huh?"

"Sex?" Tyrone repeated with a little more force. "Do you have sex?"

John shrugged. "We have."

"Is she any good?" Tyrone asked, then quickly changed his mind. "Don't answer that! Did she tell you that she was married?"

"Yeah," he answered. "She has mentioned it. Are you her husband?"

Tyrone disregarded the question. "Do you know a Martha Riggs?"

"My mother's name is Martha Riggs," he answered, regarding Tyrone with an inquisitive look.

"Is that right?" Tyrone grabbed the phone off the table behind him, pressed speaker phone, then placed it in John's lap. "Call her!"

"We don't need to involve her in this," John insisted.

"She's already involved," Tyrone said, pressing the barrel of his gun to John's knee. "Now, call her!"

Reluctantly, John deferred and dialed the phone number.

"Hello?" his mother answered on the second ring, sounding uncomfortable.

"Hey, mom!" John greeted, his voice akin others. "It's me."

"Mrs. Riggs," Tyrone took over. "There's a guy there with you. Let me speak to him!"

"Okay."

"I'm here," the guy immediately came on.

"Is everything cool?" Tyrone asked.

"Yeah," he answered. "I'm just waiting on the word."

"Stand by," Tyrone told him, concluding the call, then placing the phone back onto the table.

"Please, don't hurt my mother!" John pleaded with tears streaming down his face.

"She'll be okay," Tyrone answered. "All you have to do is stop seeing Lisa."

"It's over!" John raised his hands in a surrendering gesture. "I swear!"

"My man!" Tyrone patted him on the knee, then stood, looking around. "Nice place you have here! Where's the safe?"

"Safe?"

Tyrone leveled his gaze on John. "You do have a safe, right?"

John wavered.

"Don't lie!" Tyrone pressed. "If I find one, I'll cut you up and stuff you inside of it! Then, I'll let my man have his way with your mother. He loves old women."

John gave in. "I have a walk-in closet upstairs, in my bedroom. You'll see three large paintings hanging up. The safe is behind the second one."

"Combination?"

"Eleven, twenty-three, nine."

"Check it out!" Tyrone told Charles, then reclaimed his spot on the edge of the coffee table. "So, John, tell me more about this secret affair."

***

Charles had doffed his mask by the time he made it to John's bedroom. Entering the commodious walk-in closet, he spotted the three portraits. Pulling the second one down and leaning it against the wall, he applied the combination, then pulled the door open on the small safe.

There were four neatly stacks of bills. On top of the bills was a white, letter-size envelope from the Linkton County Health Department, which was the first thing Charles grabbed. The letter had already been opened. He extracted the folded document, which was the results from an HIV testing that read: POSITIVE.

"Damn!"

Chapter 7

When Charles returned to the living room with the money in a pil-lowcase and the envelope in his hand, Tyrone was still sitting on the edge of the table, talking to John, and Block was still stationed by the window.

"What'cha got there?" Tyrone regarded Charles.

Charles handed him the envelope, then sagely stepped back. Ty-rone eyed the company's appellative on the front of the envelope before extracting the contents. Everyone was watching him, but no one could see the angry contortions of his face behind the mask. They definitely couldn't feel the anger that redoubled inside him as he reread 'HIV Testing Results: Positive'.

"What's this!" he bellowed, flinging both letter and envelope at John, causing him to flinch in fear. "You're dying?"

"N-Not really," John stuttered. "I—"

"Shut up!"

Tyrone got up and made for the bathroom, where he closed the door, doffed his mask, and studied his reflection in the mirror as a million thoughts ran through his mind. With the back of his hand that held the gun, he wiped at the tears that streamed down his face.

They had been seeing each other for over a month, he thought. *That's more than enough time to contract the disease.* And, if she had taken on this infirmity, then it was possible that she wasn't aware of it. Tyrone had not used a condom on Lisa since Ebony was conceived, and he and Lisa had been sexually active within the past month So, if Lisa had, indeed, come down with this ailment …

Bile rose to his throat, unabated. Not able to parry it, Tyrone dropped to his knees over the toilet and allowed the contents of his stomach to pass through him. He remained in this position as his stomach disencumbered another load. Once he was sure that he was over his vomiting spell, he flushed the toilet, then got to his feet.

Laying the gun and mask on the sink, Tyrone turned on the wa-ter before taking off his gloves and shoving them into his pockets. After splashing water on his face and drying his hands on his clothes, he put his gloves back on. Grabbing the gun and mask off the sink, he—with no intentions of putting the mask back on—exited the bathroom, and made for the living room in a menacing stride.

Entering the living room, Tyrone approached and shot John in the head. Not taking a second to regard the corpse, he pressed speaker phone, followed by redial.

"I'm here," the guy answered on the first ring.

"Take her out!" Tyrone ordered.

***

It was dark when Charles pulled the Ford into the park, parking beside Tyrone's car. The money from John's safe had come up to a little over thirteen thousand dollars, in which Tyrone had split four ways. Ever since leaving John's house, he was still debating if he should head on home or get a hotel room for the night. And Lord knows he couldn't stand the sight of Lisa right now. Not with the thoughts that were currently running through his mind.

At the moment, he was still indecisive, but he knew that he had to get out of the truck so that his men could handle another one of his affairs.

"Look," Tyrone finally spoke, "go ahead and handle that other thing. I'll make contact tomorrow."

"Are you alright?" asked Charles.

"I will be," Tyrone answered before dismounting.

***

"He acted like he was concerned about you," Tonya, who was lying across her bed clad in pink pajamas, said to Carlos over the phone. "He claimed that he was going to send you some money."

"I'll never see that," Carlos replied.

"He acted like he was mad at me because I'm the reason you're in there," she told him.

"Don't worry about that, baby," he told her. "As a matter of fact, when I get out of here, we need to move."

"Can we move to Atlanta?" Tonya asked, smiling.

"Is that where you wanna go?"

"Or, up North."

"I'd rather move to Atlanta," he said. "It's closer."

"It is," she agreed. "Don't you still have to go to court, even if I don't go?"

"I should," he answered. "Just don't let them scare you into coming."

"Scare me?" she inquired.

"They'll tell you that they'll lock you up if you don't show," Carlos told her.

"Don't worry, baby!" she assured. "I won't let them scare me."

***

"Who is it?"

Tyrone, who was now back into his dress suit, had decided that he wouldn't go home tonight. A hotel room would have been peaceful, but he didn't want to be alone. Therefore, he decided to drop in on Jackie, who he hadn't been with in almost two weeks.

"Tyrone," he answered.

The apartment door opened to Jackie, the woman who'd hit Danny Blake's Lexus in the parking garage last week. She was cloaked in a blue robe, pink house shoes, with a multi-colored scarf wrapped around her hair.

"Hey!" she greeted with a broad smile.

"You got company?" he asked.

"I do now," she answered, stepping aside. "Come on in!"

"I need a place to crash for tonight," he said as he entered, handing her a wad of bills.

She regarded the money in her hand as she closed the door. "You don't have to pay me for that," she told him.

"Say 'thank you', or give it back!"

"Thank you!" Jackie asserted, placing the bills into the pocket of her robe.

***

April Copeland had to work late, again, so her mother had picked her son up from school and kept him until she'd gotten off. Now, as she pulled up in front of her house, with her son in tow, she assumed that Bruce's aunt and friends were throwing him a welcome home party, considering the groups of people that were standing in their yard and on the porch, all drinking, smoking, and confabulating.

April's supervisor had offered her the day off, but after hearing the 'not guilty' verdict of the jury, work seemed like the only thing that would take her mind off the fact that Cedrick's killer had gotten off the hook. Well, it had worked, up until now.

"Come on, baby!" she now said to her son.

Upon exiting the car, April retrieved the mail from the mailbox. As she and her son moved toward the house, April casted a glance at her neighbor's house, and just as she'd expected, Bruce, who was parlaying with a group of men in the yard, was watching her.

She quickly diverted her attention as she neared the door. As she nervously fumbled with her keys, she didn't see the black Ford Explorer pull up in front of Bruce's house with the rear window three inches down, and the barrel of an AK-47 peering out of it.

"Ooh, Momma!" her son exclaimed, pointing. "My teacher got one of those trucks!"

As soon as April turned to see what her son was trying to show her, the gun erupted. People were now running and screaming. On instinct, April grabbed her son and fell to the surface of the porch.

Suddenly, the gunfire ceased, and the SUV sped off. A female screaming caused April to lift her head and look back over at the Martins' residence. She saw people slowly approaching a body that lay stationery in the grass, and immediately realized that it was Bruce Martin.

So, the masked man had kept his promise.

Chapter 8

The following day, Tyrone phoned and informed Avery Stewart that he was not coming in. He received confirmation from Charles that Bruce Martin was no more. Upon leaving Jackie's apartment, Tyrone ventured off to a furniture store, where he purchased the necessities that he would need for the guest room in their house, which is where he will be staying until he comes up with something more appropriate. And he still couldn't get over the thought that he may be infected with the HIV virus, which is why he plans to schedule an appointment to be tested as soon as possible.

Now, it was after 6PM, and Tyrone was in his bedroom, sitting on the edge of the bed, watching the news. A male and female were reporting from the news stations. The male did the coverage on Bruce Martin, who was acquitted of murder, then murdered less than five hours after being released.

The female did the reportage on John Carpenter, who was found dead in his own home from a gunshot wound to the head, after neighbors claimed to have heard the sound of a weapon being fired. Subsequently, Martha Riggs, the mother of John Carpenter, was found dead in her home with a fatal gunshot wound to the chest cavity, when detectives arrived to inform her on the demise of her son. There were no leads on any suspects for either of the killings. Blah, Blah, Blah.

Switching off the TV, Tyrone exited the room, making for the bathroom. Seeing the door closed, he lightly tapped on it. "Ebony?"

"I'm still taking a bath," his daughter sounded from beyond the door.

"Okay, sweetheart."

Tyrone had to drain his bladder, but only had two options: Wait for Ebony to finish with her bath or use the adjacent bathroom in the main bedroom. He had succeeded in avoiding Lisa all day, but right now, duty calls.

He made it to the main bedroom where the door was open. Lisa was sitting Indian-style on the bed, watching TV. As she blew her nose on a tissue, he noticed tears streaming down her face. Noticing him standing there, she fought to compose herself.

"Ebony still had the bathroom held hostage," he told her. "Can I use yours?"

She nodded. As Tyrone entered, moving towards the bathroom, he glanced at the television set and saw that she was watching the news.

Don't worry, Tyrone thought as he entered the bathroom, *you'll be joining him, soon.*

***

Thursday finally arrived, and Tyrone was ready to clear the last three cases off this month's calendar so he could get started on next month's. Now, as he sat at the States' table with assistant district attorney Michelle Johnson, and the bailiff escorted Ellen Martinez's client out of the side door, Tyrone's mind was on Lisa. He wasn't mad at the fact that she was cheating—hell, he did the same. He was mad at the fact that she could have contracted this incurable disease, and inadvertently passed it on to him. Well, she'd better hope that's not the case, because ...

"The next case is the State versus Carlos West," Judge Lathan promulgated, bringing Tyrone out of his reverie. "Is the victim here?"

"I haven't seen her, Your Honor," Tyrone answered, checking his watch.

"Is the defendant here?" Lathan wanted to know.

"He's here, Your Honor."

Lathan turned to his other court officer. "Bailiff, will you please check outside for a Ms. Tonya Smith?"

The Bailiff made for the entrance as Martinez gathered her things at the defense table, then made for the entrance. Attorney Sara Jennings approached the defense table and began setting out her implements.

"Good morning, Ms. Jennings!" The judge acknowledged her.

"Good morning, Your Honor!" She replied, smiling.

"How was your vacation?"

"It was nice," Jennings told him. "I got a lot of rest."

"That's good!"

At that time, the second Bailiff returned. "She's not out there, Your Honor," she informed, just as the male officer re-entered the room from the door he'd went through.

"Thank you!" Lathan said, then regarded the court-appointed attorney. "This is a plea and arraignment, right?"

"Yes, Your Honor,' Jennings answered, taking a seat.

"Does the defendant wish to plead?"

"He wishes to plead not guilty."

Lathan looked to the male officer. "Bring in Mr. Carlos West!"

The Bailiff left back through the door. At that time, Tyrone noticed that Michelle Johnson was perusing documented photos of Tonya Smith from the case file.

"If a man did me like this," she finally spoke in a hushed tone, "he wouldn't make it to jail. I swear."

"I wonder why she didn't come," Tyrone said almost to himself.

"He probably scared her into not coming," she replied.

"Perhaps," Tyrone mumbled seconds before the bailiff returned with Carlos West, who was clad in the county jail's jumpsuit, with his hands cuffed in front of him

"How are you, Mr. West?" The judge greeted, once the inmate was seated beside his attorney.

"I'm okay," he gave with a shrug.

"I hear that you're pleading not guilty. Is that correct?"

"Yes, sir."

"Were you offered a deal of some sort?"

"No, sir."

Lathan redirected his attention. "State, what is your offer?"

Michelle Johnson took the initiative. "Twenty years for aggravated assault, five years for the possession of a firearm, and five years for burglary, to run consecutively.

"Is your plea still the same?" Lathan asked West. "Not guilty?"

"Yes, sir," West answered with a little more confidence.

"Okay," the judge replied. "I'll sign off on the indictment. The State will sign. Your attorney will sign it, then bring it out to you for your signature. Fair enough?"

"Yes, sir."

***

Tyrone entered the cafeteria where he knew Sara Jennings would be, and just as he hoped, she was seated at a table alone, eating a sandwich. "May I join you?" He asked, upon approaching the table.

"Sure," she answered, wiping her mouth.

Tyrone took a seat across from her. "Carlos West," he asserted.

"We can't discuss that, Mr. Davis."

"The victim didn't show," Tyrone resumed, disregarding what she said. "Why?"

Jennings shrugged. "I don't know. He was the one that told me she wasn't coming. I've never seen, nor spoken with the victim."

"You wouldn't lie to me, would you?" He asked, eyeing her.

"No, I wouldn't!" She caught an attitude. "I wouldn't have sex with you, tell you that I'll call—and *don't*— and then, when I see you, walk past you like nothing ever happened. I wouldn't do that!"

"I hope not!" He said, getting up from the table and heading for the exit.

***

Tyrone had approximately twenty-eight minutes left of Judge Lathan's one-hour recess when he pulled into Apple Tree apartments where the only people that seemed to be out were a couple of residence, maintenance men, and a few tenants. Parking and dismounting, he crossed the lot and approached apartment number six, which he'd memorized from the case file, and rapped on the door with his knuckles.

"Who is it?" A woman's voice sounded beyond the door, momentarily.

"Tyrone Davis," he replied. "From the district attorney's office."

There was a short period of silence before Tyrone heard the sound of security locks being disengaged, and the door opened up to the woman who didn't look like she was the abused victim he saw in the crime scene photos.

"Tonya Smith?" Tyrone asked, holding up his state identification.

"Yes," she answered, tugging on the strings of her gray house coat. "That's me."

"Can I come in?"

She stepped aside, allowing him entrance. After taking several steps, Tyrone stopped and looked around the mediocre but tidy living room while listening out for any movement that would indicate that someone else was inside the apartment. Tonya Smith closed the door back and took a seat on the sofa.

"You can have a seat," she told him

"No, thank you!" he declined. "I won't be here long. However, I came by to check on you because you didn't show up for court this morning. Is there a reason why you didn't show? You did get a subpoena, right?"

"Yes, I got one," she answered.

"So, what happened?"

The woman shrugged. "I couldn't do it."

"You couldn't do what?" Tyrone asked, already knowing what she was implying.

"I don't want to testify," Ms. Smith told him.

"Perjury!" He prompted, ready to play the card he'd played many times before.

"Huh!"

"That's ten years," he went on. "You can parole in eight for good behavior."

"I can't go to jail for nothing!" Tonya protested.

"Perjury is a felony," he told her. "You gave a false statement to the police and had an innocent man arrested for assault."

"I didn't lie to the police!" She contradicted, raising her voice.

"So, Carlos West did assault you?"

"Yes, but we put that behind us."

Tyrone pulled a small tape recorder from the inside pocket of his blazer, rewound the tape a little, then pressed play.

"Huh!"

"That's ten years. You can parole in eight, for good behavior."

"I can't go to jail for nothing!"

"Perjury is a felony. You gave a false statement to the police and had an innocent man arrested for assault."

"I didn't lie to the police!"

"So, Carlos West did assault you?

"Yes, but we—"

Tyrone stopped the tape and put the recorder back into his pocket. "That's all I need to convict Carlos," he told her. "Whether you show up or not, he goes to prison. Now, you have to decide if you'll be joining him or not. It's your call."

***

Carlos was exhausted when he made it back to the jail from the courthouse, so he decided to repose for a few hours, but he had only been in his bunk for a little over thirty minutes when he was called out for an attorney visit.

Being that he'd already signed the indictment at the courthouse, as Carlos now sat in the small visitation booth, awaiting his attorney, he could not think of anything that she would want to talk to him about. *This has to be something good*, he thought. However, that thought was immediately granulated when Tyrone entered on the other side and sat down.

"What's up, Carlos!"

"Hold on!" Carlos said, getting to his feet. "Aren't you that prosecutor?"

Tyrone shrugged. "One of 'em."

"Naw." Carlos was shaking his head. "You're the one on my case. I can't talk to you!"

"You got it all wrong," Tyrone told him. "I'm the one you *should* be talking to. I got your life in *my* hands. Are you ready for trial?"

Carlos smiled. "You can't have a trial without the victim. She's not coming."

"I see that," Tyrone replied, nodding. "I have a deal for you, Carlos."

"Nope!"

"You haven't even heard the proposition yet."

"I'm good."

Tyrone studied Carlos for a moment before saying, "You think you got it all figured out, huh? You think that you can beat the system. Can't nobody beat the system. Do you know why, Carlos?"

Carlos didn't respond.

Tyrone stood, locking eyes with him. "Because I *am* the system, and I've never been beaten! By the time you get out, dinosaurs will be back from extinction! I can show you better than I can tell you!"

***

Tonya was lying on her bed with her face buried in her pillow, crying. Carlos had warned her that they would try to threaten her into coming to court, but he didn't tell her that they had a charge for people who brought cases against somebody and didn't follow through with them.

She couldn't even remember the name of the charge, but she wasn't trying to be hauled off to prison to serve ten years—eight for good behavior. And for what? She hadn't done anything wrong.

Just then, the telephone began ringing, startling her. Tonya lifted her head and looked over on the nightstand at the caller ID. It was Carlos. She didn't even know what to tell him. All she could do was drop her head and cry some more. Eventually the phone stopped ringing.

***

It was almost dark when Tyrone made it home. Upon entering the house, he heard Lisa and Ebony in the kitchen talking. In lieu of stopping there, he made for his bedroom where he had to use a key to get in. Once he'd relieved himself of his briefcase and coat, he entered the kitchen where Ebony was seated at the table doing her homework, and Lisa was standing at the stove cooking with a pair of sunglasses on her face.

"Hey, daddy!" Ebony beamed.

"Hey, baby!" He kissed her on the cheek. "You doing homework?"

"Yes," she answered. "My teacher gave us some hard homework today."

"Hard work is never too hard for smart people," he told his daughter. "Don't forget that!"

"Okay."

Lisa grabbed a white, letter-sized envelope off the counter and handed it to him. Tyrone pulled out the folded documents and unfolded what he already figured to be divorce papers.

"I'll contact my lawyer tomorrow," he told her, only receiving a nod as he left the kitchen.

***

Carlos didn't want to think that something was wrong. He called Tonya earlier to no avail, which is the first time she had not answered the phone. It was bad enough that he was still livid about that assistant district attorney and his frivolous threats.

Dinosaurs?

Please!

It's been over an hour since Carlos had tried to reach Tonya. Now, as he dialed her number, he remembered that she didn't start her job at the bank until Monday. And even if she had already started, she would definitely be home by now.

However, once again, his call went unanswered. Now, he was wondering if she was with another man, but something was telling him that it was something else.

Something worse.

Chapter 9

It was Friday, and Tyrone already knew how he was going to spend his day. It was definitely not going to be holed up inside a courtroom all day. The first thing he had to do was see Judge Lathan, which is why he was now knocking on the door of Lathan's chambers.

"Who is it?" The judge answered.

"Davis."

"Come in!"

With documents in his hand, Tyrone entered, closed the door behind him, and approached the desk where the older man was seated, jotting something down.

"What's on your mind?" Lathan asked.

"Sign this court order," Tyrone told him, handing over the documents.

Lathan read the heading. "To search and seize? Who—"

"Just sign the order!" Tyrone said, not in the mood for queries.

"Alright," Lathan gave in, singing the documents and handing them back. "What time is your first case?"

"Monday," he answered, heading for the door. "I have paperwork to catch up on today."

***

Carlos, who still hadn't gotten another cellmate since Philly was transferred to prison, was lying on his bunk when his cell door was pulled open and two Linkton County Deputies entered.

"Get up, Mr. West!" One of the deputies ordered.

Not knowing what to think, Carlos sagely sat up, slipping his feet into his Nikes. The men didn't give off any bad vibes, but they were deputies and not detention officers, which wasn't good at all.

"Just step outside for a few seconds," the other deputy said.

He followed Carlos outside the cell where Carlos noticed that the other inmates were lined up along the opposite wall. He and the deputy stood outside the cell while the other one searched through Carlos' things, seconds later, exiting with a bundle, which was Carlos' mail.

"Got it," the deputy asserted.

"Why are you taking my mail?" Carlos asked, astounded.

"Court ordered," he answered as they walked away.

***

"Morning, fellas!"

Christopher Reid, another assistant district attorney, was the last person that Tyrone expected to run into as he and Danny Blake got off the elevator. With his sandy-brown hair parted, and stylishly combed to one side, the prosecutor was clad in a tan, three-piece suit and burgundy necktie.

"Hello, Reid!" Blake greeted him. "How's it going?"

"I can't complain," Reid answered. "Case after case. You know how it is."

"Of course."

"Tyrone Davis!" Reid regarded Tyrone with a plausible smile.

"Christopher Reid!" Tyrone replied minus the smile.

Reid said, "I'm quite sure you've heard that my uncle's retiring and I'll be taking his place."

"Avery Stewart is your uncle?" Danny seemed surprised.

"Do you not see the resemblance?" Reid asked, tilting his head as if to reveal his affinity to the lead district attorney.

"I do," Tyrone offered.

Reid smiled. "You do?"

"Yeah," Tyrone replied. "You both have the wits of a mosquito."

Reid burst into laughter. "I like that, Davis! In fact, you're a better comedian than you are a prosecutor. A mind is a terrible thing to waste," he added as he walked away, shaking his head.

"So, that's how he gets all the high-profile cases," said Blake.

"I guess so," Tyrone replied, now pegging Christopher Reid as a cardinal threat to his future position.

***

After the deputies left, Carlos couldn't bring himself to rest. Therefore, he forced himself to watch TV with the other inmates. He tried to contact Tonya twice today but still didn't get an answer. This really irked him because this has never happened before. For some reason, he had a strong feeling that the prosecutor on his case had something to do with all of this.

Almost three hours into half-watching the television, an officer came over the PA system, announcing that Carlos had an attorney visit, which immediately caused him to think that the prosecutor was back to mentally torment him, but Carlos planned to speak his mind this time, which is why he entered the visitation area in a menacing stride.

However, when he entered the small booth, his anger seemed to subside as he laid eyes on Sara Jennings who was smiling back at him.

"I was just in the neighborhood and decided to stop by," she told him. "Are you okay?"

"Hell no!" He answered, flopping down on the stool.

"Calm down, Mr. West!" She told him. "I'm doing all I can for you."

"Do you have your cell phone with you?" He asked, while his mind raced.

"Yes, I have my—"

"Call my girl for me!" He cut her off.

"Okay," the attorney said, pulling her cellular from her briefcase that was on the floor, beside her feet. "What's the number?" Dialing the digits Carlos gave her, Sara listened to the ringing until the voicemail came on. "Leave a message?" She asked.

"Just hang up," he said, shaking his head. "Something's not right. Can you stop by and check on her for me?"

"I can do that when I leave here," she told him. "I have the address."

"Thank you!"

"No problem."

"That DA came by yesterday," he apprised her.

"Tyrone Davis?"

Carlos nodded. "Yeah. Said he had a deal for me."

"What kind of deal?"

"I don't know," he answered, shrugging. "I turned it down before he could say."

"Did he threaten you?" The attorney wanted to know.

"Not really," replied Carlos. "Just check on Tonya for me."

***

Upon leaving the jail, Sara Jennings kept her promise and drove out to Apple Tree, the apartments Tonya Smith lived in. Remembering the apartment number, she approached the door and knocked. Not receiving an answer, she tried again. After waiting a few more seconds with no answer she headed back toward her car. As she did, she came upon another female who appeared to be returning home from work.

"Excuse me," Sara approached.

"Yes?" The woman stopped.

"Do you know a Tonya Smith?"

"I don't know anybody," she answered. "I'm new to the community."

"Oh! I'm sorry!"

"That's okay," the woman said, walking away.

***

In the parking lot of a grocery store, Tyrone had his car parked further away from those of the shoppers and employees and was leaning against the trunk when a dark-green BMW pulled up beside him. Laura, a blonde-haired, white female, dismounted, clad in gray jeans and a black sweater.

"Hi, baby!" she greeted, wrapping her arms around his waist.

"How are you?"

"I'm fine," she answered. "Still working hard."

"That's good!" He told her. "I have a job for you."

***

Upon leaving work, assistant district attorney Christopher Reid was walking through the parking garage when he came upon a blonde woman who was wearing white leggings and a mini fur coat. She was bent over in the hood of her BMW.

"Need any help?" Chris asked, approaching.

She straightened her pose and regarded him with ocean-blue eyes. "Um, yes," she answered. "Could you start it for me?"

"Sure."

Sitting his briefcase down, Chris climbed behind the wheel of the car and turned the ignition. The car started right up.

"My hero!" She exclaimed, clapping her hands.

Chris stood, smiling. "Well, I'm no Spiderman, but I am friendly."

"Don't get too friendly!" She said, with a raised eyebrow. "I carry mace."

"Whoa!" Chris raised his hands in a surrendering gesture. "Is it safe to introduce myself?"

"Sure."

"I'm Christopher Reid," he said, offering his hand. "You can call me Chris."

"I'm Laura," she replied, shaking his hand.

"And what kind of plans do you have for this cold Friday night?" He asked. "I mean, if you're not attached to anyone."

"I'm attached to my car," Laura replied. "And the only plan I have is to curl up in front of the television and watch old western movies."

"That has to be boring."

"Not really," she answered. "I love John Wayne!"

"Well, I'm no John Wayne," Chris offered, "but I can sure rustle up a good meal."

"Can you, really?"

"I can," he replied, "but I prefer dining out. Join me tonight?"

Laura smiled. "I guess I could."

***

It had gotten dark and the rain was showing no sign of letting up. At Tyrone's behest, he and Charles met up at a small restaurant just outside of Linkton County where they were now seated across from each other.

"I'll do it," Charles was saying, "but I gotta know if you mean what you say. A person would do and say anything when they're mad."

"I'm not mad," Tyrone answered, his gaze out the large window.

"Upset?" Charles ventured.

Now, Tyrone regarded him. "You haven't left yet?"

"Alright," Charles gave in. "But there's no coming back from this."

"Just don't hurt my baby!" Tyrone told him. "And go alone!"

Tyrone reverted his attention out the window, indicating that this meeting was over. Charles took heed to the gesture, and made his exit.

***

As planned, Chris and Laura ended up meeting each other at Kindred's for dinner. Chris had donned a fresh dress suit, and his date opted for blue jeans and a white, long-sleeved blouse.

Now, they were seated across from each other in the partly-crowded restaurant, awaiting their orders while soft jazz music played in the background from some unseen stereo system.

"Mmm!" Laura exclaimed, after biting into a breadstick. "This is good!"

"I think they have the best breadsticks in the world!" Chris told her. "Better yet, I think they have the best food in the world!"

"I can tell that you come here often."

"This is like a regular dinner spot," he replied. "You can pretty much come as you are and associate with every day people."

"I see."

At that time, Calvin, their waiter, returned with a bottle of champagne in a silver bucket of ice and poured them both a glass of the white wine.

"Thanks, Calvin!" said Chris.

"You're welcome, Chris!" he replied, then nodded to Laura. "Ma'am."

Laura nodded in reply. Once Calvin went his way, she and Chris clinked their glasses together before drinking.

"So, what is it that you do, Chris?" Laura finally asked.

"I'm an assistant district attorney."

"You're kidding!"

"Nope."

"You send people to prison?"

"No," Chris answered. "The judge sends people to prison. I just defend the people who've become victims of crimes."

"You sound as if you're good at what you do," she offered, with a wink. "I sell car insurance."

"How do you sell car insurance?"

She took a sip of her drink before answering, "We go from door to door, business to business, trying to get people to switch over to us. Or, if they don't have insurance, we use our gift of gab to sell them some."

Chris raised an eyebrow. "The art of seduction?"

"If that's what it takes," she answered. "I've had guys offer to buy insurance if I slept with them."

"It wouldn't be any different if you were selling Girl Scout cookies," said Chris. "I mean, can you blame them?"

"I don't," she answered, noting the compliment.

"What insurance company is this?"

"Hal's," she answered, downing the rest of her champagne.

***

Charles pulled up in front of Tyrone's house in a red Cadillac CTS and killed the engine. By now, the rain was torrential, and for the umpteenth time, he was wishing that Tyrone had chosen someone else for this job.

It's not like he'd never done this before, because he has. It's not like he's going to regret this mission, because he wasn't. It's not like he was worried about going to jail, because he knew that as long as he was under the employment of the notorious assistant district attorney Tyrone Davis, he was not going to see the insides of anybody's prison. It's just that he didn't know how Tyrone—despite what he'd said— would feel afterward.

However, a deal is a deal, which is why, after surveying the area, he got out of the car, slipping the hood of his coat over his head for the sake of the rain. As he neared the house, his eyes darted from window to window to make sure no one was expecting him.

Making it to the front door, he looked around once more before pulling out the spare key that Tyrone had given him, and sagely disengaged the locks. Once inside, he re-activated the alarm, donned his ski mask, pulled out his handgun, and began screwing the silencer into place.

***

After retrieving their coats and umbrellas from the check-out desk, Chris and Laura exited the restaurant and stood under the marquee as the rain continued its perpetual pour.

"This is really a nice restaurant!" Laura commented. "In fact, if you would have brought me here blindfolded, I would have sworn they had valet parking."

"Who needs valet parking when you have a valet escort?" Chris asked.

Laura raised an eyebrow. "And what does a valet escort do?"

"They escort you to your car," he answered, opening his umbrella. "Shall we?"

"Sure." She joined him under his umbrella, and they crossed the lot to her BMW where she used her remote to disarm the alarm and start the engine. Once she opened the driver's door, she turned to face Chris. "Thank you very much!" Laura said, smiling.

"You're more than welcome!" He replied, locking eyes with her. "Can we do this again some time?"

Laura tilted her head as if she was considering this. "Well, I did enjoy myself, and you did conduct yourself as a gentleman. I think a second date can be arranged."

"Great!" Chris let out. "Call me, later?"

"Depends on how tired I am after I shower."

"Okay."

Laura saw it coming. As soon as Chris leaned in to kiss her, she held her purse up to parry it. "That would definitely kill your chance for a second date." She said with a smile and a wink.

***

Charles knew what he had to do, and he planned to do it as quick as possible without harming Tyrone's *baby*, though he was still wondering how he was going to do this and concentrate on damaging the locks on the back door, to make it appear as if someone broke in, while the daughter is crying and screaming for her mother.

However, as he furtively moved about the house, he was surprised to see that both mother and daughter were napping at this time of the night. The mother was asleep on the living room sofa, and the daughter was asleep in her room.

Taking this into consideration, Charles made the subversion of the locks his first priority in which he conducted with efficiency, using a flat-head screwdriver. Leaving the back door ajar, he picked his gun up off the floor and made for the living room where Lisa now had her back to him. Charles stood in the threshold long enough to take a deep breath, then moved forward.

***

Tyrone was still gazing out of the window at the rain as his mind conjured a million and one unfathomable thoughts. He already knew how he was going to play the media once this was over. Plus, he wasn't worried about an alibi because the employees at the restaurant were very conversant with him.

The bell on the door dinged, pulling him from his reverie. Tyrone diverted his attention toward the entrance where a man had entered with his daughter, who appeared to be about five years old. He watched as she ran and jumped upon a stool at the counter, landing on her knees.

"What did I tell you about jumping on those stools like that!" a female waitress behind the counter chided.

"I'm sorry, momma!" Her daughter replied, making a face that Tyrone found funny.

"Give me some sugar!" Her mother said, leaning over the counter, and kissing her on the lips. "Have you been good?"

"Yes."

"Am I invisible?" The father, who was standing beside his daughter, asked.

"Do you hear somebody talking?" The mother asked her daughter, and they burst into laughter.

Watching the family induced Tyrone to realize what he'd overlooked while planning Lisa's demise. After a quick glance at his watch, he grabbed his cell phone off the table.

***

Charles didn't know why he was cautiously approaching Lisa as if he feared her awakening and seeing him. He knew that he would plug her before her brain cells could order her mouth to open wide enough to produce a scream.

As he got within four feet of the woman, whose back was still to him, he stopped and leveled his gun to the back of her head, but for some unknown reason, he was hesitating. Perhaps, it was because she was a woman, and he'd only killed two men before. No, that couldn't be it. He'd already been paid. The locks had already been damaged. It was time for Lisa Davis to meet her maker!

But, before he could execute the move, his cellular vibrated in his pants' pocket, causing his finger to ease off the trigger, though it should've been doing the complete opposite. That pretty much let him know that he needed to go ahead with the plan and get out of there so he could catch the call, which was probably from Cora, whom he'd been expecting to hear from. However, instead of pulling the trigger, he absently pulled his phone from his pocket and saw Tyrone's number on the screen.

"Yeah?" He whispered into the device.

"Pull back!" Tyrone said.

"What's wrong?"

"Where are you?"

"I'm right here," Charles answered, with his gun still trained on Lisa, who stirred but kept her back to him. "All I have to do is pull the trigger."

"Don't do it!" Tyrone told him. "Pull back!"

***

It's been five minutes since Tyrone had gotten off the phone with Charles. He decided to go ahead and finish his meatloaf and mashed potatoes before making off. As he consumed his meal, his cell phone vibrated atop the table.

"What's the matter?" He said upon answering it.

"I wish you would've told me that before I drove all the way over there!" Charles replied.

"You were right," Tyrone told him. "A person would do or say anything when they're mad. I mean, I'm still mad, but I have to think about my daughter." Saying that caused him to look toward the counter at the family. The daughter had bitten into a cupcake, and the mother was wiping the icing off her face. The father, who was now seated beside his daughter, drinking a Coca cola, was watching his family with admiration.

"Well, you need to hurry up and fix the locks on the back door!" Said Charles.

"You'd already did that?"

Charles replied, "Yes. When you called, I was less than five seconds away from pulling the trigger."

"Look, just keep the money," Tyrone told him. "I'll catch you later." Concluding the call, Tyrone paid for his meal, then exited the restaurant, hurrying to his car being that he didn't bother to take his umbrella inside. The moment he slid behind the wheel of his car, his phone vibrated again. "What's the word?" He answered after checking the caller ID.

"In the bag," Laura's voice came through the earpiece.

"That's good!" Tyrone commented. "I knew you could do it."

"I guess I'm irresistible."

"That's why you're on my team," he told her. "So, when can I expect that?"

"Tomorrow night."

"That's perfect!"

***

After changing the locks on the back door and disposing of the old ones, Tyrone made for Ebony's bedroom where she was still asleep. As he stood over his daughter, he couldn't help but think of what kind of life she would lead behind the loss of her very own mother, and whatever life she chose would be all his fault.

After kissing her on the forehead, he eased out of her room, closing the door behind him. Getting to the living room, he entered and stood over Lisa, who was asleep, with her back to him. At that moment, his mind was blank. He knew that he was part of the reason why she wanted a divorce. He knew that he wasn't the perfect husband, just as Lisa wasn't the perfect wife.

That's life, he thought, pulling a white envelope from the inside pocket of his leather coat and placing it on the coffee table. Then, he exited the living room, thinking of Laura.

Chapter 10

It was Saturday, and it seemed as if Spring was beginning to show it's 'true colors', being that the sun was out, and the wind was much less intense.

Tyrone didn't have too much planned for today. Lisa had taken Ebony to a movie theater where they were going to watch two movies, then migrate to the mall. Tyrone's plans only consisted of business, which is why he was now parked in front of Wayne Griffin's house.

"What's the quantity?" Wayne, who was seated in the front passenger seat, asked.

"I don't know yet," Tyrone answered. "Are you worried that it might be too much?"

"Never!" Wayne replied. "Truckload. Boatload. Bring it! Let's get it over with!"

Tyrone laughed. "Alright, big man!"

"I'm the black Bill Gates of the drug game!" He boasted.

"Yeah, I hear you," said Tyrone. "The drop will be on Monday. I'll pick up on Friday."

"Everything?"

"Everything."

***

Laura, who was clad in a pair of blue jeans and a gray lightweight sweater, was leaning against her car that was parked in the mall's parking lot when Chris pulled alongside her in a gray Porsche 911 Turbo, which is something she did not expect, though she took a second to admire the expensive piece of machinery. "Nice car!" Laura commented upon climbing into the passenger seat.

"Thanks!" Answered Chris, who had on a pair of stone-washed jeans and a dark-green Polo shirt. "I only drive it on the weekend."

She shot him an accusing look. "When you're out cruising, looking for babes?"

He smiled. "No!"

"Liar!" She countered, smiling back.

***

Chris pulled onto a dirt road which led up to a ranch, where he came to a stop in front of the white, weather-stained house, parking behind a beige Ford pick-up.

"So, this is where you grew up?" Laura asked, taking stock of the extensive tract of land.

"Hard to believe, huh?"

"Yeah," she answered, eyeing him. "You don't seem like the average country boy."

"Well, welcome to my world!" He said, cutting the engine. "Shall we?"

The warm, Spring breeze assailed them the moment they climbed from the car. After taking a brief second to fill her lungs with the fresh air, Laura slung the strap of her pocket book over her shoulder, then rounded the Porsche, just as the front door opened, and Chris' mother, Mrs. Reid stepped out onto the porch, drying her hands on a towel.

"Hey, Momma!" Chris greeted her as he and Laura ascended the stairs to the porch.

"Hey, baby!" She returned, embracing her son. "How are you?"

"I'm fine," he answered. "How are you?"

"I'm better," she replied, then regarded Laura. "And, who is this pretty, young lady you have with you?"

"Momma, this is my new friend, Laura," he responded, then, "Laura, this is my mom."

"Nice to meet you, Mrs. Reid!" Laura held her hand out, but Mrs. Reid embraced her as she'd done her son.

"It's nice to meet you too, Lisa."

"*Laura*, Momma!" Chris rectified.

"Laura," she repeated.

"Yes, Momma," Chris said. "I'm going to show her around."

"Okay. Will you be staying for dinner?"

"Probably not."

"Yes," Laura insisted, elbowing Chris in his side.

Mrs. Reid smiled. "Great! I'll set out two more plates."

"We'll see you then, Ma'."

Mrs. Reid re-entered the house as Laura and Chris crossed over to the barn. The large door was already standing open, so they entered, walking past stalls of cows and chickens, until they came upon the horses.

"So, who is Lisa?" Laura finally asked, when they stopped in front of one of the stalls containing a horse.

"You," he answered, now regarding her.

"What!"

"Short-term memory loss."

"Oh!" She replied. "I'm sorry to hear that."

"She'll end up calling you another name," he told her. "Just go along with it."

Laura nodded. "I can do that."

"Have you ever ridden a horse?"

***

After the horse-back riding and target practicing, Chris and Laura made it back to the house just as Mrs. Reid was finishing up with dinner. Chris and Laura washed up and joined Mrs. Reid at the kitchen table where they dined on barbeque chicken, rice, corn, and bread rolls.

"How was it, sweetie?" Mrs. Reid asked after seeing that Laura had finished her meal.

"It was great!" Laura answered. "What's your secret recipe for the barbeque sauce?"

"That recipe had been passed along our family for many of years," she answered.

"Just like this ranch," Chris offered.

"Just like this ranch," Mrs. Reid repeated, smiling at her son.

"And, you live here all alone?" Laura wanted to know.

"Of course not!" Mrs. Reid answered. "I have all of my animal friends to keep me company."

"When is the last time you've heard from Kevin?" Chris asked his mother.

"He came by and milked the cows for me," she answered. "I've been having a hard time with the cows."

"Momma, I think you should consider the retirement home."

"I'm not going to die in a retirement home when I have my own home to die in!" The older woman voiced, before abruptly getting up from the table and rushing from the room.

"Can you blame her?" Laura asked Chris. "I mean, I'd rather die in my own home, too. Why take her away from something that she holds dear to her? This is her life. To take this away, that alone, would kill her."

Chris sighed. "I know."

"Then, why do it?"

"Lori!" Mrs. Reid called out from another room.

They both looked at each other. Chris nodded as if to tell her to answer.

"'Lori' is pretty close," Laura told Chris, smiling. "Sounds better than 'Lisa'."

"Lori!" Mrs. Reid called again.

"Would you answer her!" Chris prompted.

"Ma'am?" Laura answered.

"Come here, please!"

"Yes, ma'am," she answered, standing.

"I'll get the dishes," Chris told her.

Laura entered the living room where Mrs. Reid was standing in front of the fireplace, looking at the array of pictures on the mantle. Laura felt the warmth of the lit hearth as she approached and stood beside the older woman.

"This is my family," Mrs. Reid told her.

"Who is that?" Laura asked, pointing to a picture that contained Mrs. Reid, Chris, two other men, and another, much younger woman.

"That's my husband, Henry," she answered. "Christopher and Kevin's father. That's my older son, Kevin, and that's my daughter, Kelly. She's at some college in Colorado."

"And, your husband?"

"He's in a better place."

"I'm sorry to hear that."

"We all have to go someday," said Mrs. Reid. "When the Lord says, 'Come', we must drop everything, and follow him."

90

"That's true."

Mrs. Reid grabbed a gold pocket watch off the mantle and opened it. "This belonged to Henry," she said. "He's had it ever since I've known him." Closing it, she held it out to Laura. "I want you to have it."

Laura was in awe. "Mrs. Reid, I can't accept that! That's something you should give to one of your children."

"Please, accept it!" The older woman insisted. "I'm sure you'll take care of it."

After a few more seconds of hesitation, Laura accepted the watch and just stared at it.

***

Back in the Porsche, Chris and Laura traveled the highway in silence. The only sound inside the car was the radio playing *Suds in the Bucket* by Sara Evans.

However, Laura wasn't listening. Her mind was clouded, which was not good at the moment. She knew what she had to do, but, for some reason …

"Your mother has her mind made up about not leaving her ranch," Laura finally spoke.

"Yes, she does," Chris replied. "I don't want to do it, but Kevin pretty much has the say-so on that."

Laura pulled the pocket watch from her purse. "She gave me this."

"She gave you my dad's watch?" Chris asked, taking a quick glance at it.

"Trust me," Laura started, "I declined. I think you should hold on to it."

"I have enough things to remind me of him," Chris told her. "We left that to my mother, and she passed it on to you. Keep it!"

"I guess I will," she said, running her thumb over the smooth surface of the watch.

After retrieving her car from the mall's parking lot, Laura trailed Chris to his house where he parked in his two-car garage beside a burgundy Cadillac Escalade, and Laura pulled into the driveway, parking short of the garage.

Laura didn't budge until Chris dismounted and motioned for her. Once she entered the garage, Chris pressed the button to close the door. Entering the house, he punched in his alarm code, causing the lights to come on.

"Nice!" Laura commended, looking around.

"Drink?" He asked.

"Bathroom."

"Follow me!"

She followed him through the hallway and up the steps to the bathroom where she entered, then turned to face him.

"Need any help?" He asked, leaning against the door frame.

"Not this time," she answered, giving him a wink before closing the door in his face.

"I'll fix us some drinks," Chris said through the door. "You shouldn't have a hard time finding the living room."

"I shouldn't."

Easing the lid down on the toilet, Laura sat on it and pulled her cell phone from her purse. She bit down on her bottom lip as she stared at the device in her hand. *There's no turning back now*, she thought, then dialed Tyrone's number.

***

With the lights dimmed, Chris was sitting on the living room sofa, sipping champagne from a glass and watching the fish swim around the fish tank mounted in the wall as he listened to the soft music coming from the stereo.

At that time, Laura entered, wearing a red lingerie set with black lining and laces. Seeing this, Chris almost choked on his drink, coughing a little, and placed his glass on the table next to the glass he poured for her.

Approaching, she grabbed the glass he'd sat down, and swallowed the rest of the champagne. Placing the glass back onto the table, Laura placed her hand on Chris' forehead, and pushed him, pinning his back to the cushion. She then mounted him, threw her arms around his neck, and began kissing him.

***

Tyrone was standing in the middle of the dim-lit warehouse with Block, who was dark-complexioned, 6'2", and 260 pounds, when Laura entered the side door, followed by Charles, who locked the door back and took up post there.

"Done?" Tyrone asked Laura as she approached.

"Not yet," she answered.

"Not yet!"

"He wouldn't let me put it on," she said, stopping in front of him.

"So, you didn't get the semen?"

"Of course, I got the semen," she answered, pulling a small paper bag from her purse. "It's still in the condom."

"My girl!" He exclaimed, smiling. Then, he put his right arm over her shoulders and held his left arm up as if making a presentation. "Ladies and gentlemen!" Tyrone spouted. "I will like to introduce you all to the modern-day Bonnie and Clyde. What'd you think, Block?" Before Block could answer, he turned Laura and himself to face Charles. "What'd you think, Charles? Bonnie and Clyde?"

"No," Charles answered, shaking his head. "Beauty and the Beast."

"Beauty and the—" Tyrone stopped short, then smiled. "I like that! Charles, you get a bonus! This is the beginning of Beauty and the Beast!" To Laura, he asked, "What'd you think, Beauty? Deal, or no deal?"

"Deal," she replied, flashing an implausible smile.

Tyrone turned to Block. "Flashlight?"

"Got it," Block answered, producing a flashlight, testing it.

Tyrone turned Laura in the direction of the restroom that was further along the warehouse. "That's the restroom right over there," he said, pointing. "There's no light, so my man is gonna hold the flashlight while you handle your business."

"I can hold the flashlight myself," she protested.

"Do as I say; and not as I do!" Tyrone said, slapping her on the behind. "Hurry up!"

Reluctantly, Laura made for the restroom, followed by Block. Tyrone watched as they approached the entrance. Laura stepped aside to allow Block to enter first with the flashlight. Then, she took one last look in Tyrone's direction before disappearing into the dark restroom.

Something's not right, Tyrone thought as he stared at the entrance. He'd been dealing with Laura for over a year, after he had sabotaged her trial, where she was charged with conspiracy to the murder of her husband. Barbara Hutchins was prosecuting the case, and he was prosecuting that of Laura's boyfriend, who'd actually committed the murder, being that their defense attorneys had moved for a severance of trials.

However, ever since he'd had Laura under his 'employment', she'd been overly resigned to his requests, no matter how parlous they seemed. And, not once had she ever failed to follow through, nor had she ever shown any signs of defecting.

Until tonight!

Tyrone turned and approached Charles. "Something's not right."

"You think she's wired?" Charles inquired.

"No," Tyrone answered, now watching the restroom. "She gave me a fake smile. I know *fake* when I see it. Are you strapped?"

"Yeah."

"Let me see it!"

Charles pulled his black Glock 40 from the waist of his pants and handed it to Tyrone, who cocked it, and moved in the direction of the restroom. As he neared it, Laura emerged, followed by Block. Wasting no time, he shot Laura in the forehead then turned the gun on Block, injecting two slugs into his chest. Leaving them for dead, he turned and retraced his steps. Approaching Charles, he aimed, and ridiculed his chest with the rest of the bullets that were left in the cartridge.

Chapter 11

When Tyrone came to, he realized he was still standing in the same spot, watching the restroom. He looked back at Charles, who was leaning against the door, talking on his cell phone. Diverting his attention back towards the restroom, he saw Laura and Block emerging and heading in his direction.

"Done?" Tyrone asked, once they approached.

"Done," answered Laura.

"So, how was the date?"

"It was nice," she answered. "He took me to the ranch that he grew up on. We went horse-back riding, and target practice. Then, we had dinner with his mother."

"His mom lives on the ranch?"

"Yes," Laura answered, giving him a suspicious look. "She's a very nice lady."

"You already know what you have to do," Tyrone said, disregarding the look. "But, before you do that, we need a bruise."

"A bruise?"

"On your face."

She made a face. "How big of a bruise?"

"Not too big," Tyrone answered, nodding at Block. "Just enough for evidence. Stand still!"

Block, who had pulled a black glove over his right hand, moved toward Laura. She began backing up.

"Laura!" Tyrone snapped, causing her to flinch and stop in her tracks. "This will only take a second. Stand still! Go ahead Block!"

"Don't move, okay?" Block told her.

Laura was clinching her purse in a death grip as Block towered over her 5'8", 154-pound frame. Again, he ordered her not to move, then swung his right arm, punching her in the left eye. She let out a shriek as she fell backwards to the ground, blacking out.

***

When Laura awakened, she found herself lying across the backseat of her car. With the headache of the century, she pulled herself into a sitting position, holding the left side of her face that felt abnormal to her touch. That's when she glanced into the rear-view mirror, and saw that the left side of her face was swollen, and her left eye closed.

Looking around, she saw that she was parked across the street from the police station, and for some reason, her headache seemed to intensify as she stared at the building that appeared ominous at this time of the night.

Seeing her purse on the seat beside her, she grabbed it and felt an extra bulge in it. Opening it and seeing a white, letter sized envelope, she pulled it out and opened it. There was a large stack of bills inside. Pulling them out, she flipped through them, which were all one-hundred-dollar bills.

As she placed the bills back into the envelope and was about to place the envelope back into her purse, the faint glint of the gold pocket watch caught her attention. She pulled it out and rubbed her thumb over the smooth surface, thinking about Mrs. Reid. She was a very nice lady, and Laura wouldn't even dream of causing her any heartaches or pain, although what she was called upon to do would definitely induce those effects.

But she couldn't just take the money and skip town because she was certain that Tyrone would track her down somehow. Or, would he?

***

Officer Tanisha Coleman had a deluge of paperwork to complete, which had her tied up well beyond shift-change. At this time, she was done and ready to get home to her fiancé. After filing her documents away, she threw her book bag over her back and said goodnight to some of the third-shift officers as she made for the exit.

As she neared the double-doors, a Caucasian female faltered in, holding the left side of her face that was swollen. Her blonde hair was in disarray, and her blouse was ripped at her right shoulder, revealing the top lining of her right breast.

"Oh, my God!" Tanisha cried out, rushing over to assist the woman. "What happened?"

"I was raped!"

***

"I'm coming! I'm coming!" Chris yelled out as he descended the stairs, tying his robe.

After Laura left, Chris showered, ate a light snack, then climbed into bed. It had taken him almost thirty minutes to fall asleep, only to be awakened by the constant ringing of his doorbell.

"What the…!"

After peering through the transom, he opened the door to three uniformed cops, and two cameramen from different news stations with their cameras and bright lights in his face.

"Mr. Christopher Reid?" one of the officers inquired.

"Yes, sir," he answered, using his hand to shield his eyes from the bright lights.

"Mr. Reid," the same officer spoke, "you have the right to remain silent. Anything you—"

"What the hell's going on?"

"—used against you in the court of law. You have the right –"

"I know my rights!" Chris bristled. "What am I being arrested for?"

"Aggravated battery, and rape."

Chris' heart dropped in his stomach. He just knew that this highly professional law enforcement officer had things all misconstrued, although he did refer to Chris by his full name. But who could he have violated in such a manner, when the last person he's been with, sexually, was Laura, which was one hundred percent consensual?

***

After driving and leaving an unconscious Laura in front of the police station, Tyrone returned home and helped himself to the remnants of the dinner that Lisa cooked, being that she and Ebony had already eaten and gone to bed. Then, he showered and retired to his own room, with the intent to watch the news.

He knew that, in Linkton County, when there's a high-profile case involving a government official, news correspondents would be on the scene from the arresting to the conviction of the official.

Well, that time finally arrived. Now clad in pajama pants and a white tank top, Tyrone was sitting on the edge of his bed, watching the news as they were showing footage of Christopher Reid, fully dressed, being ushered out of his home to an awaiting squad car. A female reporter was covering the story.

"This footage was taken just over an hour ago, at the home of one of Linkton County's assistant district attorneys, Christopher Reid, the nephew of District Attorney Avery Stewart. Mr. Reid was charged with aggravated battery and rape. At this time, the victim's identity is being withheld, but we'll—"

Tyrone switched the TV off, placed the remote on the bed beside him, then lied back with his hands interlocked behind his head. "Look out, King Kong!" He voiced, reflecting on his victory of eliminating Reid as a candidate for the district attorney's position.

Chapter 12

"I mean, I was in shock when I saw it!" said Danny Blake, who was seated across Tyrone's desk from him. "And, I still don't believe he did it."

"You're sounding like a public defender, again," Tyrone replied, shaking his head.

"It's true!" Blake persisted. "As much as I hate his guts, I still can't bring myself to believe he'd do something like that."

"So, if this case was handed to you," Tyrone ventured," what would you do?"

"Everything in my power to win!" Blake responded with might and main.

"So, you will be sending an innocent man to prison?"

"I'll be doing my job."

Tyrone smiled. "Now, you sound like a prosecutor!"

***

"You look rough!" Avery Stewart offered as he entered the small visitation booth, opposite of Chris who was already seated, clad in a jail-issued uniform and unshaven.

"Did you find anything?" Chris wanted to know.

"That's her real name," Stewart answered, taking a seat, "but she doesn't work for Hal's Insurance."

"I can't believe this!"

"I received word that she was still in the hospital," the older man went on, "but, when I got there, I was told she'd checked out at seven fifty-eight this morning. I was able to use my credentials to get her address, and drove out to her place. There, I got no answer."

Chris was shaking his head.

"I hope you told me everything."

"I did," Chris replied, not liking his uncle's tone of voice. "You don't think I did this, do you?"

"I just hope you didn't," he answered. "Your mother doesn't know about this yet."

"Keep it that way!" Chris pleaded. "She doesn't need this on her heart."

"I know."

"And, why didn't I go to court this morning?"

Stewart answered, "Judge Rebecca Cross has been sick with the flu since Thursday."

"She's new," said Chris. "Are you on good terms with her?"

"We've met," he answered, "but never had the chance to get acquainted. Why?"

"I need a bond!"

"Don't worry!" Avery told him. "You'll get that. Just keep your nose clean. Do they have you in general population?"

"Not right now," he answered. "What time is it?"

Avery checked his watch. "Eleven-forty. I have to get back to the office."

***

"So, Wayne Griffin ratted out his suppliers to have his case placed on the dead docket?" Judge Lathan asked, as he scanned the documents Tyrone had given him.

"Yeah," Tyrone answered, looking down at the judge, who was seated behind his desk.

"But, it was off the record," Lathan pointed out. "You know the procedures. And, how do we know if this information is substantial?"

"I checked it out."

Lathan now regarded Tyrone. "You checking it out is not sufficient evidence, Mr. Davis!"

Tyrone had already expected this. He pulled a card-sized envelope from inside his blazer, and tossed it onto the desk. Putting down the documents, Lathan extracted a stack of photos from the envelope, and perused them. They were pictures of the two drug dealers from Woodbine Street in transaction.

"They're not swelling bean pies," Tyrone asserted.

***

Today was Tonya's first day working at the bank, where she was one of three cashiers. She immediately became friends with Sharee, one of the other cashiers, who she worked alongside and conversed with until lunch time. However, she didn't expect for the manager to offer to take her to lunch.

"Whoa, Kemosabe!" Bobby, the bank's manager, who was seated across the table from Tonya, let out, as he watched her attack her sandwich. "You seem hungry."

She took a sip of her lemonade before answering. "I was rushing this morning, and skipped breakfast."

"That is so sad," said the Caucasian man with dark hair that was slicked to the back. "Now, I've skipped dressing, but never breakfast."

"Dressing?"

"Of course," Bobby complied. "I was half-way to work when I realized I had no clothes on."

"No!"

"That's what I said," he responded. "But I did eat breakfast."

Tonya shot him an incredulous look. "That's not true."

"Okay, I lied," he admitted. "But it can happen."

"I don't know about that," Tonya replied, laughing.

"You have a pretty smile!" Bobby offered, resting his forearms on the table.

"Thank you, Mr. Stevens!"

"Please," he held a hand up, "call me Bobby. It's my prerogative."

This tickled Tonya. "You just don't stop, do you?"

"I guess not."

"Well, you've made my day."

"I'm happy to hear that."

***

"That number's been changed," Sara Jennings apprised Carlos before placing her cellular back into her briefcase beside her feet.

Carlos was shaking his head. "Something's not right!"

"Your case is set up for trial on the eighth," she told him.

"Of next month?"

Sara nodded.

"That's in two weeks!" He exclaimed. "How in the hell are we going to have trial if the victim's not coming?"

"Mr. Davis won't set a trial date unless he's sure that he's going to win," Sara answered. "And he always does. Somehow, he's gotten in touch with Tonya."

"I see," Carlos said, dropping his head.

"Do you have any other way that I can contact her?"

After seconds of cogitating this, Carlos lifted his head to regard his court-appointed attorney through the glass of the visitation booth. "I think I do."

***

Chris was already seated in the visitation booth when Tyrone entered on the other side, closing the door.

"Hello, my friend!" Tyrone greeted him with a broad smile, disregarding the plastic chair.

"I'm not your friend!" Chris avowed, suspiciously eyeing him.

Tyrone's smile quickly faded. "You're right. I can never be friends with a rapist!"

Chris lunged from his chair. "I didn't rape her!"

"Down, boy!"

"You don't know a thing!"

"I know enough," Tyrone replied. "I also know that you'll see the insides of a prison before I will."

"Oh, I'm not going to prison!" Chris contended.

"Suicide is not the answer."

"Screw you, Tyrone!"

"Now, that's not nice!"

"I'll be out on bond in no time," Chris promised.

"Negative!"

"You can't stop that!"

"We'll see," Tyrone said, checking his watch. "Goodnight, Christopher!" He turned, opened the door to leave, then turned back to face Chris who was visibly fuming. "And, if you drop the soap," Tyrone added, "pick it up. If someone else picks it up for you, you owe them." Then, with a cynical smile, he made his exit.

***

The rest of Tonya's day seemed to fly by. Now, it was time for her to retire to her apartment, but she didn't want to leave without saying goodnight to Bobby, which is why she was now approaching his office, where he was seated behind his desk, talking on the phone. Not wanting to disturb him, she waved.

Acknowledging her, Bobby covered the mouthpiece of the phone receiver with his hand. "I'll see you in the morning," he told her. "And, make sure you eat breakfast."

"I will," she replied, smiling. Waving once more, Tonya made her exit, heading for Carlos' four-door Chevy Malibu.

Before she could use the key to unlock the driver's door, Sara Jennings, who was parked next to her in a red Mitsubishi Eclipse with tinted windows, rolled her window down. "God gave me the gift to not forget a face," Sara spoke, regarding Tonya through gold-rimmed sunglasses.

"Excuse me!" Tonya turned to face her.

"How are you, Ms. Smith?"

"You again!" Tonya asserted, realizing that this was the same woman who'd approached her in the parking lot of her apartments last week, asking for her. "Who are you?"

"I'm Sara Jennings," she answered. "Public defender for Carlos West."

"And?" Tonya caught an attitude.

Sara went on. "And he wanted me to get in touch with you because he couldn't. It seems as if you've changed your cell phone number and put a collect block on your home phone."

"That's exactly what I did," Tonya admitted. "Is it a crime?"

"No," answered the attorney. "But he wanted me to check on you because he felt that something was wrong."

"Everything's wrong!" Tonya replied as tears welled up in her eyes. "I did wrong. He did wrong. I've paid for my wrong. I'm not going to jail for anybody!" The tears streamed down her face as she unlocked and opened the driver's door. Then, she turned back to face the attorney. "I'm sorry!"

"I understand," was all Sara could come up with. This was one of those times that made her wonder why she'd chosen this profession. Now, she had to figure out how she was going to break this to Carlos.

Playa Ray

Chapter 13

Returning home from his runs, Charles pulled up in front of the house and saw his mother standing on the porch, talking to Tasha, which seemed a bit odd to him. Cutting the engine and concealing his gun, Charles climbed from his Suburban and moved towards the house, wondering about Tasha's presence, being that she's a smoker and would only show up here when she's trying to cop cocaine from him. "What's up?" he asked, upon approaching.

"The folks ran in on Redd and Tommy," Tasha apprised him.

"What folks?"

Tasha answered, "LPD, FBI, DEA, and every other alphabet you can think of!"

Charles gave her an incredulous look. "When?"

"That was about ten-something this morning."

"They just left about twenty minutes ago," Ms. Harvey finally spoke.

"Man, they got weed, cocaine, guns, bullet-proof vests. Everything!" said Tasha.

Charles was silent. Perhaps, this is what Tyrone meant when he said that he would handle that.

***

That night, Laura, wearing dark sunglasses and a green Oakland A's ballcap, entered her condominium, carrying a paper bag full of groceries. Leaving the bag on the kitchen table, she headed for her bedroom. The moment she flipped the light switch in her room, she gasped and immediately stopped in her tracks.

She did not expect to see Tyrone sitting on her bed, and she definitely did not expect to see the big guy— whatever his name was who'd swollen the left side of her face— standing in the far corner with his arms folded over his chest.

"Welcome home, beauty!" Tyrone spoke.

Laura didn't respond.

"I take it that you're not happy to see me," he said, getting off the bed and approaching her. "Why haven't you returned my calls?"

"I was going to," she managed. "I— this whole thing—" She flinched when he reached at her face.

"It's okay," he whispered.

Tyrone removed her hat, revealing a disheveled ponytail. Then, he removed her sunglasses to get a look at her face which was still a bit puffy, though her eye was now open.

"I look horrible!" She cried out, looking towards the floor.

"Yes, you do," Tyrone answered, lifting her chin.

"You said a *small* bruise, Tyrone!"

"You've been drinking," he acknowledged, smelling the alcohol on her breath.

"I have," she admitted, "but I'm not drunk."

"What else have you been doing," he asked, with a raised eyebrow. "Any drugs?"

"No."

"No drugs?"

"No."

Tyrone turned and tossed the hat and sunglasses on the bed. He, then, opened the drawer of the nightstand and pulled out a small, silver tray that contained powdered cocaine, a razor, and a rolled-up bill. "So, this isn't yours?" He questioned, now facing her. "Who left it? The tooth fairy?"

"It's mine," Laura admitted. "I tried it, and I didn't like it. That's why it's still there."

"Block, throw this out!" Once Block had taken the tray and left the room, Tyrone asked, "Did they give you any medication?"

"Some cream, pain pills, and antibiotics," she answered.

"Are you using them?"

She nodded.

Tyrone approached and kissed her on the left cheek. "Get well! I'll see you in court tomorrow, okay?"

She nodded, again.

Block returned with the now clean tray and handed it to Tyrone who handed it to Laura. Then, they made their exits.

***

It was Tuesday morning, and Judge Rebecca Cross was ready to get back on the bench after being sick with the flu since Thursday.

It was still dark out when she exited her house, approaching her green Cadillac Deville. As she got to the car and was fumbling with her keys, a masked man rushed up from behind her, clamped a gloved hand over her mouth, and pressed the barrel of a gun to the side of her head, causing her to drop her keys and briefcase.

"Don't struggle and you won't be harmed!" He threatened. "Got it?"

She nodded.

"Are you familiar with assistant attorney Christopher Reid?"

Another nod.

"Does he have a bond hearing in your courtroom this morning?"

She gave another nod.

"He will be denied, right?"

Cross didn't respond.

"Right!" The man repeated, putting more force on the barrel.

She nodded.

"If anyone hears about this visit, the next one will be very unpleasant. Got it?"

Another nod.

"Now, when I release you, don't look back! Count to ten, then proceed on with your day. Okay?"

She nodded.

The man released her and backed away. Rebecca remembered the man told her to count to ten, but she was so scared, she didn't know which number to begin with. Therefore, she just closed her eyes and made a silent prayer.

For Christopher Reid.

***

Inside the courtroom, Christopher Reid was seated at the defense table with his attorney, Jason Scott, an older white man. Assistant district attorney Sally Whitfield was seated at the State's table. Judge Rebecca Cross was already on the bench. Laura was seated on the second row behind District Attorney Avery Stewart, who was seated directly behind Reid and his attorney.

Ellen Martinez and Sara Jennings wanted to show their support, which was why they were seated on the back row. At that time, Judge Cross scooped up the documents in front of her and began reading from it.

"In the State versus Christopher Reid," she started, "Mr. Reid is charged with aggravated battery and rape. This is a hearing to determine whether or not the defendant is eligible for a bond. Representing the defendant is attorney Jason Scott. And, for the State, is assistant district attorney Sally Whitfield."

Tyrone checked his watch. He was sure that Reid's hearing had already begun, and he wanted to attend to make it seem as if he was showing support. Plus, he told Laura that he would be there. He just didn't expect for his appointment at the clinic to take as long as it has.

He thought he would make the short drive from the courthouse and be back within twenty minutes, but that wasn't the case. He'd been sitting in the waiting area now for over thirty minutes.

"Mr. Tyrone Davis?"

"Yes," Tyrone answered, regarding the nurse who emerged from the service door.

"Right this way, sir," she said.

Tyrone placed the magazine that he was perusing back on the table and entered the door ahead of the nurse who directed him to an examination room.

"Have a seat, please!" She told him. "And, how are you this morning?"

"I'm fine," he answered, taking a seat on the exam table. "How are you?"

"I'm great!" She replied with a broad smile. "I got married over the weekend."

"Congratulations!"

"Thank you!" She regarded her chart. "HIV test. Would you be taking the swab or the painful needle?"

"Whichever is faster."

***

"Thank you, Ms. O'Neal!" Judge Cross said to Laura, who was seated on the witness stand. "You may step down. It's your choice if you'd like to leave or stay for the results."

"I'll stay," Laura replied.

Leaving the witness stand, Laura dropped her head to keep from glancing over at the defense table. Just as she re-took her seat, Tyrone was let into the courtroom by one of the bailiffs. Taking a seat beside Danny Blake, which was directly behind Laura, Tyrone cast a glance at the defense table and noticed Chris giving him the evil eye. He nodded.

"Mr. Scott?" The judge went on.

The attorney got to his feet. "Yes, Your Honor?"

"Why should your client be granted a bond?"

"Your Honor," Scott began, "my client has been employed as an assistant district attorney for the Linkton County Superior system for more than eight years. Mr. Reid doesn't have any kind of criminal history, nor does he suffer from any kind of mental health illness. Therefore, we kindly ask the court to set a reasonable bond for the accused."

"Any objections from the State?" Judge Cross asked when the attorney re-took his seat.

The prosecutor slowly rose to her feet. "Not really, but on behalf of the victim, who still seems a bit shaken up from the ordeal, I have to. She fears for her life, and it's common for a victim of such an offense to feel that way, knowing that their assailant is, or is about to be released back into society. That's how she feels, and being that she's the one who actually endured the pain and suffering of this terrifying act of violence, her feelings should be respected."

"Alright," the judge said as the prosecutor sat. "I'm going to rule in favor of the victim, and deny bond for the accused. I'm also going to bound this case over to the Superior Court of Linkton County. Court is adjourned." After striking her gavel to confirm the dismissal, Judge Cross got up, and quickly withdrew to her chambers.

Chris looked back at Tyrone who winked at him. Then, he watched as Tyrone, Laura, Danny, Ellen, and Sara got up to leave.

As they did, Tyrone placed his hand on the small of Laura's back. To the naked eye, this would be looked upon as an innocent gesture, but Chris knew better. He already knew he'd been set up. Now, he was absolutely sure of who was behind it and why.

Chapter 14

"Tonya?" Bobby called out to Tonya, who was seated across the table from him in the half-crowded restaurant. She'd been gazing out of the window for some time now, clearly in her own world. Not getting a response, he tried again. "Earth to Tonya! Come in!"

Tonya now regarded him with a blank expression.

"I assume you're still full from breakfast?" He offered, noticing that she hadn't touched her lunch.

"I couldn't eat this morning," she replied.

"It seems like you can't eat, now," he pointed out. "What's wrong?"

"I'm just going through a lot right now."

"Family illness?"

"No."

"I'm not good at guessing," he told her, shrugging. "Can I buy a vowel?"

Tonya managed a weak smile.

"You can talk to me," Bobby went on. "What's wrong?"

After seconds of hesitation, she dug into her pocket book, pulled out a white, letter-sized envelope, and handed it across the table to him.

"Linkton County Superior Court," he read the heading, then shot her an inquisitive look.

***

Being that Tyrone didn't have any cases to handle today after Reid's bond hearing, he walked Laura out to her car, then retreated to his office where he made a few phone calls. He wanted to drop in on Connie, but as he was making his way up the hallway, he was approached by Michelle Johnson who was carrying a stack of folders.

"It's sad," Michelle was now saying. "Especially when you thought you just knew a person."

"I know," Tyrone replied, not really in the mood to talk about Christopher Reid's predicament. "I hope you're ready for this new schedule.

"I haven't looked at it yet," she admitted, "but I kind of have an idea of what to expect."

"Hi, Michelle!" Ellen Martinez seemed to materialize out of nowhere.

"Oh! Hi, Ellen!"

"May I borrow Mr. Davis for a few seconds?" The public defender asked.

"Sure," Michelle replied, indicating her folders. "I have to get these filed."

"Thanks!"

"No problem," Michelle replied before walking off.

Ellen turned to Tyrone. "Did I interrupt your courtship?"

"Michelle is married to a woman," he told her.

"I was being sarcastic."

"And I was ignoring you," he replied, checking his watch. "What do you want?"

"What's with this new schedule?" she asked, fanning a piece of paper in his face. "And, why did you push Robert Brooks' case up to next week?"

"I have new cases coming in," answered Tyrone. "I have to get these old cases out of the way. Why prolong?" Without giving her a chance to respond, he walked off.

***

In his office, Danny Blake was searching through the files in his file cabinet when someone knocked on the door. Slamming the drawer shut, he marched over and pulled the door open to Avery Stewart who was the last person he'd expected to show up at his door unannounced.

"Are you busy, Mr. Blake?" Avery inquired.

"Not really. Come on in!" Danny answered, stepping aside to allow the older man entrance, then closed the door back. "Excuse my office. I haven't really had time to—"

"It's okay," said Avery, holding his hands up. "It's your office. I stopped by because I need a favor."

Danny had never heard this before. "From me?"

"Yes," the lead district attorney replied. "I need you to handle Christopher's case."

"You want me to convict him?"

Avery shook his head. "No. I want you to do everything in your powers to make sure he's *not* convicted. You name the price. Money's not an issue."

A lightbulb came on in Danny's head. "It's not money that I want."

"Well, what do you want?"

"I want your position when you retire."

Avery furrowed his eyebrows. "Are you serious?"

"As a heart attack!"

He seemed to ponder this for a moment before responding. "Okay. You do that for me, and I'll make sure you get it."

"Deal!" Danny let out, shaking the older man's hand.

***

Tyrone eyed Danny who was seated across the table from him, for a moment, before replying. "So, what if the jury finds him guilty? He gets convicted, right?"

"Yeah, but—"

"Are you gonna pay the jury off?" Tyrone cut him off. "Have sex with the judge?"

"Of course, not!" Danny replied, making a face. "I don't—"

"Why not kill the victim?" Tyrone resumed. "Have you ever killed somebody before, Danny?"

"Nooo!" Danny gasped.

"If Reid gets convicted," he went on, "you don't get the position. You do know that, right?"

"Yeah, but—"

"Refuse it."

"Do what!"

"Turn it down!"

"Are you crazy!" Danny blurted out, his voice carrying throughout the cafeteria. "This is my chance to become somebody, and you think I'm just gonna throw it away? I think not!"

"Consider your options, Danny," Tyrone said, taking a sip from his bottled water.

"I have no options, Tyrone!"

"If Reid is found guilty," Tyrone started, "that ruins your chance of becoming the head DA. That leaves me and Barbara Hutchins, who hasn't won a case since John Hancock was elected. I haven't lost a case yet. I mean, it doesn't take a rocket scientist."

"I understand what you're saying," Danny admitted, "but my mind is already made. I believe that I can do it."

"If you believe in you, I believe in you," Tyrone said, although he was now considering Danny a threat to his future.

The same way he considered Christopher Reid.

***

Tonya was finally able to consume her lunch. Now, in Bobby's BMW, and on their way back to the bank, Tonya's attention was out the passenger window.

No matter how hard Bobby tried to cheer her up, Tonya could not stop thinking about the subpoena, Carlo's imminent trial date, and how she was going to depone against him without breaking down or looking in his direction.

"That doesn't make you a bad person," Bobby finally spoke. "You're the victim."

Tonya didn't respond.

"If you want to," he went on, "you can take off until you get this thing resolved."

"I think I can manage," she replied, still looking out of the window.

"I just don't want you to have a nervous breakdown on me," he told her. "I don't know CPR."

That comment won him a smile.

***

Sitting in a cell all day and alone was starting to drive Chris up a wall. All he could do was pace the floor of the small cell and constantly mull over the terrible situation he was caught up in, which only seemed to add fuel to the fire.

However, he found a bit of a relief when an officer came and got him for an attorney visit. He figured it was his uncle, but when he entered the booth, it wasn't Avery that was seated in the chair on the other side, but Sara Jennings, who was flanked by Ellen Martinez and Danny Blake.

"Hey, Christopher!" Sara greeted. "Are you okay?"

"I feel miserable!" Chris responded, taking a seat.

"Poor baby!" Sara cooed.

"Are you on bad terms with Judge Cross?" Ellen wanted to know.

Chris answered, "I've never met her until today."

"Well, she's not good on bonds," said Ellen, "considering that she's a state court judge, but she could've set you one. I don't see why she didn't."

"Tyrone!" Chris spoke in a tone that corroborated his visage.

"Tyrone, what?" Ellen inquired.

"He's behind all this," Chris promulgated. "He set me up."

"Why would you say that?" Asked Sara.

Chris answered, "He's been acting strange towards me."

"You two don't like each other," Ellen pointed out.

"It's beyond that, Ellen!"

"You think he sent this woman at you?" Ellen sounded incredulous.

"Listen!" Chris fought to keep his patience. "I met her in the parking garage, pretending to have problems with her car. That was the same day that Tyrone and I had words in the hallway. Am I right, Danny?"

"That's not the first time that you two have had words," Danny replied.

"Yeah," said Ellen. "I've even witnessed you two at each other's throats."

"I don't believe that Tyrone would stoop that low," Sara added.

"Would you all just listen for a minute?" He spoke through clenched teeth. "I know what I'm talking about. He was here yesterday, telling me that I'd see prison before he does. He even told me that I wouldn't get a bond. What happened? I didn't get one."

"Well—" Sara started.

"Listen!" He cut her off. "When the victim walked out of the courtroom, he walked with her, with his hand on the small of her back."

"I saw that," Ellen admitted.

"Me, too," said Sara.

"Me, three," came Danny.

"I know what I'm talking about, guys!"

"Did you have sex with her?" Sara inquired.

"Yes."

"With no protection?"

"I used protection."

"They claimed that your semen was found," Sara pointed out.

"It's not mine," Chris contended. "The condom didn't burst, nor have a hole in it. I put it on myself."

"Who took it off?" Ellen asked.

"I did," Chris answered.

"And, where did you put it?"

"In a small paper bag, and tossed it in the trash can in my kitchen."

"Has that trash been emptied?" Asked Ellen.

"I never had the chance to empty it," he answered.

"So, the condom is still there?"

"It should be."

"Then, have your uncle to go by and bag it for evidence," Ellen told him.

"He's already too involved," Chris replied, shaking his head. "I need you guys' help."

Ellen made a face. "I'll go, but I'm not touching any nasty condom!"

"How do we get in?" Sara asked.

"I'll sign my keys out to one of you," Chris answered.

"You can use my name," Sara told him.

"My alarm is not activated," he apprised her.

"Ouch!" Ellen offered.

"It'll take, at least, thirty-five minutes to receive the property," said Sara. "So, I'll stop by and see one of my clients while I'm here. Go ahead and fill out the property release form. Tomorrow, call the public defenders' office and ask for me or Ellen. We'll tell you what we've found."

***

Carlos had been worried sick about Tonya, which is why he didn't waste any time making his way to the visitation area when he was called out for an attorney visit, knowing that his public defender would have some information for him.

When he entered the booth, he was a little surprised to see that Sara was not seated, but standing, as if she didn't plan on staying long, but that didn't matter to Carlos. All he wanted to know was how Tonya's doing.

"Hello, Mr. West!" Sara greeted him.

"Did you find Tonya?" Carlos got to the point.

"No," she answered.

"No!" He exclaimed, now thinking that she didn't even try. "Did you go to the bank?"

"Yes, I did," she answered, then sighed. "Look, Carlos, I don't know what kind of agreement you two had, but it's over."

"What do you mean, it's over!"

"Something happened," she told him. "I don't know what, but—"

"She can't be dead!" Carlos felt the tears well up in his eyes.

"No, she's not dead," she assured.

"How do you know?" He asked. "You haven't even talked to her."

"I don't think she is," Sara offered. "Maybe she's hiding. If she loves you as much as you love her, she'll come around."

***

After their visit with Chris, Sara went on to visit Carlos, while Danny and Ellen exited the building, and decided to sit in Danny's Lincoln Navigator, where they were now awaiting her arrival.

"I don't know," Ellen was saying, "Tyrone does have this demon look in his eyes at times. Scares me!"

"You!" Danny let out. "Today, he asked me if I've ever killed anyone."

"What!" Ellen now regarded him. "Why'd he ask you that?"

"I don't know," Danny answered. "He was saying something about—"

Sara's tapping on the passenger window stopped Danny mid-sentence and startled Ellen, who stifled a shriek, before letting the window down.

"What's wrong?" Ellen asked, seeing the disquieting look on Sara's face.

"I need a new profession," Sara answered, shaking her head, then holding up the set of keys. "I got the keys."

***

At 7:46PM, it was already dark out when Sara pulled into Chris' driveway, and Ellen pulled her Honda Accord in front of the house, with Danny parking his truck behind her. Dismounting, Danny and Ellen followed Sara to the front door where she seemed to linger as if she was having second thoughts.

"Anybody scared?" Sara asked, now facing them.

"I know Tae-Bo," Ellen jested.

"What if we run into someone with a gun?" Sara was being serious.

"Then, we'll use Danny as a shield," she answered, patting Danny on the back.

"Very funny!" Danny replied, looking around. "Can we get this over with?"

Sara let out a sigh, then negotiated the locks with the appropriate keys. Pushing the door open, Sara took one step, then stopped in her tracks. The bad vibe she had while en route to Chris' house had been confirmed.

The place was trashed!

***

"Yeah, that was pretty clever," said Charles, who was seated on the passenger side of Tyrone's car.

"So, you're back on deck?" Asked Tyrone.

"I had a few customers come back."

118

"Step it up!"

"What?"

"The dope."

"Make them bigger?"

"Of course," Tyrone answered. "Make my dimes look like twenties! Hell, make them look like fifties! We have more than enough."

Charles nodded.

"One month," Tyrone told him.

"Then, I'm through?" Charles asked.

"Yeah," Tyrone answered. "You're done."

Playa Ray

Chapter 15

"Tyrone, I've never asked you for anything, ever since I've known you," Ellen was saying to Tyrone as they approached the elevators.

It was well after one o'clock, and Tyrone had to get back to the courtroom, but Jakie had called moments ago telling him that she was at the park, and it was imperative that he drove out to meet her, which was where he was on his way to when Ellen approached him. "Why now?" Tyrone now asked, ringing for an elevator.

"Because," Ellen replied. "I figured this thing we have is considered a friendship, and you'd do me that favor as a friend."

"Law two," Tyrone spoke. "Never put too much trust in friends. Learn how to use your enemies." An elevator arrived. Tyrone got onto the empty shaft, then turned to face her. "Scratch my back, I'll scratch yours," he asserted, as the doors were closing.

***

Despite the time of day, Laura was still in her pajamas, being that she had nowhere to go. Now, as she brushed her teeth, she entered her bedroom, and, for some reason, walked over to the nightstand.

Opening the drawer, she stared down at the gold pocket watch that sat on the small, silver tray, before picking it up and rotating it in her hand.

***

Pulling into the park, Tyrone parked beside Jackie's Ford Explorer and got out. It didn't take long for him to spot Jackie, who was seated on a bench alone. She stood as he approached.

"Hey, baby!" she greeted with a broad smile.

"What's this about?" He asked, kissing her on the cheek.

"Have a seat!" She told him, reclaiming her spot on the bench.

"I have to get back to work, Jackie."

"I know," she avowed, "but I want you to be sitting when I tell you this."

Reluctantly, Tyrone took a seat.

Jackie took hold of one of his hands before speaking. "I don't know if it was an accident or something you intended to happen, but I'm pregnant."

"And how do you know that?"

"I just left the clinic," she answered. "I'm three weeks."

Tyrone cocked his head. "Let me guess: you haven't had sex with nobody but me, right?"

"No," Jackie admitted. "But, you're the only one I've had un-protected sex with."

***

Chris was still livid about the revelation Sara revealed to him about the trashing of his home. When he asked her if they'd recovered the used condom from the trash can in the kitchen, she apprised him that the trash can was the only thing untouched, but the condom wasn't there.

Chris relayed this to Avery who promised to stop by the house on his way home. Ostensibly, Avery had told Chris' brother Kevin because it was visitation day, and Chris had been called out for a regular visit, but when he entered the booth, instead of Kevin, he was looking at the blonde hair of a woman, who had her head down. The moment he closed the door on his side, she lifted her head and removed her sunglasses.

"You've got a lot of nerves coming here after what you've done to me!" Chris vented. "You ruined my life, Laura!"

"Chris," Laura spoke, "you're a nice guy, and this is something that should have never been imposed on you. I was just doing my job."

"Your job!"

"You wouldn't understand," she said, standing, donning her sunglasses and pushing the door open to leave.

"Laura!"

Laura stopped in the threshold and hung her head for a second before looking back at him. "I'm sorry, Chris!" she said, then made her exit.

***

"Come in!" Danny, who was seated behind his desk, answered the knock at his door.

The door opened, and Danny was, once again, surprised to see Avery Stewart, who was carrying a folder.

"Are you busy?" Avery asked, approaching the desk.

"Not really," Danny answered.

Avery handed him the folder. "Here's the case."

"Already?" Danny asked, receiving the folder.

"I want this done as quick as possible."

"I'll do my best."

"I'm counting on you," Avery said, then left.

***

Being that there were no customers, Tonya was conversating with Sharee, a dark, heavy-set woman with short, curly hair, while Bridgett, the third cashier, was out on her break.

"People don't get paid today?" Tonya now asked Sharee.

"They do," she answered, "but not on this side of town. It's mostly Tuesdays, Fridays, and Saturdays. You haven't seen anything yet. Wait until Friday and Saturday. It seems like the whole world gets paid on those days."

"I can imagine."

"I see that you and Mr. Stevens have become close friends," Sharee asserted, shooting her an accusing look. "Love at first sight?"

Tonya laughed. "It's not even like that, Sharee!"

"Hey!" Sharee threw her hands up in surrender. "That's on you, if you prefer cream in your coffee. He's cute and all, but I can't see myself having sex with a white man. Or woman."

"Woman?"

"I'm bisexual," admitted Sharee. "I mean, not to offend you, or sound like I'm coming on to you. I'm just not ashamed to say it."

"You shouldn't be ashamed of what you do," Tonya said, though she'd already been inquisitive about Sharee's sexual preference. "It's your life."

"And I live it to the fullest!" Sharee stated, ardently. "I'm a big woman, so I gotta spread my love!"

"Ms. Smith?"

They both looked back to see the manager, Bobby, standing in the doorway of his office.

"Yes?" Tonya answered.

"Can I speak with you when you get a chance?" he asked.

"Sure."

"Hell, tell him I need a raise, too!" Sharee said, when Bobby went back into his office.

"Girl, you're crazy!" Tonya laughed.

"But, for real," Sharee spoke in a much quieter tone. "His divorce just became final last month. Word is, his wife left him for a black guy."

"Are you serious?" Tonya asked, now feeling compassion for Bobby who didn't seem like the kind of man that a woman would just jilt.

"Yep," Sharee answered. "And, guess how they met?"

"How?"

Sharee smiled hard. "She was a cashier, just like you. Same register."

***

Bobby was seated behind the desk, talking on the phone when Tonya appeared in the doorway. Seeing her, he motioned for her to enter. She did, and took a seat in one of the two visitors chairs.

"That'll be fine, Ms. Harris," Bobby continued his conversation. "Okay, I'll see you then." Hanging up the phone, he asked Tonya, "How are you coming along?"

"I'm okay," she answered.

"If you need to talk," he said, "you know where my office is."

She smiled. "I'll remember that."

Bobby leaned forward, interlocking his hands on his desk. "Tonya, what do you want out of life?"

"What do I want out of life?"

"What goals have you set for yourself?"

Tonya shrugged. "I just want to be happy, stress-free, and make enough money to get by."

"That's not much," he replied.

124

"I know."

"So, what makes you happy?"

***

"In two weeks?" Tyrone asked Danny, as they walked along the hallway.

"Yes," Danny answered. "I'll have to push back a lot of cases. I may even have to place some cases on the docket list."

"I don't know, Danny," Tyrone replied. "That's a mighty bold step."

"Why is that?"

Tyrone answered, "To have a trial three weeks after his arrest would raise suspicion in the judicial system, as well as the media. According to the sixth amendment, he has the right to a speedy trial, but the motion should be filed by him or his attorney. You know this, Danny."

"Yeah. You're right," Danny responded as they approached and stopped in front of his office door. "I guess I have some more work to do."

"Handle your business!" Tyrone told him, shaking his hand. "I'll catch you later."

***

"Kevin, please don't tell mom about this!" Chris said to his brother, who was seated opposite him in the visitation booth. "Don't even tell Kelly!"

"Kelly already knows," Kevin apprised. "And you know how she runs her mouth."

"I know." Chris was shaking his head. "Did she say anything about coming down?"

"She's in the middle of some kind of exam."

"Good!"

They were silent for a moment before Kevin asked, "So, how long will this take?"

"I don't know," Chris answered. "Uncle Avery is trying to speed up the process."

"You know I've never lied to Momma."

"I'm not asking you to lie, Kevin," Chris avowed. "I'm asking you to not tell her. Don't let my situation be the cause of her death! That's all I ask."

***

In his office, Tyrone was going over the last untried cases on his calendar for the month when someone knocked on the door. "It's open," he called out, figuring it was Danny coming to tell him about some other plot he devised to get Christopher Reid's case into the hands of the grand jury expeditiously.

However, the person that entered, closed, and deliberately locked the door was not Danny, but Ellen. "You win," she told him, unbuttoning her blouse, then pulling it over her head, revealing a light-blue brassiere. Letting it fall to the floor, she began unzipping her skirt.

***

"Right over here," Sharee told Tonya as they approached her gray Lincoln Navigator where she used her remote to animate the fifth door that slowly lifted upwards.

"Girl, you got the whole Macy's back here!" Tonya exclaimed, eyeing the panoply of clothes that were hanging up and laid out on the floor of the rear compartment.

"And I can't fit my fat ass in none of it," Sharee replied.

"You can't?"

"Girl, no!" she responded. "When I get the merchandise, I let my girlfriend pick out a few outfits, then sell the rest. Go ahead and pick out something. I don't charge full price."

***

"So, what's the deal?"

"Ten years," Tyrone answered, buttoning his shirt as Ellen was getting dressed.

"Seven," she dickered.

"Eight," he shot back. "That's the lowest I'm going. You bid lower, I go higher. Deal, or no deal?"

***

Ellen was in no rush to get home, being that all she had to go home to was her cat. Therefore, upon leaving her office, she made for the Linkton County jail where she was now seated in the small visitation booth when her client, Robert Brooks, entered on the other side.

"Hi, Ellen!" He greeted her with a broad smile.

"Hello, Robert!" She returned. "Are you okay?"

"I'm still living," he replied, taking a seat. "Ready for trial."

"There won't be a trial."

"What's the problem, now!"

"I've negotiated with Mr. Davis to get you eight years," she apprised, suppressing a shudder.

"Eight years?"

"It's better than thirty, Robert," Ellen asserted. "You're nineteen. You'll be twenty-seven when you're released. You can still go to school and get some kind of degree."

Robert sighed. "Yeah, you're right. Thank you!"

"Just keep your nose clean when you get to prison."

"Can I get out early for good behavior?"

"Nobody gets out early for good behavior," she told him. "Just try not to catch any more charges. I'll try my best to come and see you."

"You will?"

"Of course, I will," she replied. "You do know my address, right?"

"I still know it."

"If you need anything, send me a letter."

"I'll do that."

"Well," Ellen started, checking her watch as she stood. "I have to get home. "I do have to work tomorrow. I'll see you on Monday."

"Okay," he said. Then, as she turned to leave, "Ellen?"

"Yes?" she answered, now facing him.

"You and my dad were like the perfect couple," he said. "What happened?"

She studied him through the thick glass of the visitation booth for a moment before replying, "Ask him."

Playa Ray

Chapter 16

Entering the courthouse, Tyrone already had his day mapped out, and his first stop was Judge Lathan's chambers where he was now looking down at the old man who was studying the documents Tyrone handed him through his very small reading glasses.

"Tyrone, you can't do this!" Lathan said, looking up from the documents.

"It's already done," Tyrone told him.

"I thought you had that rape case set for trial, Monday."

"He's copping out to eight years," Tyrone answered. "We'll get him in, first thing Monday. Then, we'll start jury selection for the assault case."

"How do you plan on getting these subpoenas delivered by Monday?" Lathan wanted to know.

Tyrone answered, "I'll deliver them myself."

"And where will you come up with a jury by Monday?"

"We'll use the same jury that we were gonna use in Robert Brooks' case."

"What about the media?"

"They'll be here."

***

"Right on time!" Tyrone said to Sara, who entered the building as he was on his way out.

"For what?" she asked as he handed her one of the envelopes he was carrying. She only glanced at it. "What's this?"

"Subpoena," he answered, not looking back as he made his exit.

***

Pulling into Apple Tree apartments, Tyrone pulled around to the rent office and parked. Getting out, carrying one of the envelopes, he approached the glass door and peered in.

There was an older black woman seated behind the desk, writing something down. Lifting her head and acknowledging him, she gestured for him to enter in which Tyrone obliged.

"Good morning!" she greeted.

"Good morning!" he responded, approaching the desk. "I'm assistant district attorney Tyrone Davis, and I was looking for one of your tenants. A Tonya Smith."

"She should be at work now," the woman informed. "She works at the Town Center Bank."

"I'm aware of that," Tyrone said, "but I don't have the time to go by there. Do you think that you can give this to her?"

"Sure," she answered, receiving the envelope. "I'm usually here when she gets in."

"Thank you."

"No problem. Are you the prosecutor that's handling her case?"

"Yes, I am."

"That Carlos was nothing but trouble!" The woman offered, shaking her head. "I've had tenants complain to me about him speeding through here at all kinds of odd hours, playing that loud music. He's even gotten into verbal disputes with a few tenants. I really didn't see what Tonya saw in him. He was—"

"I wish that I could use you as a character witness," he cut her off, not in the mood to chatter.

"What would I testify to?"

"His character. Everything you just told me."

"Oh!"

"It's too late to get you on the witness list," he told her, "but I have enough evidence."

***

"That's not true!"

"It is true, Mr. Lathan!" Ellen, who was seated opposite Lathan's desk, insisted. "You sit back and let Tyrone do and say whatever he wants!"

"You go along with everything as if *he's* the judge," Sara, who was seated beside Ellen, voiced. "Have you ever wondered why he's never lost a trial?"

"He's a good prosecutor."

"That's bull!" Ellen blurted.

Sara asked, "Who authorized this new calendar?"

"He did," Lathan answered.

"And you agreed to it?"

"Yes, I did."

"So," Sara went on, "he decided to push my trial to Monday, and you agreed to it?"

"That was all my doing."

"And why would you do that?"

"To go ahead and get that case out of the way," Lathan maintained.

"I don't believe that!" Ellen remained ornery. "You're scared of Tyrone!"

***

"You mean to tell me that you've never watched the sun set?" Bobby asked Tonya, who was seated across the table from him.

"No," she answered, taking a sip of her drink to wash down her tuna sandwich.

"That's not something you'd be into, huh?" He surmised.

"It's just something I've never had the chance to do."

"I mean," Bobby went on, "I'm no astrologist, or anything like that, but that's something I do to ease my mind."

"Does it work?"

"It does for me," he answered, glancing out of the large window, then back at her. "The sun's out today."

She smiled. "I see."

***

Judge Connie Edwards just finished with her lunch which was a portion of last night's pasta and was rummaging through her desk drawer for some white-out when someone knocked on her door. "Come in!"

The door opened and Danny Blake entered carrying a bouquet of colorful flowers. Closing the door back, he seemed to approach the desk with caution which had Connie a bit leery of his motives. "Are you busy?" He asked.

"Yes," she answered.

Danny held the flowers out to her. "I just wanted to give you these."

"For what?" Connie asked, regarding the flowers as if they were contagious.

"There was a guy out front, selling flowers—"

"And out of all the people in the world," she cut him off, "you decided to buy me some, right?"

"Right."

The judge narrowed her eyes at the big man standing before her. "Are you trying to court me, Mr. Blake?"

"N-No, ma'am," he stammered.

"Then, I cannot accept those," she replied, leaning back in her chair. "Please, close my door back on your way out."

"Yes, ma'am."

She watched Danny as he left, wondering why, after all these years, he would pull such a stunt. *What is he up to?*

***

Upon leaving Apple Tree apartments, Tyrone had a brief lunch at Burger King, then drove out to the county jail where he was now seated in the small visitation booth, when Carlos entered on the other side, looking as if he was expecting someone else.

"How's it going, Mr. West?"

"Man, why do you keep coming up here?"

Tyrone waved the envelope he was holding. "I have something for you."

"I don't have to tell you what to do with that, do I?" Carlos asked, folding his arms over his chest.

"Of course, not." Tyrone got to his feet. "I'll see you, Monday."

***

It was closing time, and Tonya was breaking her register down when Sharee approached with her pocket book, ready to make her exit.

"Well, I gotta go and pick up my baby," Sharee announced.

"Your child?" Tonya inquired.

"My boo," replied Sharee. "She runs my salon. You should stop by sometime. I'm not saying you need to, but I'm there on Saturdays and Sundays."

"Saturdays?"

132

"And Sundays."

"So, you don't work tomorrow?" Asked Tonya.

"Not here," answered Sharee. "I may eat for two, but I can't work for two."

Tonya laughed. "I hear you. I guess I'll see you Monday."

"Girl, stop by the shop!" Sharee prompted, pulling out one of her business cards and holding it out to her. "This is my shop and cell phone numbers. All we do is chill and gossip."

"I might check it out," Tonya said, accepting the card.

"Call and let me know," Sharee said, before making her exit.

***

"You mean to tell us that she came to see you after what she's done to you?" Sara asked, after Chris recounted Laura's untimely visit to her, Danny, and Ellen.

"Yeah," Chris answered.

"If that's not cold-hearted!" Ellen offered.

"Should we use that as evidence?" Asked Danny.

"We?" Chris replied. "Danny, you're the prosecutor, not the attorney for the defense."

"Danny has been trying to bond with Jude Edwards," Ellen said to Chris.

"Why?" Chris asked Danny

"Because," Danny went on to explain, "Tyrone said, in order for me to win cases, I'll have to have some kind of bond with the judge."

"Could you believe he brought her some funeral flowers?" Ellen asked, giggling.

Danny glowered at her. "They were not funeral flowers!"

"Danny, this is the wrong time to win cases," Chris told him

"Why?"

"Are you trying to send me to prison?"

"Of course not!"

"Then, save the Romeo and Juliet stuff until after my trial!"

***

It was shortly after 6PM and Tyrone was glad to be leaving his office at a decent time, being that he had a few errands to run before retiring to his home.

Now, after locking his office up, he, carrying his briefcase, was moving along the hallway when he encountered the head D.A. Avery Stewart, who looked like he hadn't slept in days.

"Mr. Davis?" Avery started, stopping Tyrone in his tracks. "What's with this assault case that was scheduled for trial on the eighth being pushed up to the first? I'm quite sure I didn't sign anything pertaining to that."

"Sure, you did," Tyrone answered, pulling folded documents from inside his blazer and handing them to him.

"I did not sign this!" Avery protested after viewing the documents. "You forged my name!"

"*You* forged your name," Tyrone insisted. "I just changed the date. Now, if you would excuse me." Tyrone deliberately snatched the papers from Avery's hand, then made for the elevators.

***

Tonya had taken Bobby up on his offer to watch the sunset with him, so, upon leaving the bank, they rode out to his favorite spot, which was a grassland, where they were now, sitting on a blanket, side by side, watching the sun as it slowly set over the small city.

"Now, that's a beautiful color!" Tonya commented, regarding the sky.

"That's what?" Bobby asked. "Orange, purple, and red?"

"The red looks more pinkish," she offered.

"Pinkish?" Bobby now regarded her. "What's that?"

"That means it looks more pink than red."

Bobby grinned. "So, if I look in a dictionary—"

"Shut up!"

"Yes, ma'am!"

They looked at each other for a moment before bursting into laughter.

***

Tyrone pulled up to Wayne Griffin's house and blew the horn. Moments later, Wayne exited the house carrying a black gym bag.

Climbing in beside Tyrone he placed the bag on his lap. "This is everything," Wayne informed, patting the bag.

"Hold on!" Tyrone reached under his seat and produced the same scanner Wayne was scanned with on their first visit.

"You don't trust me?" Wayne asked, sounding surprised.

"Nope," he answered curtly, running the scanner over the bag. "Toss it in the back!"

Wayne did as he was told.

"Hold still!" Tyrone ordered, then ran the device over Wayne's body. "Alright"

"That's it?"

"Yeah," Tyrone answered, slipping the scanner back under the seat.

"You don't wanna count it?"

"I will."

"So, it's over, right?"

"Yeah," answered Tyrone. "You're done."

***

"I just need someone who can get close to Tyrone," Chris was telling Danny, Ellen, and Sara, who were still visiting him.

"How close?" Asked Ellen.

"Close enough to record him admitting his involvement in this case," he answered.

"Danny," Sara offered, jerking her thumb in his direction.

"Me!" Danny cried out.

"You two are always hanging together," Ellen pointed out.

Danny contradicted, "Not always."

"He wouldn't tell Danny," Chris acknowledged. "I think he would tell Sara, before either of you. Sara?"

"Trust me," Sara replied, "we are not on good terms."

"You don't have to be," Chris told her.

***

Upon leaving the visitation with Chris, Danny bidded Ellen and Sara a good night, then headed home. Ellen decided to accompany Sara to her visit with Carlos, being that she was not yet ready to turn in this early on a Friday.

"That would be the best thing to do, Mr. West," Ellen now said to him.

"My mind is already made!" He replied, shaking his head.

Ellen nodded. "I can't argue with that."

"And how was he able to change the dates like that?" Carlos wanted to know.

Ellen answered, "He pretty much does what he wants. The judge is afraid of him. The head D.A. probably doesn't know what's going on."

"Are you taking the stand?" Sara finally asked.

"Should I?"

"Some jurors would like to hear from the accused," she told him, "but my advice would be not to take the stand. Mr. Davis will try his best to trip you. And, once he does, he'll make you seem like the biggest liar and the biggest criminal on this planet."

***

Finally making it home, Tyrone entered the house, re-set the alarm, then entered the living room where Lisa was sitting on the sofa, holding an open dictionary in her hand, and Ebony was seated on the floor, on the opposite side of the table, facing her.

"Okay," Lisa was saying, "spell ubiquitous."

Ebony compiled, "U-B-I-Q-U-I-T-O-U-S."

"Now spell it backwards!" Tyrone said, approaching the table.

Ebony looked up, smiling at her father, displaying prominent features of her mother.

"Spell it backwards!" He repeated.

She tried. "S-U-T, I mean—"

"Try it again!" he prompted, shooting a glance over at Lisa, who looked as if she, too, was anticipating the outcome.

Ebony gave it another try. "S-U-O-T-I-U-Q-I-B-U."

Tyrone smiled. "That's my girl! Give daddy a hug!" She stood and embraced him, as he did her. "Now, gone and prepare for your bath. I need to talk to your mom."

"Okay."

"So, the house goes to you, right?" Tyrone asked once Ebony left the room.

"I just need the house and my car," Lisa answered, placing the dictionary on the coffee table. "You can have everything else."

"What about Ebony?"

"Are you going for a custody battle?" She asked.

"I'm trying to settle everything now so we can breeze through court," he told her.

"Joint custody."

"I agree," he said. "Child support?"

"No."

"You don't want child support?"

"I'm quite sure you'll still take care of your daughter," Lisa asserted.

Tyrone nodded. "We'll have to sit her down and explain everything to her before we go to court."

"Or, after court."

***

Driving his red Range Rover, Wayne Griffin was returning home from picking up his five-year-old daughter, Crystal, who was going to spend the weekend with him and his girlfriend, Niecy. Parking in his driveway, he unbuckled Crystal's safety belt, got out, and allowed her to climb across the seat to help her down. Then, she followed him to the rear of the truck where he opened the rear compartment, pulled out her pink bookbag, and handed it to her. Putting it over her back, she started for the house where Niecy just stepped out onto the porch.

"Hey, Chrystal!" Niecy beamed.

"Hey, Niecy!"

Wayne was pulling Crystal's bike from the truck when, for some reason, he looked to his right and spotted a dark-colored Buick Regal slowly approaching, with the lights off. On instinct, he thought about his daughter and looked to see that she had stopped to tie her shoe.

"Crystal!" He let out, dropping the bike and racing towards her.

The car, which was occupied by two masked men, sped up. The passenger hung a Mack-10 out of the window and squeezed the trigger. Bullets penetrated Wayne's back as he tackled his daughter, lying on top of her. Niecy was still standing on the porch, scream-ing.

The car stopped, and the passenger got out, reloading the gun. He approached Wayne, who was regarding him with blood running from his mouth.

"Don't hurt my baby!" he said, coughing up more blood.

The gunman rolled him off of Crystal who was crying, pulled her to her feet, and pushed her towards the house.

"Come here, Crystal!" Niecy beckoned for her.

Disregarding Niecy, Crystal turned back to the scene. "Daddy!"

"Go, Crystal!" Wayne bellowed.

"Come on, Crystal!" Niecy tried again.

Reluctantly, while still looking back, Crystal made it up the steps to Niecy, who grabbed her, and buried the child's face in her chest to keep her from witnessing what was about to take place.

Now, lying on his back, Wayne shifted his attention from his family and looked up at the gunman, who was standing over him with the gun aimed at his face. He didn't know where the heat was coming from, but he knew that it would, one day, come. Wayne also knew that when it came, he was not going to beg for his life, but die the same way he chose to live.

Like a soldier!

Wayne spat blood on the man's pants' leg. "I'm ready!"

The gunman squeezed the trigger, injecting slugs into Wayne's cranium until the cartridge was empty. He, then, looked up at Niecy and Crystal who were both now looking and crying. Turning, he trotted back to the awaiting car, and they sped off.

Chapter 17

Making it to the Reids' ranch, Laura pulled her BMW up to the house, parking behind the beige pick-up. Dismounting, she climbed the steps to the porch and knocked on the door.

While waiting on a response, she turned around and took stock of the ranch that bathed under the sun's dazzling glow in spite of the light, wintry breeze, which was making its presence known at that very moment. That's when she spied Mrs. Reid inside the barn, clad in a long, wool cloak, and large, straw hat, tending to the animals. Laura descended the steps, and crossed over to the barn, where she entered, and approached the older woman, who was petting a brown horse that was feeding from a feeding bag. "Mrs. Reid?"

"Yes?" Mrs. Reid faced Laura, not seeming a bit startled that someone had come up from behind her.

Laura said, "I'm Laura. Christopher's friend. Remember me?"

"I don't think so," she answered, studying the young woman standing before her.

"You gave me this," Laura said, pulling the pocket watch from her pocketbook and handing it to her.

"Oh!" Mrs. Reid exclaimed. "I remember. Lori, right?"

"Yes, ma'am," Laura went along, considering the woman's mental condition.

"You take good care of this, Lori!" she said, handing the watch back.

"Yes, ma'am!"

"Where's Christopher?"

"He said to tell you that he couldn't make it," Laura asserted what she'd been rehearsing since the inauguration of her plan to revisit the ranch.

"He'd usually come by and help me feed the animals." Mrs. Reid sounded discontented. "I have to plant some tomatoes today."

"That's why he sent me," Laura said. "To help you with whatever you need help with."

Mrs. Reid studied her for a moment before asking, "Do you know anything about crops?"

"Not yet."

***

"I don't know why they changed it to Monday," Tonya told her mother, who was seated beside her on the sofa.

Although it was Saturday, and Tonya was supposed to be at work, the manager gave her the day off, making plans to come by later to take her to an evening bar.

"Are you going?" Tonya's mother asked.

"I have to."

"You don't have to," said her father, who was seated in the recliner.

"Shut up, Joseph!" His wife turned on him.

He shrugged. "I'm just saying."

"Don't be saying! Let my daughter do what's right!"

"She's my daughter, too, Tierra."

Tierra turned back to her daughter. "Tonya, do you need me to come with you?"

Tonya shook her head. "No. This is my situation."

"You're right," her mother deferred, patting her on the knee. "But, if you change your mind, let me know ahead of time, okay?"

"Okay, Momma."

***

It was almost dark out. After planting crops and tending to the animals, Laura and Mrs. Reid made it back to the house, where Mrs. Reid fixed them a light meal. Now, they were both standing on the front porch conversing as Laura was preparing to leave.

"So, why don't you have a telephone, Mrs. Reid?" Laura was inquiring.

"Because, I enjoy peace and quiet," she answered. "I don't even know how to operate those things."

"You do live a peaceful life up here," Laura said, relishing the way the barn looked in the light of the moon and stars, and the surrounding quietness of the place. "I think I'd be scared to live here all by myself."

140

"Scared of what?"

Laura shrugged. "I don't know. I guess I would have to get used to this kind of environment."

At that time, they spotted a dark-colored Dodge Durango making its way up the gravel road. Momentarily, it docked behind Laura's car.

After killing the engine, Kevin got out, and retrieved a large paper bag full of groceries from the back, then climbed the steps, regarding Laura's dirty clothing and the bruise on the left side of her face. "Hey, Mom!" He greeted his mother.

"Hey, Kevin!"

"Who is this?" He asked, regarding Laura.

"Oh! This is Lisa," Mrs. Reid answered. "Christopher's friend. She came by to help me with the ranch."

"Hi!" Laura held her hand out.

"Hi!" Kevin returned, shaking her hand.

"Mrs. Reid, I have to get home and change these clothes," said Laura, who did not expect to encounter Christopher's brother.

"Okay, baby. Thank you!"

"You're welcome!"

They watched as she descended the steps and got into her car. While making a U-turn and driving in the opposite direction on the uneven road, Laura was hoping that Kevin didn't mention their encounter to his brother which would not be good at all.

***

The following day, after placing a call to Sharee, Tonya showered, got dressed, ate lunch, and drove out to Sharee Styles, which was the name of Sharee's salon. Pulling into the plaza, she parked and got out, wearing red capri pants, black Air Force Ones, a black t-shirt, a black ball cap with a red 'T' on the front of it, and a pair of gold-framed Gucci sunglasses.

Clutching her purse, she crossed the lot and entered the salon that had five stations that were opposite the waiting area, where other women awaited.

At the first station, Sharee was seated, talking to a light complexioned female with blonde micro-braids pulled into a ponytail. "It's about time you got here!" Sharee now regarded Tonya.

"I had to take care of some business," Tonya told her.

"There's a reason why I'm sitting in this chair."

"And, what reason is that?"

Sharee stood. "So that you can receive this miracle healing! Take off that hat, and have a seat! This is my girl, Jasmine," she said, indicating the blonde. "Jasmine, this is Tonya."

They shook hands.

"You can meet everybody else later," said Sharee. "Have a seat! It's on the house."

***

Tyrone pulled his car up to the entrance of a small corner store. Dismounting, he activated his alarm, then headed inside, passing two, hard-looking guys who were leaning against the side of the store, giving him foul looks.

Inside, an older white male was behind the counter, ringing the orders of two black females. Therefore, Tyrone browsed around until the women left. He then moved over to the door, locked it, and turned the OPEN/CLOSED sign to CLOSED. The owner came from behind the counter and Tyrone followed him to a small storage room where there were neatly stacked boxes, and a small table that was surrounded by three metal chairs.

Tyrone took a seat in one of the chairs while the owner, A.J., retrieved a small box in which he opened, and poured a bundle of bills onto the table.

"It's real," A.J. said, seeing the way Tyrone was just staring at the money.

Tyrone finally looked up. "I saw two, unprofessional-looking bodyguards outside. Yours?"

"Oh! That's Rock and Kenny. They're my runners."

"That's exactly what they'll be doing the next time they squeeze their faces up at me like that again!" Tyrone threatened.

"They're young, Tyrone," A.J. offered. "They don't mean any harm."

"We'll see."

"I'll handle that," the forty-seven-year-old man promised. "Right now, I have a problem that needs to be solved."

"What is it?"

A.J. took a deep breath before asserting, "Carla has a boyfriend, and she's the only one thrilled about it."

"How old is Carla?" Tyrone wanted to know.

"Sixteen."

"Well, A.J.," Tyrone started, "according to the law she's legal."

"Well, according to her father, she's off limits!" he shot back. "How old is this kid?"

"Seventeen," answered A.J. "Hell, he looks twenty! Tyrone, I don't want my daughter having children at a young age."

"Yeah," said Tyrone, nodding. "I'm quite sure Romeo's not shooting dog water."

"Can you handle this for me?"

"What about your runners?"

"I need professional assistance."

"I don't know, A.J.," Tyrone said, shaking his head. "This is a kid we're talking about."

After regarding Tyrone for a few seconds, A.J. tossed the box he was holding, grabbed another box, opened it, and poured another bundle of money on the table.

"What's that?" Tyrone asked.

"Twenty."

"And, what am I supposed to do with this kid?"

A.J. looked Tyrone in his eyes. "The same thing you'd do if it was *your* daughter.

***

It had gotten dark, and Tyrone, now wearing dark clothing, was standing by a water fountain that was stopped up and filled with water. At that time, he saw the black van pull into the park. He looked around, then pulled out a two-way radio. "It's clear," he spoke into it.

"Got it," came his response.

The van turned onto the grass and slowly moved toward Tyrone with its lights off. Putting the radio up, Tyrone donned a ski mask just as the van which was driven by Charles, stopped in front of him.

Charles cut the engine and was getting out, just as the side door slid open, where Block and another guy with cornrows got out, carrying handguns. Block pulled a young, white male from the van who was blindfolded, gagged, and hands bound behind him. Tyrone nodded at his men who all donned their ski masks in response.

"Blindfold," he said, and Block removed the material from the eyes of the kid who looked as if he'd been crying. "Listen to me carefully," Tyrone told the kid. "I'm going to remove the gag. If you scream, you die. Understood?"

The kid nodded.

Tyrone nodded and Block removed the gag. "What's your name?" Tyrone asked him.

"Brad."

"Do you know a girl by the name of Carla?"

The boy shot him a quizzical look. "Yeah."

"Your girlfriend?"

"Yeah."

"How old are you, Brad?"

"Sixteen."

"He's dehydrated," Tyrone told Block.

Block forced the kid over to the fountain and pushed his head into the water. Tyrone was looking at his watch while Brad put up an effortless struggle.

"Let him up!" Tyrone ordered.

Block let the kid up and turned him to face Tyrone. By now Brad was panting.

"I know how dehydration can make a person say anything," Tyrone told him. "So, we'll try this again. How old are you?"

"Eighteen."

"Are you lying to me, again?"

"No, sir!" Brad answered sincerely.

"Are you and Carla having sex?"

Brad didn't respond.

144

"We're losing him, again," Tyrone told Block.

Brad let out a yelp as Block forced his head back into the water. The other two men were looking around.

Tyrone gandered at his watch and realized he couldn't stay at this much longer. "I gotta get up in the morning," he said. "Let him up!"

Block brought the kid up.

"Are you and Carla having sex?" Tyrone tried again.

"Yes, sir."

"Use protection?"

"No, sir."

"No protection, huh?" Tyrone held his hand out to Block who handed over his gun. Tyrone placed the barrel up to Brad's penis and poked at it as he spoke. "Stay away from Carla!" He said. "If I find out you're still seeing her, I'll shoot this off. Understood?"

"Yes, sir."

Tyrone tilted the barrel toward the ground and let off a shot. Brad cried out and almost buckled, but Block held him up. Charles and the other guy were still looking around.

"Shut up!" Tyrone told the kid. "I missed. I won't miss the next time. You got me?"

"Yes, sir," Brad answered, trying to muffle his cry.

"What's that smell?" Tyrone asked, eyeing the kid. "You messed on yourself?"

"Yes, sir."

"Take the cuffs off!" He told Block, who did as he was told. Tyrone wrinkled his nose at Brad. "You stink! Go home and shower!"

"Yes, sir," Brad answered, rubbing his sore wrists. "Can I have my bike back, sir?"

"What bike?" Tyrone asked, looking around at his men.

The guy by the van reached into the cargo area, pulled out a mountain bike, and tossed it to the ground.

"Do you know your way home from here?" Tyrone asked.

"Yes, sir," Brad answered, sagely approaching his bike.

"Be careful!" Tyrone told him, handing Block his gun back.

They watched as Brad collected his bicycle, and made off without looking back. Tyrone doffed his mask, and the others followed suit. He, then, regarded the light-complexioned man with cornrows.

"Rick?"

"Yeah?" He answered.

"Let me see your phone!"

Rick extracted his cellular from his pocket, and entered his passcode, before tossing it to Tyrone, who dialed a phone number he drew up from memory.

"Hello?" A female's voice came through.

"May I speak to Ms. Tonya Smith?"

"Speaking."

"This is Mr. Tyrone Davis," he told her. "The prosecutor on your case. Did you get the new subpoena over the weekend?"

"I got it."

"Okay. I was calling to let you know that you don't have to get up so early. The subpoena says nine, but we'll be doing jury selection and that takes hours. Get there around one, or one-thirty.

"Okay?"

Concluding the call, Tyrone tossed the phone back to its owner. "Erase that number!"

Chapter 18

It was Monday, and Tyrone was more than ready to get Carlos West's trial underway, but it was still early, and he had to handle Robert Brooks' plea and arraignment, first.

Judge Lathan was already on the bench. Tyrone and Michelle Johnson were seated at the defense table. Behind her, on the first row, sat Sara Jennings and Robert Brooks' father.

At that time, Robert Brooks, in the jail-issued jumpsuit, was escorted in by the bailiff and took a seat beside his attorney.

"Good morning, Mr. Brooks!" Judge Lathan greeted the inmate.

"Good morning!" he returned.

"I understand that you're here to take a plea. Am I right?"

Robert nodded. "Yes, sir."

The judge leveled his gaze on the young man. "You do understand that you're charged with one count of rape and one count of false imprisonment, right?"

"Yes, sir."

"Did anyone threaten you into taking this plea?"

"No, sir."

"Okay." Lathan looked over at the State's table. "State, what's your offer?"

"Ten years to serve eight, Your Honor," Johnson took the initiative.

Lathan switched his gaze, again. "Does the defendant wish to withdraw his plea?"

"Your Honor," Ellen spoke up, "the plea was supposed to be for eight years."

"And, it still is," Tyrone pitched in.

"One moment, Your Honor," Ellen said, before turning and having a brief, private conversation with her client. Then, turning back to the judge, she said, "Your Honor, my client accepts the deal."

Lathan nodded. "And I accept the plea, and, hereby sentence the defendant, Robert Brooks, to ten years to serve eight, on one count of rape and one count of false imprisonment." He banged his gavel, solidifying his ruling.

After Brooks said something into Ellen's ear, she regarded the judge again. "Your Honor? My client wants to know if the court would grant him permission to hug his father."

"I don't see why not," Lathan replied, shifting his gaze. "Any objections from the State?"

Michelle looked at Tyrone, pretty much leaving the decision up to him. He looked over at Ellen, who slightly tilted her head as if to prompt him to agree.

"No objections," Tyrone finally replied. "Under the condition that the civilian be searched for anything that can be used as a weapon or serve as a means to escape."

"Does the defendant and father agree to that?" The judge asked.

Ellen looked back at Mr. Brooks. He nodded. "Yes, Your Honor," Ellen answered.

"Well, make it quick!" Lathan told them. "We have a trial this morning."

***

It was 12:52PM when Tonya entered the Linkton County Courthouse. After clearing the security checkpoint, which only took about seven minutes, she was allowed to access the elevators. Judge Lathan's courtroom was on the third floor, according to the subpoena she received from her landlord, Mrs. Baxter, this past Friday.

Outside the appointed courtroom sat two, black, uniformed police officers— one male; one female. Unaccustomed to the procedures of anything pertaining to the judicial system, Tonya didn't know if she should have a seat on the bench with the officers or knock on the wooden doors of the courtroom, and announce her arrival.

"Are they still doing jury selection?" Tonya asked the officers.

"Yeah," the female officer answered, regarding Tonya with a look of uncertainty. "Are you Tonya Smith?"

"Yeah, that's me."

She smiled up at Tonya. "You're pretty!"

"Huh?" Tonya was taken aback by the capricious statement.

"I'm Officer McKenzie," she told Tonya, "and this is my partner, Officer Allen. We were the ones who responded to the call. Allen pulled your boyfriend off of you, but you were already unconscious."

"Thanks!" Was all Tonya could come up with.

"Hell, I pulled him off of you," Allen added, "then turned around and had to pull her off of him."

"I tried to kill his ass!" McKenzie declared, making a face. "I hate a man who beats women! I hope he gets the gas chamber!"

"He won't get the gas chamber, McKenzie," her partner tried to reason.

"You really pulled through," McKenzie told Tonya. "It's good you showed up for this. Don't let him get off that easy!"

At that time, the door to the courtroom came open, and a great number of people came pouring out of it. Tonya stepped out of their way to keep from being trampled as they mobbed towards the elevators.

"I guess they're done," said McKenzie.

***

Inside the courtroom, Carlos, who was dressed in a suit and tie, was seated next to his attorney, Sara Jennings, at the defense table. Ellen was seated on the bench behind them. Fourteen jurors— twelve, plus two alternates— were seated in the jury box.

At the rear of the courtroom, camera crews from three local news stations were set up. Assistant D.A. Michelle Johnson occupied the State's table, while Tyrone was standing at the lectern, doing a direct examination on officer McKenzie, who was on the witness stand.

"Officer McKenzie," Tyrone was saying, "what happened when you arrived on the scene?"

"When I and my partner arrived on the scene," she began, "we saw that the apartment door was standing wide open. We heard rustling in the back of—"

"Let me stopyou there," Tyrone interrupted, holding a hand up. "Now, when you say 'rustling', what do you mean by that?"

"It sounded like someone was being beaten."

"Did you hear any screaming?"

Sara Jennings was on her feet. "Objection, Your Honor!"

"Under what grounds?" Judge Lathan inquired.

"He's misleading the witness," Sara answered.

"Sustained," Lathan ruled.

"Thank you, Your Honor!" Sara gave before re-taking her seat.

"You may continue, officer," Tyrone told the witness.

"Hearing the rustling," she resumed, "we drew our guns, and entered with caution. Entering one of the rooms, we observed the victim, Tonya Smith, being beaten by her boyfriend with a gun."

"Do you see the alleged suspect anywhere in this courtroom?"

"Yes, I do."

"Can you point him out, and tell me what he's wearing?"

Officer McKenzie pointed towards the defense table. "He's right there, wearing a gray suit and red tie."

Tyrone looked to the judge. "Let the record reflect that the witness has identified Carlos West."

"Reflected," Lathan responded.

"Officer McKenzie," Tyrone went on, "was the victim unconscious when you—"

"Objection!" Sara interrupted. "Misleading the witness."

"Sustained," Lathan ruled.

Tyrone shot the judge an evil look before continuing. "Officer, what was the condition of the victim at this time?"

"She was unconscious," McKenzie answered, "and her face—"

"Let me stop you there," Tyrone said, before crossing over to his table where Michelle handed him some papers. He took them over to Sara who viewed them and handed them back. He, then, returned to the lectern. "Your Honor, I would like to publish these photos into evidence."

"Any objections from the defense?" The judge inquired.

Sara Jennings got to her feet. "Yes, Your Honor. The photos are of the victim after the attack. The contents are, well, gruesome, and could cause the jury to be bias against the defendant before hearing the rest of the case."

"Your Honor," Tyrone spoke in his own defense, "this jury was sworn in to have a fair and impartial mind to all evidence and testimonies."

"That's true, Ms. Jennings," Lathan offered. "At this time, I'm going to overrule your objection. Photos are admitted."

Sara re-took her seat. Tyrone took the photos over to Michelle who began marking them one by one with evidence stickers.

"You should have taken a plea," Sara whispered to Carlos, who didn't bother to respond.

Receiving the photos from Michelle, Tyrone approached officer McKenzie. "I'm going to show you what's been masked as State's exhibits one through four," he said, handing the items to her. "Can you tell the court what you're looking at?"

She answered, "I'm looking at photo copies of the victim, Tonya Smith, right after the assault."

"Can you describe to the jury—"

Sara was back on her feet. "Objection! Your Honor, there's no need for...—It's not this witness' place to testify, or construe the contents of those photos, considering that she's not the developer, nor did she have anything to do with those items."

"Objection sustained," the judge replied. "The jurors will get a chance to view all evidence at deliberation. State, you may continue."

Receiving the photos from McKenzie, Tyrone took them over to the table and handed them to Michelle. He, then, picked up a Ziploc bag containing a black handgun with dried blood on it, and took it over to Sara who regarded it with a nod.

Tyrone turned to the judge. "Your Honor, I would like to publish this item into evidence."

"Any objections from the defense?" Lathan asked.

"No, Your Honor," answered Sara.

"Item is admitted."

Once Michelle labeled the item, Tyrone returned to the lectern with it. "Officer McKenzie," he spoke, holding the bag up, "I'm showing you what's been marked as State's exhibit five. Can you tell me what it is?"

"A black handgun," she answered. "Glock nine."

"Can you tell me anything about this particular weapon?"

"It's the weapon that was used to assault the victim."

"Was she shot by this weapon?" Tyrone posed for clarification.

"No. She was beaten repeatedly with it."

He turned to the judge. "Your Honor, may I approach the witness?"

"You may," Lathan answered.

Tyrone approached, holding the Ziploc just inches away from her face. "Officer, there's some kind of dried-up substance on this weapon. Can you tell the court what that is?"

"The victim's blood," she responded.

"Thank you! No further questions."

Judge Lathan looked to the defense table. "Cross?"

"Yes, Your Honor," answered Sara.

Tyrone returned to his table, as the defense attorney approached the lectern.

"Officer McKenzie," she spoke, "I am Sara Jennings, counsel for the defendant, Carlos West. Were you the arresting officer?"

"Yes," McKenzie answered.

"Can you recall there being any marks or bruises on Mr. West?"

"Yes."

"Any idea where they may have come from?"

"Objection!" Tyrone intervened from his seat.

"Under what grounds?" inquired Lathan.

"Your Honor," Tyrone started, "it doesn't matter what kind of bumps or bruises Mr. West may have sustained from this ordeal. He is not the victim in this case."

"Objection sustained."

"Nothing further, Your Honor," Sara said, then made for her table.

"Re-direct?" Asked Lathan.

"No, Your Honor," answered Tyrone.

"May this witness be released?"

"Yes, Your Honor."

"Officer, you may step down," Lathan told McKenzie. "State, call your next witness."

"Your Honor," Tyrone spoke, "I was going to call Officer Allen but Ms. Jennings and I decided that we won't need him. Therefore, the State calls the victim, Tonya Smith."

***

Seated outside the courtroom, Tonya and officer Allen were engaged in conversation when the door opened, and officer McKenzie exited followed by the bailiff.

"They won't be needing you, Officer Allen," the bailiff apprised. "Ms. Smith, they're waiting on you."

Tonya and Allen got to their feet.

"Are you nervous?" McKenzie asked Tonya.

"Yeah."

"Just relax. You do know they got the news in there, right?"

"Yeah," Tonya answered, wishing McKenzie hadn't reminded her that this trial was going to be aired on national television.

"You can do it," McKenzie told her. "Do it for the women that never got the chance to face their attacker. And most of those women are dead."

McKenzie's words were still lingering in Tonya's mental as the bailiff ushered her into the courtroom and up to the stand. Carlos was watching her, and Tyrone was watching him. When Carlos finally shifted his gaze to the State's table, Tyrone winked at him.

"Direct?" The judge said, after Tonya was sworn in.

Knowing it was on him, Tyrone got up and approached the lectern. "Ms. Smith," he began, "I'm Assistant District Attorney Tyrone Davis, and I'm going to take you back to October twenty-third of last year. Did anything unusual happen on that date?"

"Yes," Tonya answered in a low tone.

"What happened?"

"I was assaulted."

"Who were you assaulted by?"

"My boyfriend at the time."

"Is that person in this courtroom?"

There was a moment's pause before she answered, "Yes."

"Can you point him out and tell me what he's wearing?"

Finally, Tonya was able to chance a glance at the defense table without making eye contact with Carlos as she pointed. "Right there, wearing a gray suit."

Tyrone regarded the judge. "Let the record reflect that the witness has identified Carlos West."

"Reflected," Lathan responded.

"Ms. Smith," Tyrone resumed, "could you tell the court how the assault took place?"

"I was at home," Tonya explained. "Carlos showed up, drunk. He was constantly accusing me of cheating on him. I ..."

As a show of compassion, Tyrone waited while she struggled to keep her composure, whereas she retrieved tissue from her purse to dab at the tears streaming down her face.

"You say that he was drunk?" Tyrone finally asked.

"Yes."

"Go on!"

"He searched my apartment," she went on, "looking to see if anyone was there."

"What was his attitude at this time?" Tyrone wanted to know.

"Angry. Furious."

"Go on!"

"I was telling him to sit down, and calm down, but he wouldn't listen."

"That's when he assaulted you?"

"Yes."

Moving over to his table, Tyrone grabbed the Ziploc bag containing the gun, holding it up for Tonya to see. "Ms. Smith, this is States exhibit five," he told her. "Can you tell me what it is?"

"A gun," she answered.

"Can you tell me anything about this gun?"

"It's the gun he used to beat me with."

"When you say 'he', who are you referring to?"

"Carlos West."

"Thank you! Nothing further."

"Cross?" Judge Lathan inquired.

Again, Tyrone returned to his seat as Sara Jennings approached the podium.

"Ms. Smith," she began, "I'm attorney Sara Jennings, and I'm representing the defendant, Carlos West. You say, at the time of the incident, you and the defendant were in a relationship. Am I correct?"

Tonya nodded. "Yes."

"How long were you two together?"

"For almost six years."

"During this relationship," said Sara, "until October of last year, have you two ever had a physical altercation?"

"No."

"So, the relationship was fine until October twenty-third of last year?"

"Yes."

Shifting her weight, Sara rested a hand on her hip and a forearm on the flat surface of the lectern. "Besides Carlos being intoxicated at that time," she spoke, "was there anything else that could have triggered this attack?"

"I don't know what you're saying," Tonya replied with a confused look on her face.

"Scratch that!" Sara told her. "When Carlos showed up at your apartment that night, how did he get in?"

"I let him in."

"Was there anyone else in your apartment that night?"

Tyrone was on his feet. "Objection! That question is irrelevant to this case."

"Sustained," replied the judge.

"Ms. Smith," Sara resumed as Tyrone re-took his seat. "My client received... Never mind. Nothing further."

"Re-direct?" Lathan asked.

"Nothing, Your Honor," answered Tyrone.

"May this witness be released?"

"She may."

Lathan regarded Tonya. "Ms. Smith, you are released. What we're about to do now is decide on if we're going to do closing arguments." Then, as if remembering something, he looked over at the defense table. "I'm sorry, Ms. Jennings! Does the defendant wish to take the stand?"

"No, Your Honor," she answered.

"Then, I suppose we can discuss this now," Lathan went on. "How long will both parties need for closing arguments?"

"Considering this is not a big case," Sara spoke up, "we really won't need too long. Five to ten minutes for the defense."

Lathan looked to Tyrone. "State?"

"Ten," he answered.

"So, we should be done with this case today, right?"

"We should," answered Tyrone.

Lathan regarded his watch. "Okay. It's two-eighteen. I'll let you all break for an hour and thirty. Everyone should be back here and seated at three forty-eight. Ms. Smith, it's totally up to you if you want to come back for the remainder of the trial."

"Okay," Tonya replied, getting to her feet.

Carlos watched her as she made for the exit with her head down. Not once did she look in his direction. However, he was done with trying to figure out what caused Tonya to change her mind about not testifying against him. No matter how specific he was in his warnings, she still allowed herself to be threatened into showing up.

***

In the restroom of the courthouse, Tonya exited one of the stalls and approached one of the sinks. After washing and drying her hands, she just stood there, staring at herself in the large mirror. She didn't know what to think of herself at that moment. She loved Carlos, but… Tears streamed down her face.

At that time, the restroom door swung open. Tonya wiped at her tears, trying to get herself together as she glimpsed through the mirror at Sara Jennings and Ellen Martinez, who were now approaching her.

"Are you okay?" asked Sara.

"Yeah, I'm fine," Tonya lied, still regarding the mirror.

"He really believed in you," Sara told her. "It's none of my business why you had this sudden change of heart, but I understand. I really do."

Now, Tonya turned to face the woman. "Could you tell him something for me?"

"Sure."

"Could you tell him that this was something I had to do?"

Sara studied her for a few seconds before answering. "Sure, I'll do that."

Without another word, Tonya passed between them and made her exit, leaving the two women exchanging puzzled looks.

***

Back inside the courtroom, Tyrone, Michelle and Sara were seated at their respective tables. Ellen was back in her same seat, but was now accompanied by Danny Blake, and Tonya made sure to plant herself on the back row, near the entrance.

While the news crews and others in attendance were chattering amongst each other, Judge Lathan emerged from his chambers.

"All rise!" The bailiff spouted. "The Honorable—"

"Remain seated!" Lathan cut him off. "Is everybody here?"

"All jurors are back," the bailiff answered. "The defendant is in the holding cell."

"Well, we have to bring the defendant in, first."

The bailiff made for the side door, using his key to enter.

Lathan regarded the attorneys. "Do we have any notions, or anything that should be brought to the attention of the court?"

"No, Your Honor," Tyrone and Sara answered in unison.

"Well," he said, finally taking his seat, "let's get this show on the road!"

The side door came open, and the bailiff brought in Carlos, who spotted Tonya in the rear. Only holding his gaze for a brief moment, she dropped her head. Once Carlos had taken a seat beside his attorney, the bailiff crossed over to the juror's room. Seconds later, the jury members entered, taking their seats.

"Ladies and gentlemen," Lathan started when they were all seated, "this part of the trial is called closing argument. The State and the defense counsel will come up, one at a time, and argue their case to you. Then, you all will be further instructed and sent back to deliberate. State?"

Tyrone got up, rounded the table, and stood in the center of the room, facing the jury. "Ladies and gentlemen," he began, "this is not a hard case to decide. You've heard from the victim. You've seen the evidence. It doesn't take a rocket scientist. That's all I'll say for now. I'll let Ms. Jennings come up and give you all the reasons why her client shouldn't be convicted of a crime that he was caught committing."

"Defense?" Lathan called out.

Satisfied with the seed he'd planted in the minds of the jurors, Tyrone headed back to his table as Sara made her way to the center of the room to address the members.

"Ladies and gentlemen of the jury," she spoke. "My client is charged with aggravated assault—a charge he should not be charged with. Why? Well, on the day of the commission of this crime, my client and the victim were a couple. True enough, Ms. Smith was beaten unconsciously, but Mr. West also received a few bumps and bruises. In a case like this, both parties are arrested and charged with domestic violence—not aggravated assault.

"I can't dispute the officer's testimony of the gun, which brought the possession of a firearm charge. It may have been his gun. At the same time, it may have *not* been his gun. There have been cases where officers of the law were found guilty of planting weapons on people, to cover up something they've done. I'm not saying that it happened in this case, but it has happened.

"As for the burglary charge, my client shouldn't be charged with burglary, unless he had broken into Ms. Smith's apartment. She testified today that she let him in. I'm not trying to convince you that a crime was not committed. I'm trying to show you that my client did not commit these particular crimes. Thank you!"

She retreated to her table as Tyrone got up to conduct his final statement, in which he did while pacing back and forth before the jury.

"Like I said, ladies and gentlemen," he plunged in. "She gave all the reasons why her client should not be found guilty for crimes he was caught committing. Now, let's run this down: Domestic violence, indeed, is a charge that couples get when they have a skirmish of some sort. Not when a weapon is involved! If a weapon is used, it's aggravated assault. Also, domestic means 'of the family, or household'. Mr. West is not of the family, and was never of the household. His name was not on the lease. That's how he was charged with burglary.

"I won't even waste my time talking about the gun situation. Officer McKenzie testified that, when she and her partner arrived on the scene, Ms. Smith was still being beaten by this psycho!" He made sure to point in the defendant's direction. "With the same gun you've seen in this trial. The one with Ms. Smith's blood dried up on. She was unconscious, and he was still beating her. He should've been charged with attempted murder!

"You should never judge a book by its cover. You know why? Look at this guy. He looks harmless. He's an animal! He preys on women! He beats women! Tonya Smith was not his first victim. The other women were too terrified to report his behavior to the authorities. Had it not been for her neighbors, Tonya probably would not have reported him.

"What do you think will happen if you let this animal off the hook? He'll hunt Tonya down and finish the job. Show Tonya that you care enough about her to protect her. All you have to do is go into the jury room and find him guilty. Then, we'll put this animal where he belongs—in a cage! Thank you!"

***

After the jurors were charged on how to proceed with the case, and sent to the jury room to deliberate, Tyrone remembered that he had to call Jackie, and made for his office, where he was now seated behind his desk, talking to her on his cell phone. "I don't know," Tyrone was saying. "We'll discuss that when we find out what it is."

"Okay," her voice flowed sweetly through the device. "Can you come by tonight? I miss you."

"I can do that."

"What time should I expect you?"

"Around seven-thirty," he answered, just as someone knocked on his door. "I'll see you then."

"Okay."

"Come in!" Tyrone called out after concluding his call.

The door came open and Danny entered with a simper on his face. He closed the door back, crossed the room, and sat down across from Tyrone, who didn't know what to make of his co-worker's visage.

"What's up?" Tyrone ventured, placing his phone down in front of him.

"I tilt my hat to you!" Danny told him. "That wasn't your best closing, but you delivered it so good! From beginning to end. I definitely like the 'animal' part. You scored big-time with that one!"

Tyrone smiled. "Thinking about using it?"

Danny shrugged. "Maybe. You know, bits and pieces of it."

"Use it!" Tyrone urged.

"Thanks! How long do you think it'll take for the jury to deliberate?"

"It's only been—" Tyrone's office phone rang. He answered it. "Tyrone Davis! Okay." Hanging up, he looked over at Danny. "They're ready."

***

Back inside the courtroom, everybody was already settled in. As Carlos was being escorted in by three officers, he caught sight of Tonya who was seated in the back, looking at him. Once he was seated beside his attorney, two of the officers stood near the table with their backs against the wall, while the third officer made for the jury room. Seconds later, the jurors entered, taking their seats.

"Well, this is it," Sara told Carlos. "I've done all I could."

"I know," he replied. "Thank you!"

Sara lingered before saying, "Tonya said to tell you that this was something she had to do."

This angered Carlos. "Is that all she said?"

"That's all."

Again, Carlos shifted his gaze to the back of the courtroom at Tonya who locked eyes with him for a brief moment before looking off toward the entrance, as if she was ready to make a break for it.

"Will the foreman please stand?" Judge Lathan spoke, getting everyone's attention, including Carlos'. One of the jurors, an older white male, stood, holding the verdict sheet. "I understand that the jury has reached a verdict," Lathan continued. "Is that true?"

"Yes, Your Honor," the man answered.

"Please read your verdict out to the court."

The foreman cleared his throat before regarding the document in his hand. "We, the jury, find the defendant, Carlos West, on count one, aggravated assault, guilty. We, the jury, find the same defendant, on count two, possession of firearm, guilty. On count three, burglary, we also find the defendant guilty."

"Thank you all for your services!" Lathan told the jurors. "You can all leave or stay for the sentencing."

A handful of the jury members gathered their things and made for the exit.

The judge waited until the bailiff secured the door before shifting his gaze over to the prosecutors. "State," he began, "is there any reason why sentencing should be postponed?"

"No, Your Honor," answered Tyrone.

"Defense?"

"No, Your Honor," Sara answered.

"Will the defendant please rise to receive his punishment?" Lathan asked. Once Carlos and his attorney stood, the judge continued. "Mr. West, with the jury having found you guilty, I, hereby, sentence you on count one, aggravated assault, to serve twenty-five years. On count two, possession of firearm, I sentence you to five years, to run consecutively with count one. On count three, burglary, I sentence you to ten years, to run concurrent with count one."

Playa Ray

Chapter 19

"Hey, guys!" Chris greeted Sara and Danny as he entered on the other side of the visitation booth.

"Hey!" they both responded in unison.

"I saw the trial," Chris told Sara. "Why didn't Carlos take a plea?"

Sara shook her head. "I have no idea."

"Hell, with all the evidence against him, there was no need for a closing argument!" Chris asserted. "But, all-in-all, you did good, Sara!"

"Thanks!"

"How's everything going, Danny?" He wanted to know.

"Slow," Danny answered. "I'm trying to get this over with as quick as possible. It may take a few months."

"A few months!"

Danny shrugged. "I don't have the kind of power over my judge like Tyrone has over his. I'm trying to develop a bond with her."

"You may have made the wrong impression with the flowers," Chris told him. "Don't appear as though you're trying to seduce her. Find something she likes and strike up a conversation on it. Convince her that you two share the same interest. You follow me?"

"Yeah."

"Do it fast!"

"Okay."

"Where's Ellen?" Chris finally asked.

Sara answered, "She had to take care of some business."

"Speaking of business," Chris started, "can you handle that for me?"

"I'll try," said Sara, knowing what he was talking about.

"Should we discuss the pay?"

"We'll do that after I get the information," she told him.

***

Being that Tyrone had to meet with Charles and Rick upon leaving his office, he drove out to Charles' home, where he was now leaning against the fender of his car, talking to Charles, who was leaning against the red-brick mailbox.

"I need a good month's run," Tyrone was telling him.

"You told me I was done in one month," Charles reminded him. "That was a week ago."

"So, you have three weeks left, right?"

"Yeah."

"I need one more week," Tyrone told him. "Can you handle that?"

Charles nodded. "Yeah."

"By that time, Rick should be ready to take over." He looked at his watch. "He needs to hurry up!"

"What about this spot?" Charles inquired. "It's booming."

"This is your spot. Keep it booming. Just use my plug."

"You'll have to let Bull know. You know he doesn't like me."

"Bull doesn't like anybody," Tyrone told him. "Hell, he don't like me. All he understands is money. That's why I let him run everything."

The sound of a vehicle's sound system got their attention. They looked to see Rick's Cadillac Escalade approaching.

Parking behind Tyrone's car, Rick killed the engine and dismounted. "What's up?" Rick greeted.

"Whenever I call you to a meeting, come by yourself!" Tyrone told Rick, indicating the female in the front-passenger seat of his truck.

"Got it!" Rick responded.

"How well do you work with Bull?" Tyrone asked him.

"It's like working with Adolf Hitler!" The guy expressed.

"Well, get used to it! In a month, you two'll be Batman and Robin."

***

Upon leaving the courthouse, Tonya drove around in circles as she wept and constantly thought about the night Carlos caught her with a guy that she hadn't known for more than three days and have not seen again since that night.

164

She'd never dreamed of hurting Carlos, but she had—twice, considering he was now about to serve thirty years of his life in prison. But he hurt her also. Just because he caught another man in her apartment, that didn't give him the right to beat her into a three-day coma. That prosecutor said, in his closing argument, that Carlos should've been charged with attempted murder.

Had Carlos really tried to kill her?

All of these thoughts had her mind in a jumble. She needed someone to talk to and her parents were totally out of the question. So, her only resort was Bobby, who promised her that, when he gets off from work, he'd meet her at the restaurant they always visited on their breaks. The same restaurant where she was now seated at a table, staring out the window at nothing, with a pair of dark sunglasses on her face.

"Tonya?"

She looked up to see Bobby standing over her, but said nothing.

"What's wrong?" He asked.

"I don't know," she answered, shifting her gaze to the untouched iced tea in front of her.

Bobby sat down beside her, taking hold of her hand. "You don't feel like you did the right thing?"

"I really don't know how I feel right now." Her voice was just above a whisper.

"Look," he said, brushing a few of her brown micro-braids from her face. "Let's go to my place. Leave your car here."

***

In one of the guest rooms of Bobby's house, Tonya was lying in bed with the covers pulled up to her chest, and Bobby was perched on the edge of the bed, looking down at her.

"Get as much rest as you need," he was telling her. "If you get hungry, feel free to eat whatever you crave. Don't worry about getting up in the morning. I'll just see you when I get home, okay?"

"I have to go to work," she reminded him.

"Not anymore."

"Why not?"

"You're fired."

As if pulled by invisible strings, Tonya's body jerked into a sitting position. "What!"

"You're fired," he repeated.

"Who fired me?" She asked, not believing her luck right now

"I did."

"Why?"

"You need the rest."

"I can't pay my bills, resting!" She pointed out. "I'll lose my apartment."

Bobby shrugged. "You're tired of it, anyway."

"Yeah, but that's all I have."

"That's all you *had*," he rectified. "Now, you have a four-bedroom house with a swimming pool. Don't worry about your ex-boyfriend's car. You can drive my BMW. It's time for a change, Tonya, and it starts here. If you want me as much as I want you—stay. If not, get dressed. I'll take you back to your car. It's your call."

***

The following day, Danny Blake was seated behind his desk, going over one of his case files when someone knocked on the door.

"It's open!" He called out.

Entering, Ellen closed the door back, and slumped down in the chair across from Danny, folding her arms over her chest.

"Cats," she said.

"What!" Danny had no idea where this came from.

"She loves cats."

"Oh!" Now, he knew. "I hate cats!"

"Not anymore."

Danny made a face. "I don't have to buy any, do I?"

"No," she answered. "Just convince her that you two share the same interest."

"I guess I can do that."

"You can do it." Ellen stood to leave. "Time is ticking."

"I know. Thanks!"

"Don't mention it."

***

Walking through the corridor, Tyrone made it back to his office, and was about to unlock his door, when Sara approached from the opposite direction.

"Are you busy?" She inquired.

"Not really."

"Can I come in?"

Tyrone unlocked the door and pushed it open, allowing her to enter, first. Closing the door back, he crossed over, and took a seat behind his desk as Sara took a seat across from him.

"What's up?" He asked.

"I spoke to Barbara Hutchins," Sara said. "She's running for the head prosecutor's position. Are you running for it?"

"Maybe. Why?"

"If you become head D.A.," she told him, "I can start winning cases. Chris just threw his career out the window by raping a prostitute. Now, how stupid is that!"

"It was a bad decision," Tyrone replied, not in the mood to discuss this with her. "Are you finished?"

"Yes, but I also wanted to apologize."

"For what?" He asked, leaning back in his chair.

"For letting my emotions get the best of me in the cafeteria the other day."

"Okay."

"Forgive me."

"I said, okay."

She seemed to linger a bit. "Can I make it up to you?" She finally asked. "My place, tonight?"

"Some other time," he said as he watched her saunter out of his office.

***

Making it to the restroom, Sara entered one of the stalls and locked it. Then, pulling up her navy-blue dress, she retrieved the small tape recorder that was strapped to her right thigh, and pressed stop.

"This is gonna be hard," she whispered to herself as she rested the back of her head on the door of the stall.

***

After Sara left his office, Tyrone realized he had to make a trip to Judge Lathan's office to discuss the succession of trials they had coming up starting next week.

Now, he was waiting at the elevators when he heard the ding before one of the two cars arrived, and assistant district attorney Barbara Hutchins, a white woman in her mid-forties. with bleach-blonde hair, stepped off.

"Mrs. Hutchins?" Tyrone stopped her, making sure to place himself in the threshold of the shaft to keep the doors from closing.

"Oh!" She let out. "Hi, Mr. Davis!"

"How are you?"

"I'm fine," she answered. "Just getting over the flu."

"Yeah, I hear it's going around."

"It is."

"I also hear you're running for the head D.A.'s position," Tyrone cut to the chase.

She looked puzzled. "Where'd you hear that nonsense from?"

"It's not true?"

"Of course, not!" She answered. "I'm not ready for that responsibility, yet."

"Oh!"

"I'm pretty much in a rush, and–"

"I didn't mean to hold you up," he cut her off.

"I'll see you around."

"Okay, take care."

"You do the same," Hutchins replied, making off.

"Always," Tyrone said almost to himself, as he wondered where Sara could have gotten that information.

***

"So, how is she?" Chris asked his brother, Kevin, who was seated on the other side of the visitation booth.

"She's fine," he answered. "Your friend, Lisa, stopped by this weekend, and helped her with the harvest."

"Lisa?" Chris didn't know anybody by that name.

"Momma introduced her to me as your friend, 'Lisa',"

Realization kicked in. "That's Laura!"

"Who's Laura?"

"The one that got me in here."

"Then, what the hell is she doing at momma's house!" Kevin bristled, visibly turning red.

"Her conscience," Chris replied. "Look, Kevin, whatever you do, don't mention this to uncle Avery. And, if you see her again, don't run her off. This might work."

"What might work?"

"If I can get her to admit," Chris began, "and testify that Tyrone Davis put her up to this, I'm out of here. Just trust me on this, Kevin."

***

"Come in!" said Judge Edwards, who was just fishing up some paperwork when someone knocked on the door of her chambers. Danny Blake entered, carrying some papers. "What now, Mr. Blake?" She inquired, with furrowed eyebrows.

"Have you thought about where you're going on your vacation?" He asked, approaching her desk.

"Not yet," she answered, eyeing the papers in his hand. "What's that?"

"Oh, some stuff from the Humane Society," Danny told her, thankful that she presented the opportunity. "I'm thinking about adopting a cat."

Her eyes seemed to double in size. "A cat! Let me see that!"

He handed her the papers.

"Oooh! They're adorable!" She cried out, as she perused the computer-generated pictures of cats of various sizes, color, and gender. "You like cats?"

"I love 'em!" He lied, taking a seat. "I just haven't had the time for one."

"I think cats are the most precious animals on earth!" Connie offered. "You have to get more than one. A cat always needs someone to play with, whether it's a sibling, or companion."

More than one? Danny thought, as Connie handed the papers back, then produced a small stack of pictures from one of her desk drawers, and handed them to him.

"Those are my babies!" she said, with sheer delight. "Sha'drach, Me'shach, and A'bad Negro."

"A'bad Negro?" Danny asked, as he slowly sifted through the pictures with a feigned interested look on his face.

"That's the black one," she answered. "He's a bad negro. He's always doing something. I always have to lock him in his room."

"He has his own room?"

"They share a room. Everything in it resembles cats: wallpaper, curtains, lamps, posters—everything!"

"Wow!"

***

"I hope you have some good news for me," Chris, who was already seated in the visitation booth, said to Danny as he entered on the other side.

"Not yet," he answered, "but I'm making progress with Judge Edwards."

"We need to work fast, Danny! I'm beginning to *feel* like a criminal!"

"I'm working as fast as I can," Danny insisted. "I have trials set up for the next three weeks. Let me see what kind of progress I've made by then."

"How's Tyrone been acting?" Chris wanted to know.

Danny shrugged. "The same. Nothing's changed about him."

"I hope Sara pulls this off."

Chapter 20

The following week brought on the beginning of the succession of trials in which Tyrone had been anticipating. Now, as cameras from the local news stations were rolling, Tyrone was standing in the center of the room, questioning crime scene investigator Richard Willis, who was on the stand.

"So, that's where you came into the picture?" Tyrone was asking the Caucasian man.

"Yes," he answered.

Turning on his heels, Tyrone approached his table, where Michelle handed him a Ziploc bag containing a small, silver handgun. He, then, regarded Judge Lathan. "Your Honor," Tyrone started, "may I approach the witness?"

Lathan nodded. "You may."

Tyrone walked over, placed the bag in front of the investigator, then backed away. "This item I just set before you, Mr. Willis," Tyrone continued, "has already been admitted into evidence as State's exhibit one. Can you tell me what that is?"

He regarded it for a split second before answering. "It's a Ziploc bag containing a silver handgun."

"Have you ever seen this gun?"

"I did the ballistics on it."

"And, what did you come up with?" Tyrone inquired.

"I deduced that this is the weapon that was used to murder eighty-seven-year-old Edna Byrd."

"And, how long after the murder did this weapon surface?"

"Almost three months."

"Thank you! Nothing further."

Tyrone collected the gun and made for his table as Sara, who was seated at the defense table with her client, a black man in a gray suit, got up, and approached the lectern.

"Mr. Willis," she began, "I'm attorney Sara Jennings, counsel for the defendant, David Mills."

"Good morning!" Willis greeted.

"Good morning!" Sara returned. "Mr. Willis, while conducting our ballistic study, did you, at any time, dust the weapon for prints?"

"I did."

"What did you find?"

"I found several prints, but they were of no value."

"Meaning?"

"Meaning that I couldn't find a particular print to match a particular person."

Sara looked to the judge. "Nothing further, Your Honor."

***

Up the hall, in Judge Edwards' courtroom, another trial was underway, and Danny was standing at the lectern, questioning officer Towns, a white female who was on the witness stand.

"At this time," Danny was saying, "did you do a report?"

"Yes," she answered.

"Did Mr. Bradford mention anything about an altercation he'd had with Ms. Perry the previous day?"

Attorney Doug Turner, a black male, who was seated at the defense table with his client, Rasheeda Perry, lunged from his chair. "Objection, Your Honor!"

"Under what grounds?" Asked Edwards.

"He's misleading the witness," the attorney answered.

"Overruled!" The judge ruled, then regarded the prosecutor. "You may continue, Mr. Blake."

Doug re-took his seat and Danny continued with the acknowledgment that he had, indeed, made progress.

"Thank you, Your Honor!" He replied, then returned to the witness. "Officer Towns, did Mr. Bradford mention the incident with Ms. Perry the previous day?"

"Yes."

"Did he say that she was the one who burned down his house?"

"Yes, he did."

"Nothing further, Your Honor."

Judge Edwards looked to the defense table. "Cross?"

***

"So, you were driving along in this car that you admitted to stealing, am I right?" Sara Jennings asked her client, David Mills, who was now on the stand.

"Yes," he answered.

"Then, you were pulled over by LPD?"

He nodded. "Yes."

"What happened, then?" Sara asked, resting her elbows on the lectern.

"I stopped," her client responded. "The officer asked for my license, and I told him that I didn't have any. He made me get out, then searched me."

"Did he find anything on you?"

David shrugged. "Some cigarettes, a lighter, and some money."

"Is that it?"

"Yes."

"Go on!"

David resumed. "He cuffed me, placed me in the back seat of his patrol car, and searched the stolen car."

"What did he find?" Inquired the attorney.

"A gun."

"Where did he find it?"

"Under the front-passenger seat," he answered.

"Did you know it was there?"

"No."

***

At the time, Danny was conducting a direct examination on Tony Bradford, a black male, who was seated on the witness stand.

"Mr. Bradford," he was saying, "what happened after the fight between you and Ms. Perry?"

"I told her to get out, and she wouldn't leave," he answered. "So, I used force. After I got her out, I locked the door and called her a cab."

"And, what was she doing now?"

"She was pacing the porch, making threats."

"Like what?" Danny questioned, casting a glance at the jury members.

"She was telling me that she had something for me, and I'll pay for this."

"Nothing further," Danny said to the judge.

***

"So, you stole the car from a shopping center's parking lot?" Tyrone was now cross-examining David Mills.

"Yes," the defendant answered.

"Which one?"

"Lee's Foods."

"And, how long have you had this car?"

"Four days."

"Four days!" Tyrone moved from behind the lectern, now standing on the side of it. "You had this car for four days and never searched it for anything valuable?"

"No."

"Wouldn't that be rare for a car thief to do?"

"Objection!" Sara challenged from her seat. "Your Honor, could you please ask the prosecutor to refrain from name-calling?"

"Your Honor," Tyrone spoke in his own defense, "the defendant already pleaded guilty to theft by taking, labeling himself a car thief."

"Objection overruled," Judge Lathan made his ruling.

Tyrone resumed. "Mr. Mills, where was the gun located in the car?"

"I don't know," he answered with a shrug.

***

"Can you tell us how this fight started?" Attorney Doug Turner questioned Tony Bradford.

"Rasheeda is always accusing me of having sex with my next-door neighbor," he answered. "On that particular day, she arrived in a cab and saw my next-door neighbor leaving my house. That was around four p.m. Rasheeda didn't say anything about it until later that night. We argued, then it escalated."

"You said she threatened you, saying that you'll pay for this, and that she had something for you, correct?"

"Yes."

"Then, the next day," Turner went on, "you came home from work to see firefighters putting out a fire that was set to your home, right?"

Tony nodded. "Right."

"So, due to the fight, and the so-called threats, you believe that Ms. Rasheeda Perry is responsible for the fire?"

"Yes."

"You don't think that your neighbor could have pulled this off?"

"He could have," Tony answered, "but I don't think he did."

There was complete silence in the courtroom as the attorney seemed to linger while regarding Tony with a puzzled expression. "Are we talking about the same neighbor that Ms. Perry was accusing you of having sex with?"

"Yes."

***

Being that jury selection had taken up most of the day, closing arguments had been remitted until the following day.

Now, Sara Jennings was slowly pacing back and forth in front of the jury panel as she delivered her closing argument. "Ladies and gentlemen," Sara was saying, "my client did admit to theft by taking of the car, but he had no knowledge of the gun that was already inside the car. The burden of proof is on the State to prove that my client had ties to this weapon. Did they prove it? No, they did not.

"My client's fingerprints were not found on the gun. There's no evidence showing that my client was anywhere near the murder scene of Ms. Byrd. The owner of the car could be the murderer. The weapon was found in *his* car. My client knew nothing of the murder weapon, so how could he have known anything of the murdered victim?"

***

Just up the hall, in Judge Edwards' courtroom, Attorney Doug Turner was pacing back and forth in front of the jury box as he conducted his closing argument. "Let's say that she did make the threats," he was saying. "Why didn't Mr. Bradford report it to the authorities? Maybe he didn't take her seriously. Maybe she never made the threats. Maybe his next-door neighbor burned down his house out of jealousy.

"Ms. Perry had reasons to believe that her boyfriend was gay. When it was confirmed, she became upset. And she had the right to be. If Ms. Perry encountered the neighbor coming out of the house when she arrived, that means the neighbor had encountered her pulling up in the cab. That could have induced him to act out of jealousy, and set fire to Mr. Bradford's home."

***

"Do you know what this guy is?" Tyrone asked, pointing at the defendant, David Mills, while conducting his rebuttal closing argument. "I'll tell you exactly what he is. He's one of the world's dumbest criminals! He's driving around in a stolen car with the same gun he used to murder an elderly white lady, almost three months ago. Why? He was probably on his way to kill another elderly person. Perhaps one of your family members. Thanks to the police, he never made it.

"Now, ladies and gentlemen of the jury, it's up to you to make sure this murderer doesn't harm anyone else. When his attorney asked where did the officer find the gun, he said under the front-passenger seat. When I asked him the same question, he claimed he didn't know. So, why should we believe that he's not a murderer?"

***

"Mr. Bradford didn't say anything about a dispute with his neighbor," Danny Blake said to the jury members as he did his final closing argument. "He never said that his neighbor made any threats towards him. It was Rasheeda Perry—his psycho girlfriend! She started this fight! She made the threats! It doesn't matter if her boyfriend was homosexual, homophobic, or home alone! That didn't give her the right to burn down this man's precious home that he worked so hard to establish!

"What else is this psycho capable of? Let's not find out. Show Rasheeda Perry that her behavior is not tolerated! We will not stand for it! Linkton County does not need people like Rasheeda Perry walking around freely. What will she burn down next? A school full of children? A retirement home? She's dangerous to society!"

While awaiting both jury panels to deliberate, Tyrone and Danny had met up in the cafeteria where they were now seated across from each other.

"I mean, it really surprised me, Tyrone!" Danny was saying. "I think I've made progress."

"My man!" Tyrone said, offering his hand across the table for Danny to shake. "Congratulations!"

"Thanks! I guess I can start my winning streak."

"Law forty-seven," Tyrone said. "Do not go past the mark you've aimed for. In victory, learn when to stop."

"Don't worry!" Danny said, winking his eye. "I've got this."

***

Back in Judge Lathan's courtroom, once the jurors had filed in and taken their seats, Lathan bidded the foreman, a young, white female, to standand read the verdict out to the court.

"We, the jury," she read from the verdict sheet, "find the defendant, on count one, possession of a firearm, guilty. We, the jury, find the same defendant, on count two, murder, guilty."

***

The jurors in Rasheeda Perry's trial had taken a little longer than those of David Mills'. However, they were now all back in their seats, and the foreman, a black male, had stood to hand down the verdict.

"We, the jury, find the defendant, Rasheeda Perry, on one count of arson, guilty."

***

Pulling into a neighborhood, Tyrone parked his car along the sidewalk amongst other vehicle, where a group of people were watching a group of men play a game of basketball on a fenced-in court.

As he was scanning the crowd of on-lookers, a female in a black, spandex bodysuit, approached the passenger side of the car.

Tyrone regarded the woman for a few seconds before letting the window down.

"Are you looking for a date?" She asked, conveying a broad smile, displaying straight, exceptionally-white teeth.

"No," he answered, trying his best not to regard her cleavage that was prominently on display, being that she was leaning into the window. "You wanna make ten bucks?"

Her smile broadened. "Of course, I do."

"Do you know Rick?"

Her smile slowly dissolved. "I don't know. Are you a cop?"

"Do I look like a cop?"

"You don't look 'hood."

"Don't let this suit and tie fool you!" Tyrone told her. "I *am* the 'hood.'"

While she stood there, looking like she was searching for something to say, Rick approached from behind her.

"Look!" Tyrone said. "You missed out on ten bucks."

She turned to face Rick who was now standing beside her. "Damn! Where'd you come from?"

"Didn't you just get out of somebody's car?" Rick asked. "Go home and take a bath!"

"Shut up!" She put on an exaggerated strut as she went on about her way.

Shaking his head, Rick climbed in beside Tyrone and rolled the window back up. "What's up?" Asked Rick.

"You tell me," Tyrone replied.

"I'm waiting on Bull, now."

"For what?"

"I'm out."

"Already?" Tyrone asked, impressed.

"Man, it's off the chain around here!" Rick told him. "I don't know what your chemist put in that stuff, but I've never seen junkies act like this!"

Tyrone nodded. "How are you and Bull coming along on communication?"

"Like an English teacher and a foreign exchange student."

Tyrone laughed. "That's bad! Just don't tell him that."

"Why not?" Rick inquired with furrowed eyebrows. "I'll shoot him just as quickly as he'll shoot me!"

***

Laura opened her door to Tyrone, who was holding a bottle of champagne in one hand and a bouquet of flowers in the other.

"Are you busy?" He asked.

***

Exhausted from their sexual romp, Tyrone was lying on his back, and Laura was lying with her head on his chest, and the covers pulled up to their waists as Dixie Chicks' *Travelin' Soldier* played softly in the background.

Reaching over to the nightstand, Tyrone grabbed his glass that was still half-full of champagne, took a sip, then held it out to Laura, who had to lift her head to take a sip from it. After downing the rest, Tyrone placed the glass back onto the nightstand and began stroking Laura's bare shoulders.

"Do you feel bad about that?" He asked.

"About what?"

"The last job."

She lifted her head and locked her ocean-blue eyes onto his. "No. Why would you ask me that?"

"You haven't been yourself, since," he pointed out.

Laura broke eye contact. "I've just had a lot on my mind."

"Like what?"

"Some personal things."

"So, you're not going soft on me?"

"Never!"

Playa Ray

Chapter 21

The following week brought on another publicly broadcasted trial for Tyrone Davis who was now standing in the center of the court-room, administering direct examination on a teenaged white girl who was seated on the witness stand.

"How old are you now, Kelly?" Tyrone asked.

"Seventeen," she answered.

"How old were you when this started?"

"Fifteen."

"Did you tell your mom what her boyfriend was doing to you?" The girl nodded. "Yes."

"And, what did she say or do?"

"She cursed me out and told me to stop lying."

"Can you tell the court what he was doing to you?" Tyrone posed, leaning on the lectern.

Kelly cleared her throat before answering. "He used to kiss on me, and touch me."

"Where did he touch you, Kelly?"

"Between my legs."

"He does this while your mom is at work?"

"And, sometimes, when she's asleep."

"Did he ever force himself on top of you?"

Ellen Martinez, who was seated at the defense table with her client, Ted Russel, sprang to her feet. "Objection, Your Honor!" she spoke. "Misleading the witness."

"Overruled!" Judge Lathan responded without giving Tyrone a chance to rebut.

"Has he ever forced himself on top of you, Kelly?" Tyrone resumed when Ellen had re-taken her seat.

"Yes," the girl answered.

"How did he get caught?"

"I told my teacher, Mrs. Kennedy, and the principal, Mrs. Bell. They called the police."

"Who are you living with now?"

"My aunt Clair."

Tyrone looked toward the judge. "Nothing further."

***

In Judge Edwards' courtroom, another trial was underway. Danny, who was standing in the center of the room beside a cart that contained a T.V. set and VCR, was questioning detective Jeffery Atkins, a white male who was on the witness stand. "So, all you did was pull the tape?" Danny was asking.

"That's all," answered the government official. "The clerk said that the suspect didn't wear a mask."

"There's a tape inside this VCR," Danny told him. "Is it the original tape, or a replica?"

"The original."

"So, when I show this tape to the jury, what will they see?"

"The actual robbery," Atkins answered.

"Of the pawn shop?"

The man nodded. "Yes."

Danny looked to the judge. "May I, Your Honor?"

"Any objections from the defense?" she asked.

Attorney Sam Drake, who was seated with his client, Marcus Thomas, got to his feet. "Your Honor," he spoke, "I haven't had a chance to view it, recently."

"When did you last view it?" Edwards questioned.

"Last year."

"I'm quite sure it's the same tape, Mr. Drake."

The attorney clasped his hands together. "Well, there have been cases where—"

"Are you making an objection?" She cut him off.

"No, Your Honor," he said, sitting.

The judge regarded Danny. "You may proceed, Mr. Blake."

***

"I'm Zack."

Carlos, who was gazing out of the steel-grated window of the prisoner transportation bus in deep thought, turned to face the white guy seated beside him, with his hand extended. "Huh?"

"I'm Zack," the man repeated.

"Carlos." They shook hands.

182

"Murder?" Zack asked, eyeing Carlos' clothes that were still stained and partially stiff with Tonya's blood.

"Assault," Carlos answered, hating the jail's policy of not allowing prisoners to transfer from their facility in jail-issued uniforms.

"Me, too!" Zack became animated. "I found out that my sister's husband had been beating on her, so I took a Louisville Slugger and beat the crap out of him! And, guess who called the cops?"

"Who?" Carlos asked, as mental pictures of what he'd done to Tonya haunted hm.

"My sister!" Zack answered, his eyes the size of saucers. "I'm trying to help *her*, and she calls the cops on *me*!"

***

Now, standing behind the lectern, Tyrone was questioning Heather Whitfield, Kelly's mother, whose wide frame seemed to fill up the small box of the witness stand. "Ms. Whitfield," he was saying, "why do you think your daughter would lie about something like that?"

"Kelly's always lying!" Heather insisted forcibly. "She doesn't like Ted, so she curses him out and calls him names."

"So, you don't think your boyfriend would commit such a crime?"

"No, I do not!"

The courtroom was silent as her words—and the caustic tone of them—hung in the air.

As Tyrone stared at her with contempt, he couldn't help but wonder if she had aided this sexual abuse against her own flesh and blood. He cleared his throat. "Ms. Whitfield," Tyrone resumed. "If your daughter and boyfriend were drowning, and you could only save one of them, who would it be?"

Ellen was on her feet. "Objection, Your Honor!"

"Nothing further," Tyrone announced, feeling like he'd already planted the seed in the minds of the jurors.

***

"I hear this is a pretty rough place," Zack said, as the bus pulled through the electrical fence that was ridiculously shrouded with sharp razor wire.

Carlos didn't respond.

"First time?"

"Yeah," he finally spoke. "You?"

"Second," Zack told him. "On my first bid, I learned how to make shanks out of anything. If you feel that you'll need one down the line, get at me. The first one's on me."

"I'll remember that."

The bus finally came to a stop, and Carlos averted his attention out the window where prison guards stood around, armed with assault rifles. One of the guards unlocked and opened the security gate that separated the prisoners from the transporting officers.

"Alright, you low-lifes!" The older white officer, who looked as if he had a whole bag of chewing tobacco stuffed into one side of his mouth, gave a voice. "Welcome to my territory! When I order you scumbags to get off my bus, you will move like you have a purpose, and line up on the side of the bus, facing those officers out there. If one of you as much as sneeze the wrong way, they'll shoot you down, no questions asked! Now, get off my bus!" He backed off the bus and watched with satisfaction as the prisoners poured from the bus, as if running from danger.

***

Back inside the courtroom, Tyrone was conducting a direct examination on Clair Oliver. "Ms. Oliver," he was saying. "You are Heather's sister, am I correct?"

She nodded. "Yes."

"So, that makes you Kelly's aunt, right?"

"Yes."

"And, she's currently staying with you?"

"Yes," the woman responded, nodding again.

"How many children do you have?" Tyrone posed.

"Four, including Kelly."

Tyrone chose to switch gears. "How did this incident affect you?" He asked.

"It hurt me to my heart!" She expressed, shooting a glance over at the defense table. "It's hurting me now, just to know that I'm in the same room with him, right now!"

"Keep your composure," Tyrone advised, then paused to let her collect herself. "Can you continue?"

After taking a deep breath, she said, "yes."

Tyrone went on. "Your sister didn't believe Kelly when she informed her about the incident. Any idea why?"

"That man had Heather wrapped around his finger! She would jump off the top of this building, if he told her to. To her, Ted is never wrong. She puts him before her very own family."

Tyrone looked to Judge Lathan. "Your Honor, may I request a break?"

"How long are we talking?" He inquired.

"Thirty minutes."

"I'll make it an hour," Lathan told him. "Are you done with this witness?"

"Yes."

Lathan looked over to the defense table. "Ms. Martinez, will you be cross examining this witness?"

"Yes, Your Honor," she answered.

"Listen up, people," Lathan addressed those in attendance. "We're taking a recess. I'll need everyone back in exactly one hour. Ms. Oliver, I'll need you back in that same exact seat to be cross examined by Ms. Martinez."

***

Tyrone eased into Judge Edward's courtroom, and took a seat on the row next to the last. Charles, who was seated behind him, passed him a small, folded piece of paper, in which he unfolded. All it said was: 'Red shirt. Yellow shirt.'

Handing the paper back over his shoulder, Tyrone looked toward the jury box, immediately spotting two black men, who were seated beside each other—one wearing a yellow shirt, and the other in a red one. Tyrone nodded, then directed his attention to Danny who was questioning a Chinese man.

"Mr. Chin," he was saying, "do you see the man that robbed your store, in this courtroom?"

"Yes, I do," he answered with a nod.

"Can you point to him and tell me what he has on?"

"Over there," Mr. Chin replied, pointing towards the defense table. "Blue shirt."

"And, how sure are you about that?"

"I no forget face," he answered in broken English.

Danny looked to the judge. "Let the record reflect that the victim has identified the defendant, Marcus Thomas."

"So reflected," she responded.

***

Judge Edwards ended up adjourning a little before five o'clock. While she was instructing the jury members on not speaking to anyone about the case, Charles made his exit.

Now, he was standing in front of the courthouse as if he was awaiting a ride when a group of people with stickers on their shirts that read 'Jury Member', exited. He spotted the two men he'd targeted in the back of the throng.

Once the flock passed him, Charles followed. People branched off— some heading for the parking garage, and others continuing towards the bus stop. The two men were headed for the bus stop.

"Fellas?" Charles said, wanting to stop then, before they made it to the bus stop, and out of the earshot of the others.

Simultaneously, they turned around. Then, seeing that he was talking to them, they stopped.

"What's up?" Asked the guy in the yellow shirt.

"You boys wanna make some money?" Charles asked.

"How much?"

"Fifteen hundred, a piece."

After exchanging skeptical glances, the one in the red shirt asked, "What do we have to do?"

***

Though Judge Edwards' courtroom had already concluded for the day, trial was still in motion in Judge Lathan's courtroom where Ellen Martinez was still questioning Clair Oliver.

"Heather claims that Kelly is always lying," Ellen was saying. "Is that true?"

"People lie everyday," Clair offered with a shrug. "If your daughter revealed something like that to you, would you believe her?"

"I'm not at liberty to answer that," Ellen replied, moving from behind the lectern. "Has Kelly ever lied to you?"

"Of course, she has. That doesn't mean she's lying about this."

"But, she has lied to you, right?" Ellen wouldn't let up.

"Yes."

"Nothing further," the attorney said to the judge, then returned to her table.

Lathan looked to the State's table. "Re-direct?"

"No, Your Honor," Tyrone answered.

"We're a little past quitting time, so we'll wrap this up and continue at nine tomorrow morning."

***

In her chambers, Connie Edwards had just finished up her paperwork for the day. She grabbed her purse, and, as she approached the door to leave, somebody knocked. She opened the door to Danny, who was carrying his briefcase.

"Ready?" He asked.

"Yes," she answered, almost forgetting he'd offered to walk her to her car.

Danny stepped back to allow her to enter the corridor, and lock her door. When she turned to face him, Danny was holding up a small, stuffed cat.

Smiling, she playfully snatched it from his hand. "I have three of these, Danny."

"You do?" He appeared hurt.

"Yes, but I can make room for one more," she said, and began walking with him flanking her. "Have you bought any toys, yet?"

"Toys?"

"For the cat," she told him. "It's like bringing home babies. You gotta have everything set up. Especially food."

"I guess I'm moving kinda slow," he admitted, sheepishly.

"Don't they come home today?"

"Tomorrow," he answered, still hating that he'd taken Ellen's advice and adopted two kittens. 'Just in case she decides to come over,' she'd said.

Connie looked at her watch. "Well, you better run on down to the pet store and handle your business before they close!"

***

Carlos and three other new arrivals, dressed in prison uniforms, and carrying their folded linen in their hands, entered a two-tier cell block with metal bars, and were taunted by other inmates who were whistling, and announcing 'fresh meat!'

A balled-up piece of paper hit Carlos on the top of his head. Looking up towards the top range, he saw his old cellmate, Philly, who was holding his arms out, palms up, as if asking what happened. All Carlos could do was shake his head.

***

"I'm just worried about them flipping the script," Charles said to Tyrone, who was seated with him on his mother's porch.

"Don't worry about that," Tyrone told him, looking out at the setting sun.

"Why not?"

"It's your word against theirs." He now regarded his protege. "That's what they call 'hearsay'. Nobody gets convicted of hearsay, unless *I'm* trying the case. You feel me?"

"Yeah."

"Just stick to the plan," Tyrone advised. "Nobody in their right mind would turn down an offer like that. Money talks."

***

Carlos, after getting his things squared away in his cell, journeyed off to Philly's cell, where they were now sitting on the bottom bunk, confabulating.

"Damn, son!" Philly was shaking his head. "I thought she was gonna stick to the script."

"So did I," Carlos replied, but deep down inside, he knew that prosecutor had something to do with Tonya's change of heart.

"Have you spoken to her?"

All Carlos could do was shake his head no.

At that time, a tall, muscular white guy entered the small cell, with no shirt, winning himself a wary look from Carlos. Acknowledging the look, Philly took the initiative.

"Yo, Hard Time," Philly spoke up. "This is my homeboy, Carlos."

"What's up?" Hard Time greeted, offering his hand.

"I can't call it," Carlos answered, shaking his hand.

Philly went on. "Carlos, this is my cell mate, Hard Time, the coolest white boy in the state. Well, until you get him mad."

Playa Ray

Chapter 22

The next day, trial resumed in Judge Edwards' courtroom. The jury members were back in the box, but the two that mattered to Charles, who was seated at the rear of the courtroom, were the two he'd made the deal with on yesterday.

Today, one was wearing a black shirt and the other had on a blue one. Like the others, they were giving attorney Sam Drake their undivided attention as he paced before them while doing his closing argument.

"I know you've all heard the axiom: 'Don't believe everything you hear'," the attorney was saying. "And, I'm quite sure you don't believe everything you hear. However, I know that we all trust our eyes to the best of their abilities. If we were out walking, looking in separate directions, and you turn to me, saying that you've just seen a U.F.O, how can I contend with that? You trust your eyes!

"But, believe it or not, we'll see things in our lives that are not what they appear to be. Such as mirages, hallucinations, or just plain ol' trickery. The video that you all viewed yesterday had been altered. The perfect example of trickery!"

***

Over in Judge Lathan's courtroom, Tyrone was standing behind the lectern, examining the defendant, Ted Russell.

"Why would this seventeen-year-old girl," Tyrone was saying, "who was fifteen at the time, have so much hatred towards you, that she would compose such a fictitious story about you molesting her?"

"I don't know," Ted answered, nonchalantly, with a slight shrug of the shoulders.

"You don't know?"

"Nope."

Tyrone just stared at Ted for a moment, hoping that his visage didn't display the hatred he had for this riff raff, who should be facing the death penalty for what he'd done. Clearing his throat, Tyrone continued. "I'm no shrink," he said, "but I would like to know how could a poor excuse for a man be so sick in the head, that he would force himself on a child."

Ellen Martinez sprung to her feet. "Objection, Your Honor! He's badgering my client!"

Tyrone didn't know what had come over him but he immediately wheeled on the attorney. "Badgering!" He blurted. "How about we roll the electric chair in here, right now, and strap him in!"

"Your Honor," Ellen pleaded, "prosecutor is being highly inappropriate at this time!"

"If I molested a child," Tyrone continued, "would that be more appropriate for you, Ms. Public 'Pretender'?"

"Hey!" Judge Lathan shouted, furiously banging his gavel. "If you two don't stop this tirade, right now, I'll hold you both for contempt of court!"

"You wouldn't dare!" Tyrone shot back, shooting a menacing look in the judges' direction.

Somebody gasped. Other than that, the courtroom fell silent. Everyone's faces were frozen in shock, except for that of Judge Lathan, who appeared more embarrassed than anything, and Tyrone, who looked as though he was ready to physically assail the judge. At this point, he was totally oblivious to the three lenses of the news cameras that caught it all.

Finally, Lathan slowly rose to his feet. "Bailiff?" He spoke. "Make sure everyone stays put! Mr. Davis? In my chambers, right now!"

***

Entering his chambers, Judge Lathan left the door standing open. He was standing in front of his desk with his arms folded over his chest when Tyrone entered seconds later, slamming the door shut. "What the hell was that, Tyrone!" Lathan bristled.

In a few brisk strides, Tyrone was in Lathan's face, accompanied by his index finger. "Don't you ever threaten me like that again!"

"We were on national television," Lathan pointed out.

"I wouldn't give a damn if we were on National Geographic!" Tyrone retorted. "Do that again, I'll snatch your tongue out and feed it to you! Understand?"

With wide and apprehensive eyes, Lathan nodded.

***

Back in Judge Edwards' courtroom, Danny was pacing the floor as he conducted his closing argument. "You would be a fool to believe that this tape was altered," he said to the jurors. "Why would anyone want to frame this guy? I mean, who is he? Roger Rabbit? He's nobody! Well, he's a petty thief. But, in my book, he's a nobody."

***

Tyrone was back in his seat at the State's table. The room was still quiet except for the indistinctive chatter of the jurors and the camera crews. At that time, Judge Lathan entered.

"All rise!" The bailiff called out.

"As you were," Lathan told everyone as he re-claimed his own seat. "First, I want to apologize to the court for the outburst. It shouldn't happen again. Now, if we can pick up where we left off, Mr. Davis, you may continue with your examination."

"No further questions," Tyrone offered.

***

Carlos awakened from his sleep to see his cellmate, Deandre, and two of his friends gathered by the bunk, looking at some papers. A bit curious, Carlos sat up and saw that they were looking at the pictures of a battered Tonya from his discovery packet. "What are y'all doing?" Carlos voiced.

Deandre turned to face him. "What's it look like we're doing, coward!"

"Coward!" Carlos took umbrage.

"A coward is a man who beats women," Deandre said matter-of-factly. "That's how my coward-ass dad killed my mom!"

"You can't be going through my stuff, Deandre."

"I can do what I wanna do! This is my cell!"

"This is my cell, too."

"It *was* your cell!" Deandre asserted, flinging the papers at Carlos, causing them to scatter, some falling to the floor. "Get out!"

"Do what!"

Deandre looked at his cronies. "Am I speaking Chinese?"

He wasn't expecting an answer. He turned and swung, punching Carlos in the face. Before Carlos could react, the three of them snatched him off the top bunk to the floor, where they began punching and kicking him.

Philly and his cellmate, Hard Time, were standing further down the range when they saw other inmates gathering around the cell.

"Carlos!" he exclaimed.

Philly raced toward the scene, followed by Hard Time and two other inmates. By the time they reached the cell, the gang had brought Carlos out, endeavoring to toss him over the railing.

Philly tackled the pack, causing them all to fall to the floor. Hard Time pulled Philly up, and Philly helped Carlos to his feet as his assailants recovered. Carlos' face was swollen while blood exuded from his nose and blistered lips.

"Yo fam, what's up?" Philly asked Deandre.

"I want him out of my cell!" Deandre replied.

"Why?"

"He's a coward! He beats women!"

"They went through my stuff!" Carlos vented.

Philly already knew what needed to be done. He turned to Carlos. "Look, pack your stuff. We'll walk you to the door. When you get to medical, tell the lieutenant you wanna sign up for protective custody. You won't make it in here."

***

Back in Judge Lathan's courtroom, Ellen Martinez was standing in front of the jury box, delivering her closing. "Now, we all know that children lie," she was saying. "When we were children, there were things we've lied about. I'm quite sure we all have stolen something when we were children. We were all looked upon as our mommy's and daddy's little angels. We could do no wrong.

"Kelly was her mommy's little angel until she told the biggest fib that a child could ever tell. In fact, that's what we'll call this case: 'Kelly's Biggest Fib'. All she does is lie. You've heard that from her mother, and who knows Kelly better than her own mother? Her aunt, Clair, even admitted that Kelly has lied to her.

"Let's look at the evidence: No sign of forced entry. No semen found in or on Kelly. Not even in her bed, where she alleges this all took place. She has never liked Ted, so she came up with a way to get rid of him. It's called 'Kelly's Biggest Fib'."

***

In the jury room adjacent to Judge Edwards' courtroom, the jury members viewed the evidence and were now casting their votes. Once everyone jotted down their votes on separated scrap pieces of paper, they pushed them to the center of the table, in one pile, where the foreman, an older white man, collected them and looked them over.

He let out a frustrating sigh. "Okay. We have ten 'guilty' votes, and two 'not guilty' votes. People, we can run through the video again. My opinion shouldn't have any effect on your opinions, but come on, people. The evidence is irrefutable." He began passing out more scrap paper. "We'll try this again."

"I'm sticking with my verdict!" said the guy in the blue shirt.

"So am I," said his friend who was seated beside him.

***

"It doesn't matter if she's told a few lies," Tyrone said, while doing his rebuttal closing. "She's not lying about this! This sick-minded, poor-excuse-for-a man, fondled her! Your children lie. If your child told you something like this, being the true parent that you are, you would take immediate action. Well, today, Kelly is your child. It's time to take action!"

***

Charles was still seated on the back row when the jurors filed into the courtroom. Once they were all settled in, Judge Edwards summoned the foreman to his feet. The older, white man, complied.

"I understand that you all couldn't reach a verdict," Edwards spoke. "Is that correct?"

"Yes, ma'am," he answered.

"Thank you!" The judge turned to the presiding attorneys. "I, hereby, declare this trial a mistrial, due to hung jury."

Danny was crushed. He regarded the now former jurors with an incredulous look as they slowly made for the exit. Satisfied, Charles moved amongst the group as he, too, made his exit.

***

Tyrone's mind was elsewhere as the jurors filed into the court-room He was pulled from his reverie when the judge asked the fore-man to stand and read the verdict out to the court. That's when he looked over at the black woman who began to read from the verdict sheet.

"We, the jury, find the defendant, Ted Russell, on one count of child molestation, guilty."

***

Making it outside the courthouse, Charles and his two tempo-rary employees stopped in front of the building, allowing the rest of the group to proceed on.

"When y'all get to the bus stop," Charles told them, "look in the trash. It's in a brown paper bag."

"Fifteen a-piece, right?" One asked.

"That was the deal," Charles replied, then made for his truck.

***

"I can't believe they fell for that 'trickery' stuff!" Danny was saying, as he and Tyrone were walking through the car garage, headed for their cars. "Somebody paid them off, because there's no way in hell they could believe that tape was altered!"

"Some people are easily persuaded," Tyrone offered, though he was secretly celebrating Danny's loss.

"They probably knew him," Danny said pensively, still com-plaining about the two jury members who refused to find Marcus Thomas guilty.

"It's a small world." Tyrone wasn't making matters any better. "But, don't fall apart. That's not the case that's going to change your life."

"I still need to build my credibility, just in case things take a wrong turn," Danny said, as they made it to his truck, and stopped.

"Right now, you're the perfect candidate for the position. Your trials are publicized, and, on top of that, you win them all. You're undefeated!"

Tyrone smiled. "I'll take that as a compliment. Thank you!"

"You deserve the title for your hard work," Danny went on. "I feel I deserve the title for the effort that I put into this job to achieve it."

"And, that's what I like about you, Danny."

"Thanks!" Danny checked his watch. "Look, I gotta go and pick up some cats."

"Cats?"

"Adoption."

"Oh! I'll see you in the morning."

***

"That was some real dramatic stuff!" Chris said to Ellen, who was accompanied by Sara on the other side of the visitation booth.

"Judge Lathan is afraid of Tyrone," Ellen let on.

"Yeah, and now the whole world knows it," said Sara.

"So, he's not falling for any of your pick-up lines, huh?" He asked Sara.

"He has a trial set for every week," she answered. "He's busy, but I'm still trying."

***

It was already dark when Tyrone pulled up in front of A.J.'s store. He'd already been home, showered, eaten dinner, and helped Ebony with her homework. He watched TV with his daughter until it was almost time for him to make his meeting.

Now, he dismounted, armed his alarm, and entered the store under the watchful eyes of Rock and Kenny, A.J.'s runners, who were stationed out front. A.J. was behind the counter, and there were no customers. Tyrone made for the back room.

"Did you lock the door?" A.J. asked, stopping Tyrone in his tracks.

Saying nothing, Tyrone turned and made for the door as A.J. headed for the back room. Getting to the door, Tyrone flipped the sign to CLOSED, turned the lock, then turned it again, leaving it unlocked.

When he got to the small room, A.J. was holding a small box, and standing by the table, where there were four bundles of bills that were bound with rubber bands, on top of it. Tyrone pulled out one of the old, metal chairs and sat down.

"This is it," A.J. promulgated. "Our final deal."

"Yeah. This is it."

"Five whole years."

Tyrone cocked his head. "Has it been that long?"

"Hell yeah!" A.J. responded. "You're the best business partner I've had, ever since I've been dealing."

"I'm glad to hear that. Have you heard anything from Romeo?"

A.J. looked genuinely confused. "Who!"

"The kid."

"Oh!" A huge smile spread across his face. "I don't know what you did, but I heard that his family moved back to Michigan two days later."

"Good news for you, huh?"

"The best news I've heard in years!" He answered. "I don't like to see my Carla upset, but she'll get over it."

"Yeah, she will."

At that time, they heard the sound of tennis shoes scuffling on the floor of the store. A.J. looked at Tyrone who remained calm as if he hadn't heard a thing. Just then, Rock and Kenny were forced into the room by two men in ski masks, carrying handguns. The third man—who Tyrone knew was Block, for his size—entered behind them, carrying a duffle bag in one hand and a can of gasoline in the other.

The two men forced Rock and Kenny, who were bound with handcuffs, to the floor. A.J. turned to Tyrone, who regarded him with an inscrutable look.

"Tell me it's not so!" He insisted.

"It's not so," Tyrone answered, coolly.

"Then, what the hell is this, Tyrone!" A.J. demanded, gesturing toward the scene.

"It's all a part of your imagination. Now, shut up, and get on the floor!"

There was no mistaking the look on A.J.'s face. He was hurt. Reluctantly, he did as he was told, and lied face-down beside his men. Once he was cuffed, Block handed the duffle bag to Charles and retreated to the front of the store. Charles stepped over A.J., and began tearing boxes open, filling the bag with money and cocaine, while Rick stood sentry.

Tyrone stood and began stuffing the money from the table into his pockets. While doing so, he tossed one of the bundles of bills, hitting A.J. on the head.

"Don't do this, Tyrone!" A.J. pleaded.

"It's already done, A.J.," Tyrone told him. "Don't worry, I'll see you when I get to hell. Just save me a seat."

With that, he stepped over Rock and entered the front of the store where Block was pouring gas all over the place. Without altering his momentum, he nodded at Block, grabbed a bag of potato chips from a nearby rack, and made his exit.

Playa Ray

Chapter 23

The following morning, Tyrone was seated behind his desk, sifting through the contents of a manila folder, when someone rapped lightly on the door.

"Come in!"

He sighed inwardly and closed the folder. Sara entered, closing the door back. Leaning back in his leather chair, he watched as she took a seat across from him.

"Good morning!" She said.

"What is it?" Tyrone asked, feeling uneasy of her abrupt appearance.

"I just came by to see how you're doing," she purported.

"I'm okay."

She seemed to linger for a moment, before saying, "I still have those magic fingers, if you need a massage."

Tyrone raised an eyebrow. "Are you coming on to me?"

"I'm just offering a friendly massage," She told him. "You can make whatever you want to make of it."

***

Carlos had taken Philly's advice and signed up for protective custody. After medical personnel purveyed him with pain medication and ice packs for his injuries, they placed him in a solitary cell that had no windows. The steel door had a food tray slot that was locked from the other side, and a small window that was obscured by a metal plate. Officers would periodically slide it open in a feigned show of doing a security check.

Now, Carlos, clad in a pair of boxer shorts, was doing push-ups on the concrete floor beside his bunk, when he heard commotion coming up the hallway. He could hear the sound of heavy boots plodding on the sleek waxed corridor floor, but they weren't as loud as the voice of an inmate, who was being *escorted* to lock-up.

"Y'all don't know me!" He was yelling. "I'm Hannibal Lecter! I'm the real killer! I don't care about another charge! I'll be out of here in no time!"

Carlos heard the cell door next to him slam shut. He listened as the officers removed the restraints, slammed the tray slot, and trooped back up the hallway.

***

Upon his break, in lieu of getting something to eat, Tyrone made the short drive out to the Linkton County Clinic, to make his appointment with Dr. Green. He was now seated in the waiting area, skimming a boating magazine. At that time, Dr. Green, an older white male, came through the service door.

"Mr. Tyrone Davis?" He inquired, after referring to a folder he was carrying.

Tyrone looked up from his magazine. "Right here."

"This way, sir."

Placing the magazine back onto the table, Tyrone followed the doctor to the appointed room, and took a seat upon the exam table. The doctor closed the door and opened the folder he possessed.

"You're here for the results from your H.I.V testing," the doctor acknowledged. "Are you nervous?"

"Not really," Tyrone answered, truthfully.

"Okay, your results are negative."

"Thank you!"

"Would you like to take another test?"

The question caught Tyrone off guard. "Why would I do that?"

"Not trying to insinuate anything," the doctor started, "But the disease doesn't always show up in the first testing. That's why I always recommend an immediate second testing. It's up to you."

***

Completing his sets of push-ups, Carlos began doing sit-ups. He was in the middle of his last set, when he heard the guy next door, speaking through the exhaustion vent above the sink.

"Hey! Next door!"

Carlos stopped and looked up at the vent. He was not for making new friends. He just wanted to be left alone while he got his thoughts together on what he was going to do. He sure as hell didn't plan on being locked in this cell until it was time for him to go back for his new trial hearing.

"Hey! Next door!"

Carlos shook his head as he got up off the floor. For some reason, he felt this guy was not going to stop calling for him. Giving in, he stood up on the toilet so he was able to speak through the vent.

"What's up?" Carlos asked.

"Do you have some shine over there?" The man inquired.

"Shine?"

"Some fire."

"No, I don't have any fire," Carlos replied, figuring this guy was some nut case.

"You don't smoke?"

"No."

"Damn!" He let out. "How long have you been over there?"

"Since yesterday." Carlos was ready to get back to his workout.

"Have you been at this prison for a while?"

"Three days."

"Three days!" He seemed surprised. "That's how long 'I've' been here." There was a pause. "Is that Carlos over there?"

"Yeah," Carlos answered, slowly, not knowing what to think. "Who is that?"

The guy laughed. "Damn! I sat beside you on the bus."

"Zack?" Carlos asked, a smile spreading across his face

"The one and only!" Zack spouted. "What the hell are you doing over there?"

"I got jumped by my cellmate, and two other dudes."

"And they locked you down?"

"I signed P.C."

"Are you injured?" Zack wanted to know.

"Hell, I'm over here looking like the Elephant Man!" Carlos said, smiling.

"Ouch!"

"What'd they get you for?"

"Some guy told me that he was going to rape me," Zack relayed with no emotion.

"What!"

"Yeah," Zach went on. "Grabbed me on my ass when he said it."

"So, you're on P.C.?"

"Hell no!" Zack let out. "I had already made three shanks when I first got to the cell block. As soon as we got back from the chow hall today, I went straight to his cell with the two that I already had on me. You should've heard him screaming! One of his friends came to his rescue. Now, they're both in the hospital."

Carlos laughed. "You went off like that?"

"Hell yeah! You should've seen the looks on everyone's faces, when I emerged from the cell like Michael Myers, all bloody!"

"Did they charge you?"

"Yeah, but I don't care. I'll be respected from now on."

"Yeah."

There was a pause, before Zack spoke again. "Carlos, you can't stay on P.C. forever. You got to get back out there, seek revenge. Get at least one of 'em. Don't worry about the charge. It'll run concurrent with your sentence. In prison, it's all about respect, but you got to take it. Nobody respects a coward."

Carlos sighed. I guess I'm not built for this."

"Well, you better start building!" Zack told him. "You work on you, and I'll work on your sword.

"My sword?"

"For when you get back out on the battlefield."

***

Tyrone decided to take Sara up on her offer. She did have magical fingers that worked miracles on his muscles, and he was definitely in dire need of a massage. Plus, since he felt Sara had some kind of ulterior motive, he was more than ready to find out what it was.

Now, at Sara's home, Tyrone, with his shirt off, was lying across her bed. Sara, was in a purple panties and bra set straddling him and squeezing massaging oil on his back. Closing the top, she placed the bottle on the bed, and began massaging the oil in at his shoulders.

"How's that?" She asked.

"Feels good."

"Am I still the best?"

"For now," he answered, though he was already feeling the tension evaporate.

"I can settle for that."

Tyrone decided to test the waters. "This doesn't have anything to do with next week, does it?"

"The trial?" Sara replied. "Of course, not! I won't even mention that. However, I am thinking about taking on another profession."

"Like what?"

"I'm still thinking," she answered, working her hands down to the small of his back. "I need something less stressful. Hell, I would sell drugs if I knew that I wouldn't get caught."

Tyrone laughed. "Yeah, right!"

"All white people didn't grow up in the suburbs with silver spoons in their mouths," she asserted with an attitude. "And I'm not as innocent as I appear. I've done things."

"Like what?"

"I used to date a drug dealer, years back," she said. "I've done and witnessed horrible things that I can't really speak on. He's the one who came up with the bright idea of sending me to law school. First, I had to wing myself away from heroin. I kind of miss that life. If I could do it all over again, I would."

"You still haven't told me what you've done," said Tyrone. "What makes you *not-so-innocent*?"

"Well," she started. "I've lured other drug dealers into hotel rooms to be robbed by my boyfriend and his gang. I've transported drugs out of town, by bus."

"You ever killed anybody?" Tyrone tested.

"No, but I did stab somebody."

"Why are you telling me all this?"

"Because I need some extra money, and I know that you can help."

"What makes you think that?"

"Let's just say that I have a hunch."

Tyrone didn't reply. Now, his suspicion of Sara's ulterior motive had intensified. She was definitely up to something, and Tyrone had gotten away with too many misdeeds to get caught up now. *But who is she working for?* He thought. FBI?

"Look," he finally spoke, "I'll tell you what. Fix us some drinks, and we'll discuss that when you get back."

"Okay."

When Sara left the room, Tyrone lingered a few seconds, before getting off the bed, and searching the room. He grabbed her purse off the dresser and rummaged through it. Seeing nothing out of the ordinary, he sat the purse down, went over to the nightstand, and opened the drawer, eyeing the contents. Closing the drawer, he stood, looking down at a large, framed picture of a smiling Sara, and an older woman that could possibly be Sara's grandmother, that sat atop the nightstand.

On instinct, he tilted the picture toward him, and took a second to eye the small tape recorder that sat securely behind the frame, before picking it up, and seeing that the record button was pushed down.

Chapter 24

Laura pulled into the parking lot of her condominium, and parked. After retrieving a bag of groceries from the back seat, she crossed the lot, and came upon Scott, one of the residents, who was seated on a plastic milk crate, working on his motorcycle.

"Hi Scott!" Laura greeted, stopping beside him.

Scott looked up. "Oh! Hi, Laura!"

"What's wrong with it?" She asked, indicating the bike.

"Nothing. I just did some adjustments to the chain. You still want to take it for a spin?"

"I will, someday."

"You always say that," he accused with a smirk.

"I've been busy, lately. Right now, I have to make some phone calls. You just keep that bike in good condition."

She smiled, ruffled his sand-brown hair, then sauntered off, knowing he was watching. And, indeed, his eyes were glued to her backside that was accentuated by her tight-fitted jeans.

"God, you deserved an Oscar for that one!" He said, shaking his head.

***

Tyrone was sitting on the edge of the bed, when Sara returned with two glasses of Chardonnay, in which she handed one to him, then sat up on the bed, Indian-style.

"I'm ready," she told him.

"You have to be more specific," he said. "How much money are you trying to make?"

"A lot," she replied, taking a sip from her drink.

"What are you trying to do?"

"I can transport," she said, "But I'd rather not deal with drugs right now. I want to do set-ups."

"Yeah?"

"I saw you leave out the courtroom with that woman who had Reid arrested. That was clever."

Tyrone smiled. "You think so?"

"Hell, yeah!" Sara let out. "I was tired of hearing him boast about being the next head District Attorney. I hope he gets raped in prison!"

Tyrone laughed. "I can't believe I'm hearing this from you."

"You could've paid me to do the job," she said, taking another sip. "How much does that pay, anyway?"

"From twenty to fifty."

"Thousand?"

"Yeah, depending on the target."

"What did Reid's hit cost?" She wanted to know.

"Thirty."

"Wow! Can you put me on to something like that?"

"I'll see," he said, looking at his watch. "I got to go."

"You can't stay a little while longer?" She appeared desperate.

"Not tonight," he answered, passing her the glass that he hadn't taken one sip out of.

She sat there, watching as he put his shirt back on, still holding both glasses, Sara got off the bed, and followed Tyrone to the front door.

"I guess I'll see you, tomorrow," she said, as Tyrone opened the door to leave.

"I'm taking the rest of the week off," he told her. "I'll see you in trial."

"Okay. Goodnight!"

"Goodnight!"

Tyrone left. Using her foot, Sara pushed the door closed, placed the glasses on the coffee table, then ran back to her bedroom, where she retrieved the tape recorder. The record button was still pushed down, and the red light was still on, which indicated that the tape had not run out.

"Yes!" She cried out to this revelation, as she pressed stop. "Come to momma!"

Sara opened the recorder, and almost fainted. The tape was gone! Now, she was wondering if she'd taken the tape out. Of course, not! She has never taken that tape out. She'd never had any reason to.

***

That Saturday, Laura spent all morning with Mrs. Reid, feeding the animals, milking the cows, and picking tomatoes, pickles, and green peppers.

Now, as they emerged from the field, with Laura carrying a basket of their fresh picks, they saw Kevin approaching.

"Hello, ladies!" He greeted.

"Hi!" Laura returned the greeting.

"Hey, sweetheart!" Mrs. Reid greeted him with a hug. "Kevin, this is Lisa, Christopher's friend."

"How are you, Lisa?"

"I'm fine," Laura answered.

He reached for the basket. "May I?"

"Sure." She allowed him to take it off her hands. Thanks!"

"Now problem."

***

"In prison, this is what they call *fishing*." Zack was telling Carlos through the vent. "I made a fishing line. That's a tube of toothpaste, tied to a string made from my sheets. Go to the bottom of your door. I'll throw the line. If you can't reach it, I'll pull it back, and throw it again. Got it?"

"Yeah," Carlos answered, although he was unsure of this thing they called 'fishing'.

"Let's go!"

Carlos, in only a pair of boxer shorts, being that it was too hot for anything extra, stepped down off the toilet, approached the door, and got down on the floor, looking up under it. Being that the space was a little over three inches wide, it was tough.

"Are you there?" Zack's voice echoed through the narrow hallway.

"Yeah," Carlos answered.

"Stick your arm out as far as you can."

"All right." Feeling awkward, Carlos stretched his arm out as far as he could.

"Here goes!"

Carlos heard the sound of something sliding across the floor toward his cell and stopped. He looked out and saw the tube of toothpaste, that missed his hand by an inch.

"I can't reach it," he told Zack.

"Okay. Hold on."

Zack reeled the tube back in. Seconds later, the tube came sliding down the hallway, again. This time, it slid right into Carlos' hand.

"I got it!" Zack told him.

Carlos reeled the line in, until a sharp, metal object that resemble a knife, came up under his door.

"What the hell!" He exclaimed, as he picked the weapon up by its thick handle that was ostensibly fashioned with portions of bed linen.

"Come to the vent!"

Still eyeing the weapon, Carlos mechanically got up off the floor, approached, and stepped up on the toilet.

"Carlos!" Zack called, pulling Carlos from his trance.

"I'm here," he finally answered.

"Do you like it?"

"I guess so."

***

Laura helped Mrs. Reid prepare a dinner, in which she, Mrs. Reid, and Kevin enjoyed together. Conversation was mostly about the ranch, and Chris. Mrs. Reid was always asking why hadn't he been to visit, and only being told by Kevin and Laura that he'd been very busy.

After dinner, Laura offered to help Mrs. Reid with the dishes, but she declined. Now, with her purse, Laura entered the kitchen, where Mrs. Reid was still washing dishes, and stood beside her.

"Well, I have to get going, Mrs. Reid," Laura told her.

"Okay, baby."

"I'll see you next weekend. Hopefully, if Christopher's not too busy, he will be here, also."

"That would be nice," Mrs. Reid said, drying her hands. "Tell him that I miss him."

"I will." Laura embraced the older woman. "Goodnight!"

"Goodnight, baby!"

Laura exited the kitchen. She didn't like lying to Mrs. Reid, but what was she supposed to tell her? That her son was in jail for rape? Because of her? Because of Tyrone? And, why did he ask if she was going soft on him? Could he really sense that? Well, it doesn't matter, because she has a few tricks up her sleeves. Yes, Tyrone Davis was in for a rude awakening.

Upon entering the living room, Laura saw that Kevin wasn't sitting in the recliner. Maybe, he'd went to the bathroom, she surmised. Oh, well! She made her exit, closing the front door behind her.

"Laura?"

"Huh!" She turned abruptly toward Kevin, who was seated in the rocking chair, at the corner of the porch. It was dark, so she couldn't make out his features

"That is your name, right?"

He knows! She thought but said nothing.

"Look," he went on. "Chris said to tell you that he needs to talk to you."

"About what?" Laura found her voice.

"He didn't say."

Chapter 25

It was Monday, and in Judge Lathan's courtroom, another trial was underway. Twelve jury members were in the box, a camera crew was stationed at the rear, and Tyrone was standing in the center of the room, questioning officer Paige, a white female.

"So," he was saying, "When the chase began, you were ahead of your partner?"

"He was ahead of me when the chase started," she answered

"The chase lasted for quite a while, so we had a few lead changes. I was the one to get close enough to tackle Mr. Walters."

"How did you tackle him?" Tyrone inquired. "Did you jump on his back?"

"I dove into him, catching his legs."

"Then, you both hit the ground?"

The officer nodded. "Yes."

"Where did the assault come from?"

Paige answered, "When he was trying to get out of my grasp, by yanking and jerking his legs, he kicked me several times in my face."

"Did he get away?"

"By the time he'd broken from my grasp, my partner was on top of him."

"Were the drugs found on him?" Asked Tyrone.

"We found the drugs on the ground on our way back to the car."

"Did he say that the drugs belonged to him?"

"He said that they didn't, but we saw him discard them."

"Thank you, officer! Nothing further."

"Cross?" Judge Lathan asked.

Tyrone made for his table, as Sara, who was seated at the defense table with her client, Brandon Walters, a black male, approached the lectern. She was trying her best not to make eye contact with the prosecutor, being that she was still confounded about what happened to that tape, last week.

***

In Judge Edwards' courtroom, Danny had his hands tied with his own trial. Now, he was standing at the lectern, questioning Vera Jones, a white female.

"So," Danny was saying, "You came out of the grocery store, holding bags of groceries?"

"I was pushing a cart full of groceries," she corrected

Danny raised his eyebrows at this. "Okay. What happened when you got to your car?"

"I pulled the cart to the trunk of my car, and started unloading my groceries," she answered. "That's when this guy walked up to me with a gun."

"Then, what did he do?"

"He stood beside me with a black handgun pointed at my stomach.

He told me to not scream, and to place my groceries and pocketbook into the trunk."

"Did he have on a mask?" Danny posed.

"No."

Retrieving a Ziploc bag, containing a black handgun, from his table, Danny turned, and held it up.

"This is what's been marked as States' exhibit two," he told her. "Do you know what this is?"

"It's the gun that I was robbed with."

"Nothing further."

"Cross?" Judge Edwards inquired.

Danny took his seat and nervously chewed on one of his fingernails as Attorney Greg Bush, who was all of a sudden representing the defendant, Sean Hall, approached the lectern.

"Ms. Jones," he spoke, "I'm Greg Bush, the attorney for the defendant, Sean Hall. Now, on the day of this incident, what was the lighting condition?"

"It was daybreak," she answered, "a little after six o'clock."

"Do you wear glasses?"

Vera made a face. "No."

"So, you've never had any problems with your eyes vision wise?"

"No." The look still lingered.

"Twenty-twenty?"

"Yes."

"One second, Your Honor."

Greg approached the state's table and conducted an inaudible chat with Danny and Alvin Newman. When Alvin handed him a sheet of paper, he faced the judge.

"Your Honor, may I approach the witness?"

"You may," answered Edwards.

Greg approached, placed the sheet of paper in front of Vera, then stepped back.

"Ms. Jones," Greg resumed, "What I just placed in front of you, is State's exhibit five. Can you tell me what that is?"

"A police report," she answered.

"Of your case?"

"Yes."

"Go down to where it says, *subject one*," he told her. "Are you there?"

"Yes." The witness was regarding the document before her.

"Before I go any further," the attorney said, "I want you to take a few seconds to look that over."

As Vera studied the report, Danny wondered, for the millionth time, how did Sean Hall manage to hire the illustrious Greg Bush. He wouldn't step foot inside a courtroom for anything less than twenty thousand. Hall was indigent. Perhaps, he'd contacted someone with that kind of mazuma.

"Are you ready?" Greg inquired.

Vera nodded. "Yes."

"What you've just read," he resumed, "Is the description that you gave of your assailant, am I right?"

"Yes."

"I tried to memorize it the best I could but stop me if I'm off. You said that your assailant was a black male, right?"

"Yes," she answered.

"Around five-eight to five-ten?"

"Yes."

"Late twenties?"

"Yes."

"Dark skin-tone?"

"Yes."

"Dark skin-tone?" Greg repeated.

"Yes," Vera answered though there was a hint of uncertainty in her voice.

"And this is the guy that you pointed to at the defense table, earlier, right?"

"Yes."

"I have one more question," said the attorney. "What is your idea of *dark skin-tone*?"

"Anyone who's not white."

Greg nodded. "Thank you! Nothing further."

***

"Greg Bush!" Tyrone exclaimed.

For lunch, Tyrone and Danny decided to venture to the cafeteria, where they were now seated across from each other.

"I don't know how he got the case," Danny said, shaking his head. "Hall was represented by a public defender."

Tyrone raised his eyebrows. "You know, Greg Bush is like the white Johnny Cochran."

"Don't remind me."

"He's no threat to me."

"Godzilla is no threat to you," Danny pointed out. "I can't beat this guy. I can already hear his closing."

"How was his opening?"

"Phenomenal!"

***

Back inside the courtroom, Greg Bush was pacing the floor, while conducting his closing argument.

"I'm not here to convince you that Ms. Jones wasn't robbed. Maybe she was. Who knows? If she *was* robbed, it wasn't by my client, Mr. Hall. I know that much. Where's the evidence? A black handgun with no fingerprints? That gun was found in a wooded area of the apartments where Mr. Hall resides. Do you know how many black handguns are found in those woods, a week?"

"Who's to say that this particular gun was the gun? Who's to say that the gun found last week wasn't the gun? What about the gun that was found last night? Everyone has a black handgun. My dog has a black handgun.

"But, that's not it. Ms. Jones claims that her assailant was dark skinned. I want everyone to take a look at my client. He's almost *my* skin tone. From a distance, he looks like one of my relatives. Her definition of dark skin is anyone who's not white. That could be any black person on this planet. I think that was a racial comment …"

***

When the jurors on Brandon Walters trial retreated to the jury room to deliberate, Sara contacted Ellen, and they rendezvoused in the cafeteria, where they were now sharing a table.

"Girl, I don't know what to tell you about that," Ellen was saying, shaking her head.

Sara sighed. "I know."

"Maybe, you forgot to put the tape in."

"I don't remember taking it out," Sara contradicted. "And he admitted to setting Chris up."

Ellen leaned forward, eyes wide, voice just above a whisper. "Are you serious!"

"Yes."

"On tape?"

"I don't have a tape, Ellen."

"Damn!" Ellen leaned back. "Maybe, he did get the tape."

***

Danny was slowly pacing back and forth, in the center of the courtroom, as he did his closing argument.

"You don't think Ms. Jones knows what her assailant looks like? He didn't cover his face. How hard is it to forget the face of somebody who's done something bad to you? That's kind of hard.

"If Ms. Jones thought she had the wrong man, she wouldn't have pointed him out in court, today. It doesn't matter if she called

him *dark skin,* or *purple skin.* He's darker than her! Or, in her definition, he's not white.

"Is she wrong for saying that? Of course not! Who are we to
question her beliefs? People, she was able to identify the man that
robbed her at gunpoint. That's all that matters."

***

Bobby contacted his childhood friend, Kyle Johnson, who was
a private attorney, and asked him to drive down from Atlanta, where
he was part-owner of a small law firm in the Buckhead area.

Now, they were seated across from each other, at the Deloris
Delights Restaurant, having ordered nothing but cups of coffee.

"Kyle, I don't know much about the case," Bobby was saying.
"I don't even know much about Carlos."

"But you want me to do his appeal." This was not a question.

"Yes," Bobby answered, with more force than intended.

"Okay." Kyle stood to leave. "I'll see what I can do."

Bobby didn't respond. He was thinking about Tonya, and the
lethargic mood she'd been in, ever since Carlos' trial. He didn't care
anything for Carlos, but Bobby felt that if he could get Carlos' case
overturned - or, at least, get his time dropped to a lesser sentence,
perhaps, Tonya's healing process would increase.

***

Back in Judge Lathan's courtroom, seated at his table, Tyrone
absently drummed his ink pen on the side of his head, as the jury
members filed into the jury box, taking their seats. Lathan called on
the foreman, who was a black female.

"I understand that the jury has reached a verdict," said Lathan.

"We have," she answered.

"Would you, please, read your verdict out to the court?"

She regarded the verdict sheet in her hand. "We, the jury, find
the defendant, Brandon Walters, on count one, possession of a
Georgia controlled substance, guilty. We, the jury, find the same
defendant, on count two, assault on a peace officer, guilty."

***

"That's all I can tell you, Mr. Hall." Greg Bush told his client,
who was seated beside him at the defense table.

"So, somebody just walked up, and paid you to take my case?" Hall asked.

"Basically," the attorney gave, with a mere shrug of the shoulders.

At that time, Judge Edwards entered, and everyone rose at the call of the bailiff.

"You may be seated," Edwards baded, as she took her own seat. "If we don't have any motions to entertain, we can go ahead and bring in the jurors."

"None from the defense, Your Honor," Bush announced.

"None from the state," offered Danny.

Edwards turned to the bailiff. "Bring in the jurors!"

Well, this is it, Danny thought, as he watched the court officer make for the jury room. He didn't need a psychic to tell him what the verdict would be.

"Does it bother you that Greg Bush has never lost a trial?" Alvin Newman whispered to Danny, pulling him from his reverie.

"I'm not worried," Danny replied.

"Confident?"

"No. I'm just not worried."

At that time, the jury members entered, and took their seats. Under the judge's instruction, the foreman, a white female, stood to read the verdict.

"We, the jury, find the defendant, Sean Hall, on one count of armed robbery, not guilty."

***

In the parking garage, Greg Bush was standing in front of his burgundy Mercedes-Benz, when he saw Tyrone approaching. He pulled out a wad of folded bills and handed them to Greg.

"It's all there," Tyrone said, as he kept walking.

"Tyrone?" Greg called after him. Tyrone stopped in his tracks and turned to face him. "Did you know this kid?"

"Does it matter?" Tyrone asked.

Greg shrugged. "Not really."

***

"I don't know, Danny," Connie Edwards was saying to Danny, as they exited the courthouse. "Some people just have that gift."

"If I had that gift –"

"You don't need that gift," she cut him off. "You're doing just fine."

"Thanks!"

When they made it to her Jaguar, Connie deactivated the alarm, and started the engine by remote. Danny held the driver's door open for her.

"Well, I guess I have to get home to my babies," she told him.

"Yeah, me too," Danny said, feeling awkward.

"Have they gotten used to their new place, yet?"

Danny shrugged, "They're still marking their territory."

"You have to train them, Danny. They're like dogs, but smarter when it comes to home-training."

She can't be serious. Danny thought, but said, "I'll get the hang of it, someday."

That made her smile. "Do I need to assist you?"

"I would appreciate it."

"Would Saturday be fine?"

Now, Danny was smiling. "Of course."

***

"Sara, how in the hell did you manage that!" Chris said, after Sara, who was accompanied by Ellen and Danny, told him about the missing tape.

Sara shook her head. "I don't know."

"I believe that she just forgot to put the tape in," Ellen voiced. Chris dropped his head in disbelief.

"I tried," Sara offered.

Chris lifted his head and sighed. "Yeah, you did."

"With or without that," Danny broke the silence that ensued, "We may be in luck."

"How's that?" Asked Chris.

"I'll know by Saturday, then I'll let you know, next week."

***

220

Tyrone made it home, just in time for dinner. Although he and Lisa were in the middle of a divorce, and have yet to promulgate this to Ebony, they still tried to act *normal* in her presence. Now, the three of them were seated at the dinner table, enjoying the meal that Lisa had prepared.

"Daddy, you look different on TV," Ebony was saying.

Tyrone looked over at her. "How so?"

"You look mean," she pointed out, with a grin. "It's like you're a different person."

"Well, I *am* a different person when I'm at work," he told his daughter. 'I'm dealing with bad people, and that requires me to be mean."

"I want a job like yours when I grow up," she announced.

Tyrone did not like this. "I thought you wanted to be a doctor."

"I changed my mind."

"You wouldn't like my job."

"Why not?" She asked.

"You have to be somebody that you're not," he answered. "Then, on top of that, you make a lot of enemies. You don't want to have to go through life, looking over your shoulders, knowing that one day, some bad person you've sent to prison will come back and blow your brains out!"

"Tyrone!" Lisa cried out.

"I'm telling her the truth!" He insisted. "This is a dangerous job!"

Chapter 26

The following morning, at the office of public defenders, Sara was seated at her cubicle, drinking coffee, when her phone rang.

"Sara Jennings!" She answered. "Not really. Yes, I did. Okay. I don't know." She grabbed a pen and began writing. "What's your name, again? Bar number? Phone number? Okay. Once I check you out, I'll call you, and we'll get together to discuss the case."

Sara, inadvertently, slammed the receiver into its cradle. She was, indeed, afraid. All she could think about was Tyrone, and that missing tape. Getting up, she quick-stepped to Ellen's cubicle, where Ellen was consuming a breakfast sandwich.

"Ellen!" she hissed, keeping her voice down, for the sake of anyone in earshot. "Some guy just called me, saying that he was paid to handle Carlos West's appeal, asking if we could meet somewhere to discuss the case."

Ellen took a sip of her coffee, then grabbed the piece of paper from Sara's hand, looking at it.

"I don't trust it!" Sara carried on. "It's kind of suspicious that this would happen all of a sudden. I'll check his bar number during lunch. Something's not right. I can't let −" She broke off abruptly when she noticed the look that Ellen was giving her. "What?"

"This is Kyle Johnson," Ellen said, waving the piece of paper.

'You know him?" asked Sara.

"He's the lawyer who defended that guy in that 'Halloween Massacre' case, in two thousand."

***

'What made you go off like that?" Connie asked Tyrone, who was seated in one of her conference chairs, as she was perched up on the edge of the desk, in front of him.

"I don't know," he answered, avoiding eye contact.

"You need a vacation," she told him. "Why haven't you taken one yet?"

"I haven't found the time."

"Well, you need to find it, because you're stressing. Stress is the number one cause of death. You do know that, right?"

"Yeah, but I'm not stressing," Tyrone admitted. "I just have a lot of work to do."

"Tyrone!" She grabbed his chin, and lifted his face toward her, "You're pushing for the DA's position. Now, I don't know if you're too busy to notice, but you're the only assistant DA that has proven yourself worthy of the position."

***

"Carlos! Carlos!"

Carlos was roused from his slumber by the sound of Zack's voice, coming through the vent. Stretching, he got out of bed, and climbed on top of the toilet.

"What's up?" Carlos asked, voice a bit groggy.

"Man, I just got a letter from the deputy warden." Zack informed.

Carlos sighed. "Is that what you woke me up for?"

"Of course. Check it out! It says: 'Dear Zachary Bates. I've done a thorough investigation on your incident and ascertained that you acted under self-defense. Therefore, all charges will be dismissed, and you will be released from Administration Segregation on the twelfth'. Man, that's Thursday!"

"Yeah, it is," replied Carlos. "You got lucky."

"It's not luck," Zack told him. "It's just that these people don't care about inmate on inmate violence. It's either inmate-on-inmate, or inmate-on-staff. Trust me, they don't want inmate-on-staff."

Carlos was nodding his head. "You're right."

"So, when are you signing those papers?" Zack inquired.

"I don't know."

"You can't let that go, Carlos. Are you going to spend your whole bid, running?"

"Nah," Carlos answered.

"That's what I'm talking about!" Zack let out." And, I got your back."

***

Sara had agreed to meet attorney Kyle Johnson at Deloris Delights, to go over Carlos West's case. Now, as they sat across from each other, Kyle was perusing the contents of a folder, as Sara, who was a bit relieved that Ellen had shed some light on her about the attorney, slowly sipped pink lemonade from a straw.

"So, you've already filed the motion for a new trial?" Kyle finally asked, placing the folder on the table.

"Yes. I also stated the claim for the record."

"Do you want to handle the hearing for the new trial?"

"I was going to," she answered, "But you said that you were paid to handle it."

"I was paid to handle the appeal," Kyle told her. "But, if your hands are tied, I'll go ahead and handle that, also."

"My hands are very tied," she offered, with a smile.

"Is that the trial transcript?" He asked, indicating the two manila envelopes on the table, in front of Sara.

"Yes."

"You can go ahead and file a motion to withdraw, and I'll do my notice of entry."

***

"I thought you said *next week*." Chris said to Danny, who was already seated in the visitation booth when he arrived.

"Look," Danny said, disregarding the accusation, "Hire Greg Bush to take the case."

"What!"

"Hire Greg Bush," he repeated. "He's a guaranteed win. That way, I won't look too bad in front of the media."

"It's not about you or the media!" Chris rectified. "It's about *me* looking bad. Besides, Greg and I are not on good terms."

"That doesn't mean a thing when it comes to money. Greg is all about money."

"That may be true," said Chris, "But I don't want him taking my money and blowing my trial, intentionally."

Danny simpered. "Now, why would he do that? He has a reputation to uphold. Why would he choose your case to break his impeccable winning streak?" That would be extremely asinine, if you ask me."

Chris sighed. "You may be right."

"I *am* right. Hire him!"

"I'll make the call, but I can't make him take the case."

"He will," Danny assured. "And have him file a motion for a speedy trial, immediately! I'll have it heard as soon as I get it."

"The thing is to get Judge Edwards to grant it."

"I'll work on that," Danny told him. "You just call Greg Bush!"

***

"Girl, you're paranoid," Ellen told Sara, as they walked through the parking garage, headed for their cars.

"Well, why hasn't he said anything to me?" Sara asked.

"Probably because you haven't said anything to *him*. You know how he is."

"Yeah, you're right. It could just be me."

"Going to see Chris?" Ellen asked, as they made it to her car, and stopped.

"Friday," Sara answered, looking around.

Ellen sighed. "Me too. Right now, I'm going home to eat, take a long bubble bath, and lay down."

This made Sara smile. "That sounds like a good idea! I guess I'll see you in the morning."

"Okay."

Ellen got into her car, as Sara made for her own, which was farther down the deck. She unlocked her door and opened it. Before she could do anything else, a large man in a ski mask rushed up from behind her, wrapping one arm around her waist, and covering her mouth and nose with a rag that reeked of chlorine.

Her briefcase and keys clattered to the ground, as she tried to struggle with her attacker. Two more masked men came into the picture, one carrying a small paper bag. More frightened than she'd ever been in her whole entire life, Sara kicked her feet out. She managed to connect with the steering wheel of her car, blaring the horn, hoping to get Ellen's attention. She couldn't see her for the green Chevy Suburban that was parked beside her car, obscuring her view.

The big guy pulled her back, surceasing her SOS attempt, while the other two looked around. Ellen would have heard the horn, had her music not been turned up as loud as it was. It didn't matter, because Ellen was pulling off, just as Sara began to lose consciousness.

Once her body went limp, the guy without the paper bag, helped the big guy prop Sara up in the driver's seat, then stepped back. That's when the third man walked over, knelt down, and dumped the contents of the bag into her lap, which was a black, rubber belt, a silver spoon, lighter, small bags of heroin, and a syringe.

After tying the belt around her left arm, he grabbed the spoon, and a bag of heroin, dumping the drug in the scoop of the spoon, and tossed the plastic bag onto the floorboard. Using the lighter, he set a flame under the spoon, until the drug liquidized completely. Tossing the lighter onto the floorboard, he held the syringe over his head, for the big guy to pull the top off.

Filling the syringe with the drug, he tossed the spoon onto the floor, then injected the drug into her vein. Once that was complete, he brushed the other bags of heroin off her lap, and onto the floor, while leaving the syringe in her lap and the belt intact.

The big guy handed him the keys and briefcase, in which he placed on the passenger seat. He closed the driver's door and after seeing that the coast was clear, they all retreated in the direction from whence they came.

***

Later that night, Tyrone was sitting on the edge of his bed, watching the news. They were doing a report on today's top story, where a Caucasian male reporter was reporting from downtown Linkton County's parking garage.

"It was here," he was saying, "in the parking garage of downtown Linkton County, that Sara Jennings, a Linkton County public defender, was found in her car, apparently overdosed from a high dosage of heroin. She was rushed to the hospital, where she'll undergo treatment. Now, standing with me, is assistant district attorney Barbara Hutchins, who discovered the unconscious public defender.

"Ms. Hutchins, how did you make this discovery?"

"Well," Barbara started, as the camera zoomed in on her," I was about to get into my truck that was parked beside her car, when I noticed her sitting motionless in her car. Her windows are tinted, so I looked through the windshield, and realized that something was wrong."

"Were you very familiar with the public defender?" The reporter asked.

"Yes. And this is not like her."

There was a knock at the bedroom door. Tyrone switched the TV off, and opened the door to Lisa, who handed him a white envelope.

"Court date?" He asked.

She nodded. "Yeah. I think we should explain it to Ebony afterwards."

"That's fine," he said, closing the door once she walked off.

***

The following day, Ellen entered the recovery room that Sara was housed in. There was a male doctor, and a female nurse standing over Sara, who looked as if she had not slept in days. Not wanting to interrupt, Ellen waited just beyond the door.

Sara spotted her. "Hi, Ellen!"

"Are you okay?" Ellen asked, but didn't budge.

"I feel terrible!"

"I'll have the nurse to bring you some food and coffee, okay?" The doctor told Sara.

Sara nodded. "Okay."

"Don't try to leave, again!" He said, pointing a finger at her.

"I can't feel my legs," she replied.

"Good!" The doctor said, then left the room, followed by the nurse.

Thankful that they didn't question her, nor sermonize her on the visitation rights of patients, Ellen crossed over the bed.

"Sara, what happened?"

"I don't remember, Ellen," she answered. "All I remember is waking up to a bunch of bright lights. The doctor told me, this morning, that they had to resuscitate me from an overdose of heroin. I don't use heroin!"

"Well, according to the news, you do."

"It was on the news! Sara exclaimed.

"And, in the papers," Ellen said, extracting a small newspaper article from her pocketbook, handing it to Sara. "Barbara Hutchins found you in your car, unconscious. This was right after I left you in the parking garage."

Sara was reading the article. "They claim to have found a syringe in my lap, a belt tied around my left arm, and drug paraphernalia on the floorboard of my car. That's a lie!"

"They showed the footage on the news," Ellen was reluctant to point out.

Sara looked down at her left arm. There was a piece of cotton in the fold of it, held in place by a band-aide. She pulled them off and stared at the needle-sized hole that was there. Right then, everything started to come back to her.

"This is crazy, Sara!" Ellen's voice seemed miles away. "You don't remember *anything*?"

Sara looked up at Ellen, with tears forming in her eyes. "I was attacked!"

Playa Ray

Chapter 27

"How much did you hit her with?" Tyrone asked Rick, as he watched the goings-on of the community park, from the front passenger seat of Rick's truck.

"A whole twenty piece," Rick answered.

"That's what? Two hits?"

"Pretty much."

Tyrone smiled at this soon-to-be right-hand man. "Rick, the chemist! That has a nice ring to it. Are you ready to take over?"

"When do I start?" He asked.

"Soon."

***

Sara was finally able to check herself out to the hospital. It was already dark out when she and Ellen exited the building, heading for Ellen's car.

"For some reason," Ellen said, "I had the feeling that every news station in the world would be waiting on you to come out."

"I'm just glad that the police are not waiting on me," Sara replied, looking around for any sign of potential danger, being that she was still a bit tremulous from yesterday's ordeal.

"Judge Lathan handled that for you," Ellen told her.

"Remind me to thank him."

When they climbed into Ellen's car, she started it and adjusted the air conditioner, as Selena's *"Como La Flor"* played at a low volume.

"Do you want to stop by your place to grab some clothes and hygiene items?" Ellen asked, pulling away from the curb.

Sara said, "Right now, I'm too scared to go anywhere near that place."

"What makes you think that my place is any safer?"

Sara didn't respond.

"We're about the same size," Ellen went on, "So you should be able to fit into my clothes."

"Thanks, Ellen! I owe you one."

***

The next morning, Carlos lied awake in bed, after a long, and sleepless, night. Perhaps, he couldn't sleep for thinking of Tonya. He wondered how she was doing. What was her mood at this time? How did she feel after testifying against him in a trial that left him serving thirty years of his life in prison? But, most of all, what induced her to change her mind?

Clomp! Clomp! Clomp! Clomp!

Carlos was pulled from his reverie by the sounds of heavy boots assaulting the hallway's tiled floor. Then, came the sound of a steel window flap sliding open.

"Zachery Bates!" He heard officer bark. "Pack it up! We'll be back in five minutes. Be ready!"

The boots retreated back up the hall. Smiling, Carlos got up and went over to the vent.

"Get up, Michael Myers!" He jested.

Zack came to the vent. "I'm out of here!"

"I heard," Said Carlos." Look, I'm coming out tomorrow."

"That's what I'm talking about!" His friend let out. "Yard call?"

"Yard call."

"I got your back."

***

"I know you had something to do with that!" Chris, who was standing, accused Tyrone, who was seated on the other side of the visitation booth.

"Is that what you think?" Tyrone asked, coolly.

"It's what I 'know'!" Chris shot back. "Just like you had something to do with me being in!"

"Okay. Let's say that I *am* the source," Tyrone said. "Can you prove it? Of course, not."

"You won't get away with this!"

Tyrone stood, locking eyes with him. "I already have."

"I swear!" Chris spoke, pointing a finger at Tyrone. "When I catch you, I'm going to kill you, bastard!"

"Law nineteen," Tyrone quoted, "Know who you're dealing with. Do not offend the wrong person."

***

Back in his car, and driving along the highway, Tyrone could not stop thinking about the threat that Chris made towards him. It was well-deserved, he'd admit, but it was also borderline racist, and that was not acceptable. After another moment of cogitating this, he grabbed his cellular, and dialed Laura's number.

"Hello?" She came on the line.

"Hey, Beauty!"

"Oh! Hi, sweetheart!" She spouted. "How are you?"

"I'm good," he lied, ready to get down to business. "Look, didn't you say that Chris took you to his mother's ranch?"

***

Immediately after getting off the phone with Tyrone, Laura, who was enjoying a bowl of ice cream and a pay-per-view movie before he called, rushed out of her unit, struggling to put her arms through the sleeves of her coat.

"This man doesn't stop", she thought, as she half-ran, and half-stumbled down the stairs, en lieu of taking the elevator. Tyrone didn't sound upset, but his query of the Reid's' ranch had triggered Laura's consternation. Whatever his intentions were, they were not good, and all she could think about was Mrs. Reid.

Getting to the next floor, she snatched the exit door open, and ran to Scott's apartment, where she banged on the door with her fist.

"Scott! Scott!"

Seconds later, she heard the locks being disengaged, before the door came open to a turbid-looking Scott, who was wearing a blue robe.

"Scott, I need to borrow your bike!" Laura asserted, through heavy breathing." It's an emergency!"

***

Tyrone walked into a body shop, looking around. Though everything appeared legitimate, he knew otherwise, which was the advantage he had over former offenders that he maintained contact with.

"Tyrone!" A young, Spanish guy approached. "What's happening, amigo!"

"What's going on, Perez?" They shook hands

"Nothing much," he answered. "Working hard."

"Still chopping cars?" Tyrone asked, with raised eyebrows.

"Nooo!" Perez denied. "Everything's legit."

"Yeah, right!" Tyrone said, taking another tour of the place. "Look, I'm ready for that favor."

***

It was almost dark, when Laura reached the ranch. She, thankful that the motorcycle wasn't loud, drove up the gravel road, to the barn, where she stopped, and cautiously looked around. Seeing no one, she slowly accelerated through the barn, and out the other side.

Now, with the sole light incandescing, she traveled the same trail that Chris had taken her horse-back riding on, until she came out on the open range, where they had target practice. Approaching the small, wooden shack, where Chris kept his guns, she killed the engine, dropped the kickstand, and dismounted. Getting to the door, she removed the helmet. That's when she realized that, not once, had she thought about the archaic-looking security lock that was now impediment to her.

"Damn!" She exclaimed, feeling as if time was running out, but not knowing why she felt that way.

Instinctively, she began buffeting the antediluvian lock with the helmet. Then, realizing that she was only damaging the helmet, she stopped, and looked around for something more suitable, to no avail. When her eyes landed on the bike, she no longer thought about the lock, but the door of the cabin, in which she knew was quite unsound.

"Sorry, Scott!" she said, as she donned the helmet, and mounted the bike. "I'll buy you another one."

Starting the bike, Laura rode a short distance up the trail, and made a U-turn, to align the bike with her target. As she revved the motor, she absently looked around. That's when she spotted what she was looking for. To the right of her, was a large, concrete boulder.

***

It was completely dark, when Laura, with a rifle strapped to her back, returned to the barn. Cutting the engine, she got off, and pushed the bike through the extremely-dark barn, toward the front-end, guided by the distant light of the stars, and Mrs. Reid's porch light.

Reaching the entrance, she rolled the bike into a corner, propping it against the wall. Leaving the helmet on the straw covered ground beside it, she approached the doorway, pulling a pair of safety goggles from inside her coat, putting them atop her head. When she unstrapped the rifle, the animals began to stir, as if they had a sixth sense that something was about to happen. Hell, Laura herself didn't know if anything was about to happen. For all she knew, she was also moving on instinct.

Then, at that instant, Laura heard the faint sound of tires crunching on gravel. She spotted a vehicle, which appeared to be a truck, from the size of the headlights, slowly approached the house that was a good forty to fifty yards from the barn.

"Shut up!" She hissed at the animals, who were probably just as scared as she was.

Dropping the safety goggles over her eyes, Laura dropped to one knee, and watched the dark-colored pick-up through the rifle's scope, as its lights went dead. She couldn't make out the occupant, but she kind of had an inkling of who it could be.

"Don't make me do this, Tyrone," she muttered, as the truck came to a stop in front of the house.

The driver killed the engine, then got out, clad in dark clothing, and a skull cap that was pulled real low over his face. Laura still couldn't make out any features, but she could make out the dark object he carried in his hand, as he ascended the stairs.

A gun!

This prompted Laura to act fast. She locked her sight onto the center of his back, then squeezed the trigger. The bullet caused his body to freeze mid-stride, before falling backwards down the steps. The animals were in total helter-skelter, now.

Still clutching the rile, Laura trotted over to the body that had landed on the gravel, with one foot on the bottom step. Looking down she saw that it wasn't Tyrone, but some Hispanic man.

***

Laura had to drive for almost ten miles, before reaching a service station, where she had to use the 4-1-1 operative line on a payphone, to reach the local sheriff's office.

"Sheriff's office!" A male's voice boomed through the earpiece. "Sheriff Taylor speaking."

"Yes, Sheriff Taylor?" Laura spoke. "I'm calling to report shots fired at the Reid's ranch."

"Who am I speaking to?" He inquired.

"It doesn't matter who I am, Sheriff!" Laura snapped. "Right now, you need to be calling all cars!"

**

Three Sheriff cars sped up the gravel road of the ranch. When they stopped in front of the house, they all got out, and stood around the cadaver with guns drawn.

"Green, check the body!" Taylor commanded. "Sanders, check the barn! I'm going in."

Taylor jolted up the steps, as his deputies tended to their duties. He'd been knowing the Reids for more than thirty years, and he knew that they, like everybody else in the county, never locked their doors.

Therefore, without knocking, he entered the house, gun aimed. Everything seems normal. Still, he checked every room in the house, until he came upon Mrs. Reid's bedroom. The door was standing wide open, and Mrs. Reid was lying in her bed with the covers pulled up to her chest and her eyes closed. Lowering his gun, Taylor sagely approached the bed, and looked down at the frail-looking woman.

"Mrs. Reid?"

She opened her eyes. "Yes."

"Are you okay?"

**

Over an hour later, in the living room, Mrs. Reid was seated in her recliner, while Avery, Kevin , Sheriff Taylor, and the two deputies stood around, talking.

"Something strange is going on," Avery was saying, shaking his head.

"So, you found the shotgun that was used on the guy, in the barn?" Kevin asked Taylor.

"I did," Sanders answered. "There were also a pair of safety goggles."

Taylor said, "it looks as if whatever he had planned, someone put a stop to it. I can't say what his intentions were, but he was armed."

Kevin turned to his mother. "Momma, do you know anything about a shotgun being in the barn?"

"There are no shot-guns in my barn, sweetheart," she answered, sweetly.

"Momma, I'm sorry, but you have to move!" He told her. "You can stay at my place."

"He's right, Beth Anne," Avery gave voice.

"I am not leaving my home," she said, with no inflection of anger.

"It's not safe here," Avery persisted.

Mrs. Reid smiled. "Don't worry, my angel will not let anyone harm me."

Playa Ray

Chapter 28

The next day, it was yard call, and Carlos, who'd been released from protective custody two hours ago, emerged from the building behind four other prisoners. He stopped short of the entrance and took stock of the fenced-in perimeter.

There was a basketball game, in which other prisoners were lined along the fence, watching. Other prisoners were walking around. There were a handful of prisoners in the workout section, lifting weights, including Deandre, and the two guys who'd aided him in assailing Carlos.

A few feet away from them, Carlos spotted Zack, who was smoking a cigarette, and watching him. Then, his tall, lanky friend pulled a skull cap over his head. Carlos did the same, then set off in their direction. At this time, Deandre was on the bench. As Carlos neared, Zack dropped his cigarette, grounding it out with his boot, then shoved his hands into his pockets, just as Carlos had his. His right hand was gripping the weapon that Zack made for him.

Deandre sat up. Carlos' grip tightened. Deandre stood, stretching. Carlos slid the shank out of his pocket. Deandre spotted him but, before he could react, Carlos drove his make-shift blade into his side. They both fell over the bench, to the ground. Carlos was on top of Deandre, stabbing and punching him. One of his cronies tried to assist him but, before he could reach for Carlos, Zack, with a shank akin to Carlos', came from behind, and drove it through the side of the guy's neck.

The man yelled out in pain, as he went down. Zack kept walking, blending in with a group of guys that were tearing away from the scene.

***

"And his name is Carlos West?" The swarthy complexion female prison guard asked, regarding her computer screen.

"Yes," answered attorney Kyle Johnson, who'd finally taken the hour and half drive to the prison Carlos was housed. She pointed. "If you would walk through those –"

She broke off, as an alarm sounded. Then, almost instantaneously, a male's voice boomed through her radio that sat on the desk. "We have a ten-seventy-six; West side yard! Ten-seventy-six; West side yard."

"Sir!" The officer spoke. "You may have to come back next week."

"What's going on?" Kyle wanted to know.

"A riot," she replied. "We have to shut everything down."

As officers rushed past them, in full riot gear, Kyle thought about the unnecessary drive he'd taken. All he could do was shake his head.

***

"I can't believe this!" Chris cried out, after Kevin informed him of the shooting at the ranch that left a dead man lying in front of his mother's front door.

"They found the rifle at the entrance of the barn," Kevin went on. "Somebody saved momma."

"How did the Sheriff know about it?"

"Taylor said that some female called and notified him about it. Said she wouldn't give her name. But, in order for her to know about the shooting, she had to have been on the ranch at the time."

"Laura!" Chris said, almost to himself.

***

After hearing of the demise of Perez, on the Reid's ranch, Tyrone called a meeting with Charles, Block, and Rick, at the park, where they were seated. Tyrone was pacing back and forth, as he did in trials, when presenting his arguments to a jury.

"I still can't figure this out," he was saying. "I didn't use the phone. He couldn't have been wired, because he didn't know I was coming. But, yet and still, somebody knew that he was coming."

"Hell, the old lady probably killed him," Rick offered.

"I doubt that, Rick," Tyrone replied, stopping to face his goons. "I know foul play when I smell it!"

***

That Saturday, Connie Edwards spent all day at Danny's place, helping out with the new kittens. Then, once agreeing to have dinner at a nice restaurant, Connie drove home to freshen up, with the promise of meeting him at the restaurant, where they were now seated across from each other.

"You need to give them names," Connie was telling Danny.

"I still haven't thought of any," he replied.

"Don't give them names that you would give a dog, like Spike, Rover, or 'Scooby-Doo."

"Scooby-Doo?"

Connie laughed. "I'm just saying. They have to be precious names."

"I'll come up with something," he promised, ready to change subjects. "How's your dinner?"

"Great!" She answered. "I may have to order another side of potatoes. They're good!"

"Yes, they are," Danny concurred, wondering if he should, or how he should broach the subject. "Can I ask you something?"

"I'm listening," she said, forking a chunk of meatloaf into her mouth.

"What do you think about Christopher Reid's case?"

She took a sip of her wine before answering, "I really haven't given it any thought. Why?"

"I think his lawyer's going to file for a speedy trial," he told her, "and I'm not going to object to it. I want to get this case over with, as soon as possible."

"So, what are you asking?"

"For you to grant the motion and allow me to set an immediate trial date."

***

"So, he didn't sound concerned?" Sara asked Ellen of Tyrone's inquiry about her on yesterday.

Both clad in pajamas, Sara and Ellen were sitting on the living room floor of Ellen's apartment, playing cards across the coffee table, as Jennifer Lopez's *"Love Don't Cost A Thing"* played from the stereo.

"Not at all," Ellen answered.

"Did he look, or sound suspicious?"

"No," Ellen gave, with a shrug.

Sara sighed. "And you still don't think he had anything to do with this?"

"Right now, I don't know what to think."

***

That Monday, Kyle made another trip out to the prison and, this time, was granted a visit with his new client, whom he ascertained was a part of last week's disruption.

Now, Kyle was seated in the attorney's booth, when two guards escorted Carlos, who was handcuffed and shackled, into the other side, and locked him in. Once Carlos took a seat, Kyle grabbed the phone receiver, in which they were to communicate through. Carlos grabbed the other with his cuffed hand.

"Carlos West?" Kyle asked, noticing that he didn't look as though he'd been in any kind of riot.

"Yeah," Carlos answered.

"I'm attorney Kyle Johnson," he went on, "And I was hired to represent you in your motion for a new trial."

"What happened to Sara Jennings?"

"She had a slight accident, but she's okay." Kyle made sure to add. "I was here, Friday, to see you, but a riot broke out.

Today, I find out that you were the source of it. You have a new assault charge. Another guy was stabbed in the neck and died.

You weren't charged with murder, because witnesses say that a Caucasian man killed him. He got away. Did you know him?"

"Nope," Carlos answered curtly.

Kyle shrugged. "Anyway, Ms. Jennings already filed the motion for a new trial. All I did was pull some strings to get you in court quicker."

Carlos perked up. "When?"

"I don't know when," Kyle replied, "But it'll be quick. Trust me! Let's just hope that the prosecutor doesn't mention this new charge of yours."

***

Sara couldn't remember the last time she'd rode the commuter bus, which was why her ride from Ellen's place to the car rental place, seemed extremely awkward. She was hoping she'd never have to do that again, for a long time. As she entered the establishment, and approached the front desk, she was greeted by a young, white female.

"Hi!" The woman greeted her. "Welcome to Budget Rental! How may I help you?"

"I'd like to rent a car."

***

"Chris, I can't tell you more than I already have," said Laura, who was opposite Christ in the visitation booth.

"You got me in here, Laura!" Chris said, trying to contain his anger. "I deserve some kind of explanation!"

"You'll be okay," she promised, as she stood to leave.

"Laura, somebody tried to kill my mother," he finally let out. "Some unknown female saved her."

Laura asked, "Is she okay?"

"Yeah, she's fine." Chris stood, locking eyes with her. "Thanks!"

***

Driving, Charles was on his way home from Robinson & McCoy's Seafood, where he had a job interview, and managed to score a job. This was his last day working for Tyrone, and he wanted to do something legitimate for a change.

He was coming upon the Linkton County Jail, when he spotted Laura's BMW pull out of the lot and ride past him, in the opposite lane. Not knowing what to make of this, Charles grabbed his cell phone, and dialed Tyrone's number.

"Yeah?" Tyrone answered.

"You won't believe this," Charles began.

***

Laura didn't make it home, until later that night. Upon entering her apartment, she dropped her keys into the small bowl on the counter that separates the kitchen from the living room, then made for her bedroom door. She gasped, throwing her hand over her chest, as if to stop her heart from leaping out. She did not expect to see Tyrone sitting on the edge of her bed. In the dark!

"Tyrone, you got to stop doing that!" She said, shaking her head.

"Let's take a ride," he told her.

Parked outside, in the black van, Charles and Block watched as Tyrone and Laura exited the building and made for Tyrone's Mercedes. Charles waited until they pulled out of the parking lot, before starting the van, and trailing them as planned.

"So, how was your weekend?" Tyrone asked, keeping his eyes on the road.

"It was okay," she answered.

"Do anything spectacular?"

"No."

Tyrone made a right turn onto the next street. That's when Laura leaned forward and spotted the all-too-familiar van in the right-wing mirror. She'd already spotted the van in the parking lot, when she and Tyrone emerged from her building.

"Have you talked to Ebony yet?" She asked, in an attempt to keep the conversation going, while formulating a plan.

"About the divorce?" Asked Tyrone.

"Yeah."

"Nope," he answered. "We decided that we'll do that after court."

"I can imagine how she'll feel, hearing that her mom and dad are separating."

"She'll get over it," Tyrone said. "I'll make sure she knows who's responsible for the breakup."

"Have you thought about where you're going?"

"I just bought a new house, Saturday."

"Oh!"

Laura leaned forward, pretending to scratch her ankle, and peered into the right-wing mirror, at the van that had kept at a considerably close distance. Seeing that Tyrone was nearing a traffic light that was red, she eased her hand down to the buckle of her seatbelt.

The moment the car stopped, Laura, as quick as she could activate her limbs, unbuckled the seatbelt and grabbed the door handle and bolted from the car. She was thankful that she'd worn tennis shoes, as she scampered up the sidewalk.

Throwing the car into park, Tyrone got out, and looked at Charles and Block, who were sitting there in the van, as if they hadn't seen a thing.

"What the hell are y'all waiting for!" He asked, agitation in his voice. "Get her!"

His men bolted from the van, and gave chase, leaving the van where it sat. Getting back into the car, Tyrone sped up the street, and pulled up onto the curb, in an endeavor to cut Laura off, but she bolted across the street, dodging vehicles, as his men tried to keep up. Pulling his car off the curb, Tyrone drove farther up the street.

***

"I swear, Mr. Lathan, I was set up!" Sara said to Dennis Lathan, who was seated across from her at the Daila's Diner. "I've never done drugs a day in my life!"

"And you believe that Mr. Davis had something to do with it?" He asked, slicing into his custard pie.

"I *know* he had something to do with it!"

"Sara, you know I can't take any kind of action without proof."

"You gotta believe me!" She pleaded. "I know what I'm talking about."

"Whether I believe you or not," he started, "I still need proof. Right now, you're in no position to march into anyone's office, and tell them anything about anybody."

She sighed. "I know."

"Right now, you're just suspended until you have your hearing with the board."

"Will you be there?"

"Yes, and I'll be speaking on your behalf."

***

Still running, Laura cut down a semi-dark alley, with Charles not too far behind, and Block lagging behind him. At the far end of the alley, she spotted Tyrone's car as it entered, moving slow. Just then, she came upon a piece of plywood that was in her path.

Stopping, she picked it up, and turned to face her pursuers. Charles slowed to a walk, letting Block catch up to him.

"Come and get me!" She yelled out, holding the plywood as if she were a baseball player, awaiting the pitch.

Then, suddenly, the side door to one of the buildings swung open, in which Rick and Bull emerged from, carrying handguns. They both took positions on each side of Laura, with their guns aimed at Block and Charles, who both stopped in their tracks, and went for their weapons.

"Don't do it!" said Rick, whose gun was trained on Charles, as Bull's was on Block.

"What's up?" Charles asked, looking confused.

"You should already know," Rick replied, as Tyrone's car stopped several feet behind them.

Exiting the car, Tyrone placed a round brimmed hat atop his head, as he approached, clapping his hands.

"Bravo! Bravo!" he was saying, "Another job well done by yours truly, Beauty and the Beast!"

Relieving Laura of the stick, he tossed it aside, then took hold of her hand, as they ceremoniously took a bow.

"I'll take it from here," Tyrone told her, kissing her in the mouth.

Laura turned, and sauntered toward the car, where she sat up on the hood to watch.

"Fellas!" Tyrone now regarded Charles and Block. "It's that time. You're done. I wanna thank you for your services. You both have been very loyal, but everybody knows that nothing lasts forever. Any last words?" No one spoke. "Okay. It's been real." He turned, and made for the car.

"Yeah," Charles found his voice, "I got some last words." stopping, Tyrone turned to face him. "Speak!"

"Law Twenty-eight—"

"Shoot 'em!" Tyrone commanded.

Charles went for his pistol that was tucked in the waistline of his pants but, before he could get the barrel high enough to get a shot off, Rick and Bull, simultaneously gunned him down. Block turned, trying to make a run for it, and both guns were turned on him, as slugs slammed into his back forcing him face-down to the concrete, lowering his gun, Rick looked over at Tyrone.

"What's 'Law Twenty-eight'?" He asked.

"Enter action with boldness," Tyrone answered, regarding Charles' lifeless body with admiration.

"Well, he did that!" Rick commented.

"What now?" Asked Bull, who was 5'6, and 210 pounds.

Tyrone turned to him. "You got that shipment ready?"

Playa Ray

Chapter 29

The next day, in her chambers, Judge Connie Edwards was sitting at her desk, applying nail polish to her fingernails, when someone knocked on the door.

"Come in!"

Danny Blake entered, carrying documents. After closing the door behind him, he approached the desk.

"Date?" He asked, regarding her orange-coated nails.

"Not that I know of," she responded. "What'cha got?"

"The motion for speedy trial, filed by attorney Greg Bush, for the defendant, Christopher Reid," he said, holding the papers out to her, but she held her hands up, reminding him of the still wet polish. "Sorry!" Danny offered, retracting the documents. "So, how fast can you hear it?"

"Within two weeks, I guess," Connie answered.

"Two weeks!" Danny exclaimed.

"There's a possible chance that we can get it done, next week," she reconsidered.

"How about tomorrow?"

"That's impossible!"

"All it takes is one phone call, and a court order," he told her. "I'll call Greg Bush and draw the court order."

"What's the court order for?" She inquired.

"To have Mr. Reid put on the court list for tomorrow. You sign it, and I'll fax it over to the jail."

She regarded him with narrowed eyes. "I'll do it this time. Just don't make it a habit."

Danny smiled. "Yes, ma'am!"

***

"Trust me on this, Chris! I got it!" Danny said to his friend, who was seated on the other side of the visitation booth, with a worried expression on his face.

"I sure hope so!" Chris replied. "But, are you sure that you can have me in trail by next week?"

"No," Danny answered, truthfully. "But I'm confident in my argument. Plus, I've already subpoenaed forty-seven people for jury selection, Monday. She doesn't know this."

"When did you subpoena forty-seven people?"

"Last week," replied Danny. "If she doesn't agree to Monday, I'll have to make forty-seven phone calls."

***

That following morning, the only people in the courtroom were Judge Edwards, Danny Blake, who was accompanied by Alvin Newman at the State's table, attorney Greg Bush, who was seated at the defense table with Christopher Reid, and Avery Stewart, who sat on the bench behind the defense table. Plus, there were two court officers.

"Mr. Blake," the judge was saying, "is there any reason why I should grant, or deny, motion for speedy trial, filed by attorney Greg Bush, with respect to his client, Christopher Reid?"

"Your Honor," Danny spoke from his seat, "Mr. Reid has been indicted by the grand jury. The indictment has been signed by the district attorney. The evidence in this case is as follows: DNA samples taken from the victim, matches that of the defendant, Christopher Reid. Also, testimony from the victim, given to the initial officers, and at the bond hearing of said defendant, that was heard, and denied by the Honorable Judge Rebecca Cross. The defendant pleads not guilty The state is in support of the motion, and hopes that the court grants said motion, so that this case can be set up for trial, immediately. Thank you."

The judge looked to the defense table. "Any objections from the defense?"

"None, Your Honor," Greg Bush answered.

"Okay," Connie replied. "I'm going to grant the motion for speedy trial. Does the state have a particular date he wishes to set for this trial?"

"Monday, Your Honor," Danny answered.

"Next week?"

"Yes, Your Honor," said Danny. "The defendant and his counsel will be here. I also have forty-seven civilians that'll be here for jury selection.

***

Tyrone still couldn't believe he'd let Dr. Green talk him into undergoing a second HIV testing. He'd never heard the mention of the virus not showing up in the first testing, although it was quite plausible. Besides, he wanted to make sure that Lisa had not contracted the disease, and passed it on to him. This Thursday afternoon, he was, again, seated in the waiting area of the Linkton County Clinic, pretending to be interested in the Stuff magazine. The old doctor appeared at the service door, holding a folder.

"Mr. Davis?" He asked, looking directly at Tyrone.

Saying nothing, Tyrone placed the magazine back onto the table, and allowed the doctor to escort him to the same examination room he'd been in on the previous visit. At the doctor's insistence, Tyrone sat up on the exam table, as the doctor closed the door.

"Good afternoon, Mr. Davis!" Mr. Green stood in front of him, clutching the folder to his chest.

"Good afternoon.!" Tyrone forced out, already ready to leave.

"You're here for the results from a second testing," the doctor asserted. "Are you nervous?"

Tyrone raised his eyebrows. "Should I be?"

"That's a question I ask all patients. The same question I asked you on your last visit. Remember?"

"Yeah. I'm not nervous, said Tyrone, although he wasn't quite sure."

"Okay." Dr. Green opened the folder. "On your first visit, your results were negative. I explained to you how the disease may not show up on the first testing, if, in fact, there is a disease. I recommended an immediate second testing, in which you agreed to take. Mr. Davis, here's your results."

Instead of reading the results out like he'd done on the last visit, Dr. Green turned the folder, and held it up for Tyrone to read for himself.

***

"So, you don't have a strategy?" Chris asked Danny through the glass of the visitation booth.

"No," he answered. "I'm just going to fight this case like I fight all cases. Greg Bush is every prosecutor's worst nightmare! He could win a case from home, via satellite!"

"I hope you're right about this," Chris replied. "You and Judge Edwards are on good terms, right now. I'm quite sure she'll be more than likely to take your side when it comes to objections."

"I think she'll be fair." Danny looked at his watch. "I gotta get some rest. I'm sorry that I came so late, but I'm still preparing for your trial."

"What else do you have to prepare?"

"I was working on my opening and closing," Danny replied, standing. "If I'm gonna lose in front of the media, I, at least, want to look good doing it."

Chris smiled at the big guy, as he too stood. "I can't argue with that. I guess I'll see you, Monday."

***

It was dark out, when Danny exited the building. As he made for his truck, he didn't know that he was being watched through the windshield of a black Ford F-350. Once Danny pulled out of the parking lot, the diesel fueled truck started up, and followed.

***

Being that Tyrone didn't have any cases to try, tomorrow, and he was going in late, he decided to spend the night with Jackie, taking a fresh dress suit that he would wear the following day.

Now, he and Jackie were just lounging in bed. She was lying on her back, and Tyrone was lying on his side, rubbing her bulging stomach.

"Why can't I take pain pills when I'm in pain?" She was asking.

"I don't know the specific reason," he answered, "but doctors forbid women from taking pain pills while pregnant. It may cause birth defects."

"Did Lisa crave pickles and ice cream when she was pregnant?"

Tyrone didn't answer right away. One of his reasons for choosing this *sleepover* with Jackie, was to take his mind off of Lisa, and other things he had going on. However, surely, he couldn't get upset with his twenty-four-year-old girlfriend for posing such an innocent question. It's not like she has any kind of idea or knowledge of his domestic issues.

"Yeah," he finally answered, fixing her with a smile. "Is that what you crave?"

"Nooo!" She exclaimed, making a face. "But I hear that's what a lot of pregnant women crave. Pickles and ice cream, together. Nasty! I need one of those pregnancy diet books. I guess I'll get one on my next visit to the clinic."

Tyrone said, "you'll have to cut down on grease, salt, and sugar. Eat more vegetables."

"That's what the book says?"

"Basically."

"Well, I do want a healthy baby," Jackie admitted. So, whatever it takes."

"My girl!" He said, kissing her on the cheek.

***

Still driving along the main street, Danny, happy that things were going his way, was drumming his index finger on the steering wheel, as he sang along with *"Nickelback's 'Someday'"*, that played through the speakers of his factory stereo.

Coming to a stop at a traffic light of an intersection, he was still drumming his finger on the steering wheel when something in his rear-view mirror caught his eye. Looking up, he saw the Ford truck, with its enormous steel grilled, coming upon the rear of his truck at an unreasonable speed.

"What the –"

Danny tried to turn in his seat to make sure that his mirror wasn't playing tricks on his eyes. But, before he could bring the truck into his line of vision, the left side of the Ford' steel grill crashed into the right side of Danny's truck, sending the Navigator spiraling across the intersection, and slamming into the telephone pole on the left side of the four-way pass.

Other vehicles had come to screeching halts. The Ford fled the scene but Danny, who was pinned between the driver's seat, and the steering wheel with the deflated airbag, was unaware of all of this, as his eyelids gave way, and darkness slowly overtook him.

Chapter 30

The next morning, Tyrone managed to ease out of bed, without waking Jackie. After showering and getting dressed, he re-entered the bedroom. While putting on his watch, he stood looking down at his girlfriend, who seemed to be at total peace, with one hand resting protectively on her bulging stomach.

His baby.

There were no doubts in Tyrone's mind that the baby was his, which was why, now, his stomach began to churn, and his heart began to ache for both, mother and unborn child. Though he loved Jackie more than he'd ever loved Lisa, he was highly aware that, one day, everything has to come to an end, no matter how much love is involved.

Tyrone sat on the edge of the bed, and gingerly placed his hand atop her hand that was rested on her stomach. Her eyelids fluttered, before lifting.

"Don't get up," he told her. "I'll see you tonight."

***

"Oh my God!" Ellen exclaimed, when she and Avery Stewart entered the recovery room, where Danny was housed.

Danny's arms, legs, and head were bandaged. His neck was in a brace, and his left leg and both arms were in elevated slings. As the approached the bed, they could see that his face was swollen beyond recognition, along with his eyes that were badly bruised, and seemed to be sealed shut. At that moment, a white female doctor entered.

"Excuse me?" The doctor approached the opposite side of the bed, regarding them with an inquisitive look. "Are you his immediate family?"

"Co-workers," answered Avery.

"Well, he can only be visited by his immediate family, at the time," she told them. "I don't know who made that stupid rule, but I have to enforce it. Now, are you his immediate family?"

Ellen caught on quickly. "I'm his sister, and this is our uncle."

The blonde-haired doctor smiled. "That'll work. Now, do you have any questions?"

"Is he in a coma?" And how long will he be here?" Avery took the initiative.

"Well, no one can determine the period of a coma," she replied, casting a glance down at Danny. "But, lucky for us, he's not in a coma. He's under anesthesia and it looks like he could be here for over a month. Every bone, except for his spinal cord, and right leg, is broken.

Ellen gasped. "Will he walk again?"

"I'm just an angel," the doctor offered. "I repaired him. God does the healing."

"This cannot be happening!" Avery said, thinking about his nephew's trial that was set for Monday, which was approximately three days from today.

***

"This can't be happening! Not now!" said Chris, after hearing about Danny's contretemps from his uncle, who came straight to the jail upon leaving the hospital.

"That's what I said," Avery replied. "Now what?"

"I'm going to trial, Monday!" Chris asserted, with defiance.

"How?"

"See if you can get Barbara Hutchins to step in."

Avery pulled out his cellular and dialed. After listening for a few seconds, he said, "Yes, can you page Assistant District Attorney Barbara Hutchins? Thank you."

"He'd just left from seeing me," Chris said, almost to himself.

Avery spoke into the phone, again, "Yes, Ms. Hutchins?" This is Avery Stewart. Look, I need you to step in for Danny Blake on a trail that's set up for Monday. You do? Okay. Thanks!"

"She'll do it?" Chris asked, once Avery hung up.

"No," he answered. "She already has a trial set up for Monday."

"Damn!"

"It'll have to be rescheduled," Avery told him.

"No!" Chris forced out.

"The only person left is Tyrone, and you don't –"

"Yes, I do!" He cut his uncle off.

Avery appeared shocked. "You want him to prosecute the case!"

"He can't beat Greg Bush."

"Are you sure?"

"I'm positive!" Chris answered, with a wicked snarl on his face.

***

In his office, Tyrone was seated at his desk, searching through his rolodex for his attorney's number, when there was a rap on his door. He sighed, thinking that it was probably someone else wanting to talk to him about what happened to Danny Blake, as if he cared. As if he didn't have his own problems to deal with.

They knocked again.

"It's open," he gave in.

Here we go! He thought, as Avery Stewart entered, closed the door, and approached the desk.

"Are you busy?" He asked.

"No," Tyrone answered, leaning back in his chair.

"I'm quite sure you've heard about Blake," Avery went on

Tyrone nodded. "Yeah. Hit and run."

"Broke every bone, except spinal, and right leg."

"Ouch!" Tyrone offered, with little emphasis

"Yeah, that's pretty bad," said Avery. "Look, can you fill in for him, Monday, for Christopher Reid's trial?"

"I can do that," Tyrone answered, knowing it would come to this. Avery hesitated a moment, before speaking again. "Tyrone, can I make you a proposition?"

"I'm listening."

"Blow the case, and I'll see to it that you get my position when I step down.

"Are you asking me to lose?" Tyrone asked, leaning forward, and resting his elbows on the desk.

"Yes."

"Your position is not enough for me to break my winning streak."

The head DA sighed. "Well, what *is* enough?"

"Your position, and fifty grand, up front."

"Fifty grand!" Avery exclaimed.

"Up front," Tyrone stood his ground. "Deal, or no deal?"

***

All day, Connie had been debating if she should visit Danny in the hospital. She didn't make her mind up until after she'd gotten home, showered, and realized that she was at a loss of appetite.

Now, carrying a basket of flowers, with two, small, stuffed cats, hanging from it, Connie entered Danny's room, where a white female nurse was feeding him some kind of liquid from a cup, through a straw.

"One sip at a time, Mr. Blake!" The nurse cautioned, pulling the straw back. "I know you're thirsty, but I have to follow procedures. Your lungs are feeble, right now. Too much can choke you."

Danny shifted his partially opened eyes to Connie, who approached the other side of the bed.

"Hey! She said, voice barely above a whisper.

"He can see and hear you," the nurse explained, "but he can't speak. Come on, Mr. Blake, one more sip." She placed the straw up to his mouth. "There you go! I'll be back, shortly to check on you."

When the nurse left, Connie placed the flowers on the small table beside the bed, and stared down at Danny, who was staring back up at her.

"Something told me not to come, because I didn't want to see you like this," she said, fighting back the tears that threatened to make a guest appearance. "It could've been worse."

"Hi, Ms. Edwards!"

Connie looked to see Sara entering the room. "Hi, Sara!"

"How's he doing?" Sara asked, stopping on the opposite side of the bed.

"He's alive, but he can't talk."

"Poor baby!"

***

Getting home from work, Jackie parked, and exited her truck, carrying the small bag of groceries she'd gotten from the grocery store she works at. Without much ado, she disengaged the locks, then entered her apartment. Before she could close the door, Bull, who was standing behind it, struck her in the head with the butt of his gun, knocking her unconscious. When he closed the door, Rick emerged from the rear of the apartment.

"Ready?" Bull asked.

"Let's do it!"

***

Tyrone entered Danny's recovery room, closing, and locking the door. As he approached the bed, he eyed the array of monitors that Danny was hooked up to. Then, he took stock of Danny's body, which was bandaged from head to toe.

"What's up, soldier!" Tyrone said to Danny, who was staring back up at him. "What are they about to do? Mummify you?"

Danny tried to utter something that came out as a mere grunt. Tyrone leaned closer, so he could hear better.

"What was that?"

"You... did... this!" Danny's words came out slow, and strenuous.

Tyrone straightened his posture. "Now, where would you get an idea like that from? I'm your friend, Danny. I would never hurt you. In fact, I came down here to help you." He pulled out a pair of black gloves and began putting them on. "A true friend would never let a friend suffer. Rights now, you're suffering, Danny. It hurts me to see you like this. I'm going to help you out."

Danny tried to scream at the top of his lungs, but Tyrone placed a gloved hand over his mouth.

"Don't do that!" Tyrone scolded. "You wanna be a vegetable for the rest of your life? Of course, not! Now, relax!"

Using his free hand, Tyrone pinched Danny's nostrils together, cutting off his breathing, while staring into Danny's huge, and frightened eyes, and listening to the beeping of the monitors. Moments later, Danny finally gave up the ghost, which was corroborated by the now perpetual buzz of the monitors.

Quickly, Tyrone doffed the gloves, shoved them into his pockets, and exited the room. Casually, he moved along the crowded corridor, as medical personnel rushed past him, claiming something of a Code Red in room seven. The same room he'd just left.

***

Tyrone pulled onto a dark street, parking behind the black van that was parked behind Jackie's Ford Explorer. He didn't see Rick and Bull, until he got out, when they emerged from the wooded area, just in front of the Explorer, both carrying gas cans.

Getting to the driver's door of the Explorer, Tyrone saw that Jackie was bound to her seat, with what seemed like a half a roll of duct tape. There was also a piece over her mouth. Her eyes widened when she saw him. He could tell she'd been crying. Now, fresh tears cascaded down her face.

"Are you alright?" He asked her. She nodded. Tyrone, then, turned to his men. "Let me talk to her." He waited until they crossed over to the other side of the street, and were out of earshot, before turning back to Jackie. "Baby girl, I hate to do this, but I have to. I'm sick. If I'm sick, that means you're sick. If you're sick, the baby is sick. I can't let a sick baby come into this world."

More tears streamed down her face and Tyrone wiped them away with his thumb, disregarding his own.

"It's not your fault," he continued. "It's not even my fault. I've never told you this, but I love you. I always have, and I always will." He kissed her on the forehead. "I'm sorry!"

He, now, wiped his own tears, before crossing over to where his men awaited.

"Are you good?" Asked Rick

"Yeah," Tyrone lied.

"What's the extra gas can for?" Bull wanted to know.

"The van," Tyrone answered. "I'll be in the car."

Without another glance in the direction of the Explorer, Tyrone made for his car, feeling like his legs were about to give out on him. Climbing behind the wheel, he made a U-turn, stopping a few yards away from the scene. He looked into the rearview, and, once again, his stomach churned, and his heart began to ache. Tears rolled down his face, as he watched his men douse both vehicles with gasoline.

But, when he saw the Explorer go up in flames, something inside of him snapped. He dropped his head on the steering wheel and wept.

***

Entering his home, Tyrone locked the front door back, and in a menacing stride, made for Lisa's bedroom, where the door was wide open. Stopping at the threshold, he saw that both, Lisa and Ebony, were asleep in the huge bed he used to share with Lisa, who he was now glaring at, as the anger inside him seemed to boil over. She ruined his life, and there was no way he was going to let her get away with it.

Playa Ray

Chapter 31

That Saturday afternoon, Sara entered a pawn shop, and browsed the not-so-crowded store. She already knew what she'd come for, but she didn't want to appear as if she had bad intentions, or that something was wrong , although she wasn't so sure.

Finally, she made her way to the thick-glassed counter that encased a panoply of handguns and ammunition. While she was eyeing the array of guns, the owner, an older white male, approached.

"Now, what's a nice woman like yourself doing in the gun section?" He asked.

"Maybe, I'm not nice," she replied, then pointed at a .38 caliber pistol. "How much for that one?"

***

Again, Laura spent another Saturday, helping Mrs. Reid out on the ranch. This time, they were accompanied by Kevin. After feeding the animals, and tending to the crops, Laura helped Mrs. Reid prepare a dinner for the three of them. After dinner, they all retired to the living room, where conversation resumed.

Now, Laura was standing at the front door, with her purse, ready to make her exit.

"You drive safe, baby!" Mrs. Reid told her.

"I will."

Kevin stood. "I'll walk you to your car."

"Thanks!" Laura said, opening the front door. "Goodnight, Mrs. Reid!"

"Goodnight!" She replied from her recliner. "And thank you!"

"You're more than welcome!"

Kevin followed her out, closing the door behind him. They descended the steps. Feeling that Kevin wanted to say something to her, Laura unlocked, and pulled her driver's door open, before turning to face him.

"Laura, I still don't have a full understanding of what's going on," he began, "but Chris came up with the idea of you being the one who saved our mother's life. Thank you!"

"God works in mysterious ways," she offered, smiling.

"Yes, he does." Kevin paused, before speaking again. "So, the trial is –"

"Don't speak on it!" She cut him off. "Chris will be okay. Good night, Kevin!"

"Goodnight!"

He watched as she turned her car around, and drove down the now dark gravel road, before going back inside.

***

"And you paid him!" Chris stared wide-eyed at his uncle.

"In cash," Avery answered. "That's the only way he would do it."

"I don't trust it!"

"Everything that's going on is your call," Avery reminded. "Besides, you're confident that he can't beat Bush, anyway, right?"

"Unless he pulls some kind of stunt," Chris said, leaning back in his plastic chair. "Laura plays a big part, also."

***

Laura entered her apartment and locked the door. She didn't see Tyrone's car in the parking lot, but somehow she could feel his presence. Dropping her keys on the counter, she made for her bedroom, where her feelings were confirmed.

Tyrone was standing out on the balcony, with his back to her. Leaving the light off, Laura crossed the room, dropped her purse on the bed, and stepped out onto the balcony, standing beside him.

"Enjoying the view?" She asked.

"Not really," he answered, without looking in her direction. "Where've you been?"

"Out with some friends," she said, noticing the anger in his tone.

Saying nothing, he pulled two, letter-sized envelopes from inside his blazer. They were unsealed. Pulling a folded piece of paper from one of them, he handed it to her.

"What's this?" She inquired.

"Sign the bottom, under your name," he said, handing her an ink pen. "That's for the grand jury."

"What about the grand jury?"

264

"Everybody signed the indictment, but you," he told her. "It's just saying that you're the victim."

She placed the paper on the flat surface of the railing, signed directly under her appellation that was typed. She handed it back to Tyrone who placed it back into the envelope, and handed her the folded document from the other envelope.

"This copy goes to the clerk," he told her.

"Same thing?"

"Yeah."

She signed it, then gave the document and pen back. Tyrone placed the document back inside the envelope, then handed both envelopes to her.

"Seal 'em!"

She did and handed them back.

"The prosecutor in this case was in an accident," Laura asserted. "Won't that stop the trial?"

"Not this one," Tyrone said, placing the envelopes back inside his blazer.

"Why not?"

"Because I'm taking over."

"You are?" She asked, hoping that her voice didn't betray how shocked she was by this revelation.

"Of course," he said, then appeared as if he was trying to think of something else to say, as he stared out into the night. Then, as if to himself, he said, "All fairytales have endings."

"What are you talking about, Tyrone?" She was studying the side of his face.

Tyrone turned and locked eyes with her." The end of *Beauty and the Beast*."

Laura caught the hint, but it was too late. Bull and Rick stepped out onto the balcony, both clad in dark clothing, and wearing gloves. Immediately, Bull grabbed Laura, lifting her off her feet. She screamed at the top of her lungs, as she clamped both hands onto the railing, hoping to prevent the inevitable, but Rick ended up prying her hands free, and Bull lifted her over his head, before tossing her over.

The three of them watched, as she passed six other floors, before her body contacted the concrete sidewalk below. Tyrone motioned for his men to move out, then followed them through the bedroom, dropping the two envelopes on the bed, as they made for the front door.

Chapter 32

It was Tuesday morning, and in Judge Edwards' courtroom, Tyrone was seated at the State's table, with Michelle Johnson. Attorney Greg Bush was seated at the defense table with Christopher Reid, who was looking dapper in a gray suit and red tie.

To show support for his nephew, Avery Stewart was seated on the first bench, with his other nephew, Kevin with Ellen Martinez and Sara Jennings seated behind them. Plus, the local news stations had their crews at the rear, sending out live feed to the world.

"Due to the time it took to pick the jury, yesterday," Judge Edwards was saying, "we didn't get a chance to go over any motions, or preliminary matters. Are there any motions, or preliminary matters I should know about at this time?"

Tyrone stood. "Yes, Your Honor. On yesterday, I was handed a letter, typed and signed by the victim, who, apparently committed suicide over the weekend."

"Who handed you this letter, Mr. Davis?" Asked the judge.

"The clerk," he answered. "Actually, it's a copy."

"So, the State intends to pursue this case, although the victim is unable to persecute the defendant?"

"Yes, Your Honor."

"Due to the evidence, which is a letter, allegedly typed and signed by the victim, correct?"

Tyrone nodded. "Correct"

"At this time," Judge Edwards went on, "Can the State prove that the letter is, indeed, of, and by the deceased victim?"

"Yes, Your Honor," Tyrone answered, before retrieving two pieces of paper off his table holding one in each hand. "You Honor, what I have here is the typed letter, signed by the victim, and the initial police report, also signed by the victim. I also have a handwriting expert outside the courtroom."

She looked to the defense table. "Mr. Bush, have you seen these documents?"

"No, Your Honor," the attorney answered.

As if it was his cue, the bailiff retrieved the documents from Tyrone, took them over to the defense table, and handed them to the attorney, who studied them.

"The only way I'll allow the expert to testify," Connie resumed, "is if you argue the fact that there's no comparison."

"No argument." Greg replied, handing the documents back to the officer, who returned them to the prosecutor.

The judge regarded Tyrone. "Before we go on, Mr. Davis, you can tell your expert that we won't need them."

Tyrone made for the entrance.

"You should've let him testify," Chris whispered to his attorney.

"It's a match," Greg told him. "That would be a waste of time."

"I'm ready, Your Honor," Tyrone announced, upon re-entering the courtroom, taking his seat.

Clearing her throat, Judge Edwards collected the documents in front of her. "At this time," she began, the State wishes to pursue case number three-seven-zero-eight-five-nine, Laura O'Neal versus Christopher Reid. Ms. O'Neal accuses Mr. Reid of committing the acts of rape, and aggravated battery against her. Due to the untimely death of the victim, the State wishes to proceed with said case. Are there any objections from the defense?"

"No, Your Honor," Greg answered.

"Is there anything else, before I summon the jury?" Connie inquired.

"No, Your Honor," Tyrone answered.

"Nothing from the defense," Greg offered.

The judge nodded to her officer. "Bailiff."

He withdrew to the jury room.

"I don't believe Laura committed suicide," Chris now whispered to his attorney.

"You should keep that to yourself," Greg advised.

"Why?"

"Because, when Homicide convinces themselves otherwise, guess who becomes their number one suspect?"

Chris ruminate this, as the twelve jury member's piled in, taking their seats.

"Welcome back ladies and gentlemen of the jury," Judge Edwards greeted, once they were seated. "You all are already familiar with the case. At this time, we'll be doing opening arguments. First, you'll hear from the State. Then, you'll hear from the defense. State, you may begin."

Getting up, Tyrone approached the center of the room, facing the jurors.

"Ladies and gentlemen," he started, "I'm not going to say much, right now, but I want you all to pay close attention to this case, as it unfolds in front of you. A horrible crime was committed. I'm going to prove that to you. I'm also going to prove to you that the person accused of this horrible crime, is, in fact, the person that committed the horrible crime. Thank you!"

"Defense?" The judge prompted.

Tyrone made it back to his table, as Greg Bush approached the jurors, resting an arm on the lectern.

"Ladies and gentlemen of the jury," he spoke with his easy-going voice, "I'm attorney Greg Bush, counsel for the defendant Christopher Reid. Yes, my client is accused of the offenses, but he's not guilty of any of them. I also want you all to pay close attention to this case. I'll prove to you that my client is not guilty. Thank you!"

"State, call your first witness," said Edwards, as Greg returned to his seat.

Tyrone stood. "Your Honor, the State calls Officer Tanisha Coleman."

The bailiff exited the room, returning seconds later, with the officer that first encountered Laura, when she'd stumbled into the police precinct. Now, in civilian attire, Coleman was ushered to the witness stand, where she was sworn in by the bailiff.

"Ms. Coleman," the judge took over, once the officer was seated. "Would you, please, state your full name, and spell your last name out for the court?"

"Tanisha Coleman," she answered. "C-O-L-E-M-A-N."

"Direct examination?" the judge said.

Crossing the room, Tyrone took locus behind the podium regarding the officer.

"Ms. Coleman," he said, "I'm Assistant District Attorney Tyrone Davis, and I only have a few questions for you. When you first encountered the victim, Laura O'Neal, where were you?"

"At the precinct," she answered. "I was on my way out. By the time I got to the entrance, Ms. O'Neal burst through the door, looking like she'd been attacked."

"Was her clothes torn?" Tyrone asked.

"Objection, Your Honor!" Greg Bush spouted. "Misleading the witness."

"Sustained," Judge Edwards replied.

"Thank you, Your Honor!" Greg offered.

"Ms. Coleman," Tyrone resumed. "What did you do at that time?"

The woman answered, "I helped her to a seat, got her some medical attention, and did the report."

"So, you ended up staying over?"

"Yes."

"Did Ms. O'Neal have to go to the hospital?" Asked Tyrone

"Yes, but after we completed the report."

"And you're the one who did the report?"

She nodded. "Yes."

"One minute."

Tyrone approached his table, where Michelle handed him a piece of paper. He held it up for the judge to see.

"Your Honor, what I'm holding now, is the initial police report that I would like to place into evidence."

"Any objections from the defense?" Edwards asked.

"No, Your Honor," answered the defense attorney.

"Item is admitted," said the judge.

Tyrone handed the report to Michelle, who stamped it, before handing it back.

He turned to face the judge, "Your Honor, may I approach the witness?" She nodded. "You may."

Approaching, Tyrone placed the report in front of Coleman, then took a couple of steps back.

"Ms. Coleman, I've just placed something in front of you," he said. "Can you tell the court what that is?"

"It's the police report that I did on the victim, Laura O'Neal," she answered.

"Signed by who?"

"Myself, and the victim, Laura O'Neal."

"Thank you!" He said, retrieving the report, then heading back to his table. "Nothing further."

"Cross?" Edwards inquired.

"No, Your Honor," Greg told her.

She looked at the witness. "Officer Coleman, you may be released. State, call your next witness."

"The State calls medical examiner Patricia Hartley."

The bailiff escorted Tanisha Coleman out, then returned, moments later, with a white female in a white laboratory coat. She wore black-framed glasses, and her curly, brown hair was pulled into a ponytail. She took the stand, and was sworn in.

"Ms. Hartley," Edwards said, "would you state your full name, and spell your last name for the court?"

"Patricia Hartley," she answered "H-A-R-T-L-E-Y."

Edwards looked to Tyrone, "direct?"

Tyrone got up and emplaced himself behind the podium. "Ms. Hartley, where are you employed?

"At the Linkton County Hospital," she answered.

"And what are your duties at this hospital?"

"I'm a DNA analyst."

"Do you study all DNA?" He asked. "Or a particular kind?"

"All."

"Are you the one who analyzed the DNA in this case?"

She nodded. "Yes, I am,"

"What kind of DNA was it?"

"Semen," Hartley answered.

"From whom?"

"First, from the victim, Laura O'Neal," she said. "Then, from the defendant, Christopher Reid."

"The semen found in the victim belonged to who?" Tyrone posed for the record.

"Christopher Reid."

"And how long have you been in the field?"

"For over eleven years."

"Thank you!" He said. "Nothing further."

"Cross?" The judge prompted.

Tyrone made for his table, as Greg Bush took the podium.

"Ms. Hartley," Greg began, "I'm attorney Greg Bush, counsel for the defendant, Christopher Reid. "Now, you and I both know that there's more to just walking into a laboratory, extracting DNA from both sides, looking into a microscope, and saying 'okay, this DNA belongs to so-and-so', right?"

She nodded. "Right."

"There are many procedures, right?"

"Right."

Greg shifted his weight. "Can you explain to the jury the structure of the DNA?"

"Girl, this is going to be a showdown!" Ellen whispered to Sara.

"The DNA molecule is called a Double Helix, "Hartley explained, "in which two chains of nucleotides, running in opposite directions, are held together between pairs of bases reminiscent of the rungs of a ladder, and coiled like a spring. It looks like a twisted rope ladder, or a spiral staircase. Whatever their derivation - human, animal, or vegetable - all DNA molecules have this shape."

Greg nodded his approval. "And the long threads that make up the sides of the DNA ladder, are made up of alternating units of phosphate and sugar called deoxyribose, right?"

"Right."

"Can you tell the court what a 'band shift' is?"

Hartley recited, "The banding patterns of two different samples containing the same DNA, may not line up exactly. They will be close, but not exact. A match can nevertheless be called, if the bands are in essentially the same place within a permissible degree of error."

"Did you test for band shift?" Greg posed.

"I did."

"How many ways are there to test for band shift?"

"There are two ways to test for band shift," she answered. "First, a mixed-lane sample can be run. Here, a part of the known sample, and the evidence sample are run in the same lane. If only two bands appear, the DNA is the same."

"One moment," the attorney said, before approaching the State's table to confer with the two prosecutors.

"This lady is smart!" Ellen commented to Sara.

"I wonder how much she gets paid," replied Sara, who had, all morning, done her best at avoiding eye contact with Tyrone.

After a moment of confabulating, Michelle Johnson handed Greg Bush a manila folder. He turned back to face the judge. "Your Honor," he started, "What I'm holding is Dr. Hartley's analysis report."

"Does the State wish to enter the report into evidence?" She asked.

"Yes, Your Honor," Tyrone answered.

"Evidence is admitted," she granted.

Once Michelle stamped the folder, and handed it back, Greg faced the judge, again. "Your Honor, may I approach the witness?"

"You may."

Approaching, Greg placed the folder down in front of the doctor, then returned to the podium. "Doctor," he went on, "what I've placed in front of you, is State's exhibit two. Could you tell the court what that is?"

She opened the folder and scanned the pages. "It's my initial report of this case," she answered.

Greg asked, "and, every conclusion that you've come up with, is in there, right?"

"Right."

"You admitted that you tested for band shift," the attorney said. "Is that in there?"

She nodded. "Yes."

"What about the six steps of forensic identification?"

"It's in there."

"As a scientist," he went on, "is it safe to say that you make mistakes?"

Hartley answered, "as a person, I make mistakes like any other person. As a scientist, yes, I have made mistakes."

"So, you have stumbled across what is called a false match during a procedure?"

"No procedures are infallible," she cited. "If, for example, a sample was accidentally mislabeled, and the laboratory compared two samples from the same source, believing it was comparing a sample of evidence with a sample from the defendant, the result would be a false match. Or, if the laboratory mistakenly, or carelessly added sample material from the defendant to the evidentiary sample, and the evidentiary sample was very degraded, leaving no bands on the autoradiograph, the bands from the defendant's sample in evidence lane would match the bands in the lane assigned to the defendant's sample, and again, a false match would occur."

"Okay.' Greg shifted his weight. "So, laboratories sometimes make mistakes. Is it true that a rare DNA pattern may be shared by several others, particularly by relatives of the defendant?"

"Yes."

"Nothing further," the attorney said, before returning the folder to the prosecutors, and re-taking his seat.

"Re-direct?" Judge Edwards inquired.

Tyrone stood but remained at his table." Hartley, you just agreed that a rare DNA pattern may be shared by relatives of the defendant. What about a sequential pattern?"

"The DNA from no two people, outside of identical twins, contains the same sequential pattern," the doctor replied.

"So, you're telling me that, if my sister and I are not identical twins, we don't share the same DNA?"

"You would have to be identical twins," she told him.

"Thank you!" Tyrone said, re-taking his seat. "Nothing further."

Judge Edwards looked to the defense table. "Re-cross?"

"No, Your Honor," Greg answered.

When Judge Edwards called for a recess, Ellen, Sara, Avery, and Kevin, decided to have lunch in the cafeteria, together, where they were now sharing a table.

"You know," Ellen was saying, "that Greg Bush has to be worth every penny! I mean, when does he have the time to study DNA?"

"Yeah, he surprised me there," Sara admitted, picking onions out of her tuna sandwich. "I'm still thinking about Laura. I still don't believe she committed suicide."

"None of us does," Said Kevin. "It doesn't sound like her."

"Did you know her?" Ellen wanted to know.

Kevin answered, "I've gotten to know her."

"I'm anxious to hear that letter," said Ellen, regarding Avery. "Didn't you get a copy of it?"

"I received a copy," said Avery, who, for some reason felt as if Tyrone was not going to hold up to his end of the deal, which was to blow the trial.

"What does it say?" Ellen pressed.

"It's evidence," Avery told her. "You'll have to hear it in trial."

***

"State, you may call your next witness," Judge Edwards announced, once the jurors had taken their seats.

Tyrone stood. "Your Honor, at this time, the State will put up essential evidence in this case, which is a letter, typed and signed by the late Laura O'Neal, who was the victim in this case."

"Mr. Bush, have you viewed this evidence?" Edwards questioned.

"I have," he answered.

"Any objection from the defense?"

"No, Your Honor."

She looked to Tyrone. "State, you may present your evidence."

"The evidence will be presented by Assistant District Attorney Michelle Johnson."

With the letter in hand, Michelle stood, and made for the witness stand. Before she was halfway across the room, Greg Bush got to his feet, as if remembering something.

"One second, Ms. Johnson," he said. "Can I see that?"

Stopped in her tracks, Michelle looked back at Tyrone, as if seeking permission. He nodded. Changing directions, she approached the defense table, and handed the missive over to the attorney, who read it to make sure nothing had been altered. He handed it back, and Michelle continued on to the witness stand. Once she was sworn in, Tyrone took to the podium.

"This, right here, could be critical," Greg told Chris.

"That bad?" Chris asked.

"Very!"

"Ms. Johnson," Tyrone began, "what you're holding is what's been marked as State's exhibit three. Can you tell the court what that is?"

"A typed letter," she answered.

"If you may," Tyrone resumed, "Could you read the full content of the letter, out loud, for the court?"

Michelle began to read.

"'To whom it may concern. I don't know if this letter will reach the court circuit, but I'm writing it because I don't think that I can face Christopher Reid, the prosecutor that lured me into his home to assault and rape me. Right now, I'm still shaken up. This incident has left me emotionally wrecked. It's been over a month, and I still cry at night. I still have nightmares. My life is miserable now, and I don't have the strength, or will power to go on, knowing that I've been violated by a person that prosecutes people like himself, for doing the things that he's done to me. How could I trust a man after this?" How could I trust the law? I haven't looked into a mirror since. I'm afraid to. How can I go on like this? I can't. I won't. I'm sorry! Sincerely, Laura Lynn O'Neal. And she signed it."

Michelle wiped tears from her eyes. Greg noticed that some of the jurors were doing the same.

"They got the jury," he told Chris.

"I see," Chris replied, though he maintained faith in his attorney.

"Thank you, Ms. Johnson!" said Tyrone. "You may step down."

"State, do you have any other witnesses?" The judge inquired, as Michelle made for their table, still clutching the letter.

"Your Honor, at this time, the State rests," he told her, retreating to his table.

She looked to Greg. "Will the defense be putting up any witnesses?"

"No, Your Honor," Greg answered, getting to his feet. "However, the defense calls the defendant, Christopher Reid, to the stand."

Tyrone watched Chris, as he got up, and strolled over to the witness stand. They didn't lock eyes, until Chris was being sworn in. Tyrone winked at him, though he didn't seem fazed. Once he was sworn in, Greg Bush approached the center of the room.

"Mr. Reid," Greg began, "Prior to this incident, what was your occupation?"

"Assistant District Attorney,' he answered.

"For what county?"

"Linkton County Superior Court."

"In this same exact building?" asked the attorney.

"Yes."

"And how long have you been in this field?"

"Nine years," Chris answered.

"Did you know the victim, Laura O'Neal, prior to this case?"

"I met her the day before," Chris said.

"How did you two meet?"

"I was leaving the courthouse," Chris went on to explain. "Entering the parking garage, I noticed her looking under the hood of her car and offered a hand. She asked me to start the car, and I did. The car started right up. After that, we talked for a while, and agreed to have dinner that night, at Kindred's. Leaving the restaurant, we exchanged phone numbers, then went our separate ways."

"Did you call her?" The attorney posed.

"Later that night."

"Make any plans?"

Chris shrugged. "We made plans to go to my mother's ranch the next day, and we did. I took her horseback riding and target practice. Then, we had dinner with my mother. After leaving there, we headed to my place."

"What happened there?" Greg urged.

"We got intimate," Chris said, matter-of-factly.

"So, you had consensual sex?"

"Yes."

"Let me fast-forward," Greg said, crossing over to the podium, and leaning on it. "Upon your arrival at the Linkton County Jail, were you met by medical personnel?"

"Yes."

"What did they do?"

"They stripped me down," he answered, "and searched my body for visual bruises or marks. Then, they took DNA samples. I used protection."

"You did?" Greg asked, with raised eyebrows.

"Of course, I did!" Chris bristled. "And the condom did not burst. I took it off, placed it in a small paper bag, and threw it in the trash."

"How many times did you and Ms. O'Neal get intimate?"

"Just that once."

"Nothing further," the attorney offered, before heading back to his table.

"Cross?" The judge asked.

Tyrone declined. "No, Your Honor."

"Mr. Reid, you may step down."

Chris headed back to his table, casting an evil look at Tyrone, who was also regarding him, but with an inscrutable expression.

"You mean to tell me that he passed up the chance to intimidate Chris?" Ellen said to Sara.

"He's done enough," she responded, now looking in Tyrone's direction.

"We're at the final stage of this trial," Judge Edwards said. "Would the State and defense like to go on with closing arguments, or wait until tomorrow?"

"I'd rather go ahead and do the arguments today, Your Honor," Greg answered.

She looked to Tyrone. "State?"

"I agree," he replied.

Judge Edwards regarded the jurors. "Jury members, this is where we do closing arguments. The State will come up, first, and argue his case. The defense will be next. Then, the State will close it out. State?"

Tyrone approached the center of the room, facing the jurors. "People," he began, "I won't say too much right now, but you will hear from me, again. You've heard the case. You've heard the evidence. Now, hear from the counsel of the predator, as he gives you all the reasons why this animal should be let back into society, to hunt down another victim. You will hear from me again."

Tyrone re-took his seat, as Greg Bush seemed to take up the same spot where Tyrone stood.

"Ladies and gentlemen," he started, "of course, there are some strong evidence in this case, but you have to keep an open mind. Let's go to the scientist. The DNA analysis. She admitted that laboratories make mistakes. Therefore, you can't believe every discovery that's presented to you.

"My client admitted to using protection. Why would he lie about that? Why would he not use protection on some strange woman that he hasn't known for more than forty-eight hours?" We're talking about a law student, who graduated at the top of his class. Very smart! Why would he pull a stunt like this, and end his promising career? It doesn't make sense, people!

"I think my client was set up. Look at how they met. Why was she in the parking garage of the courthouse?" She didn't work at the courthouse. She wasn't scheduled for court on that day. How do I know? Because I went back and checked the roster. As a matter of fact, she never even entered the building on that day. How do I know? I went back and viewed the surveillance tapes of that day.

She was nowhere! Except, in the car garage, pretending to have car trouble. Pretending!

"What kind of trouble would you have out of a new, two thousand and five BMW, besides a flat tire? She purchased this car, two months prior to the incident. My client was set up!"

Tyrone had a simper on his face, as he traded places with the doyen attorney.

"Ladies and gentlemen," he said, "there you have it! All the reasons why this animal should be released back into society. Set up? Why would anyone want to set him up? This man is a rapist! He's been around criminals for so long, he's become one! It doesn't matter that he'd graduated from college. Do you know how many murderers, robbers, and rapists that are in prison, who've graduated from college? Don't let that affect your opinions.

"How many other women has he done this to? How about some of the women that were found raped and murdered, with no lead on the suspect? Guess what? He's right here in this courtroom! And, if he used protection, why was his semen found inside the victim? He's a liar!

"Why would the scientist come in here and lie on him? Why would Ms. O'Neal lie on him? He drove this woman to take her own life! She wanted to be here to tell her side of the story, but she couldn't face this monster! The one that she constantly had nightmares about! Ladies and gentlemen, I want you all to go back into the jury room and do justice! Not for me. Do it for Ms. O'Neal. Do it for the victims that never got the chance to face their aggressors. Some of those women are at home, watching now. Don't let them down!"

***

"Did you really check the surveillance tapes?" Avery Stewart asked Greg Bush, who was seated across his desk from him, beside Kevin.

"Of course, I did," the attorney answered. "Did you forget that I used to be a detective?"

"No. I just didn't think that you would go that far as a defense attorney."

280

"That's what distinguishes me from the rest," Greg asserted. "I like to win."

"Yeah, you did an outstanding job out there!" Avery commented. "You nor Mr. Davis has ever lost a trial."

"Well," the attorney replied, "someone has to lose this one."

***

It took less than thirty minutes for the jury to reach a verdict. Everyone else were already back in their seats, as the jury members filed into the courtroom, entering the jury box.

"How'd I do?" Greg asked Chris.

"Better than I thought you would," Chris admitted. "Thanks!"

"You're quite welcome!" Greg replied, and they shook hands.

"Will the foreman please stand?" The judge asked, once the jurors were seated.

The foreman, a Caucasian man, stood, holding the verdict sheet.

"I understand that the jury has reached a verdict," said Edwards.

"We have, Your Honor."

"Please, read your verdict out to the court."

He recited: We, the jury, find the defendant, Christopher Reid, on count one, rape - guilty. We, the jury, find the same defendant, on count two, aggravated battery - guilty."

"Thank you, jury members!" The judge offered. "You may be released."

The jurors gathered their belongings and made their exits. At this time, Chris was beyond angry. His mind would not allow him to believe that this was nothing more than a bad dream. But it wasn't. He was actually going to prison for something he did not do. All he could think about was his mother, and how the news could be detrimental to her health.

"Right now," the judge resumed, "we're pressing for time, so we should postpone sentencing for another day."

"I agree," said Greg.

"Your Honor," Tyrone weighed in, "you have to keep in mind that this is not my assigned courtroom, and I have other cases to handle. It won't take but a few minutes for sentencing."

"You're right," the judge deferred. "Does the State have a recommendation as to what kind of punishment should be imposed?"

"The State recommends the max on both offenses."

She leered at him. "You do know that the max for rape is life, and the max for aggravated battery is twenty years, right?"

"I'm aware of that," Tyrone replied.

She looked to Greg Bush. "anything from the defense?"

"Your Honor," Greg started, "you and I both know that my client does not deserve the max. He has no record of any sort. It would be utterly inequitable to just throw the book at him on his first offense."

"Is that all?" Edwards asked.

"Yes, Your Honor."

"Will the defendant, please, rise to receive his punishment?" She said.

Chapter 33

Upon leaving the courthouse, Avery Stewart, and Kevin, decided to stop by the jail to see Chris, before Kevin headed back to his home in Savannah, Georgia.

"That's only twenty years, Chris," Kevin was telling his brother.

"I shouldn't have *that*!" Chris vented, shaking his head.

"It was your call to let Davis prosecute the case," Avery pointed out. "And I'm gonna give him a piece of my mind, first thing tomorrow morning! Plus, I'll try and get you held here, until your new trial motion."

Chris just nodded.

"How long do you think we can keep this from momma?" Asked Kevin.

"Somebody has to break it to her," Chris said, looking from his brother to his uncle.

***

"Daddy, you beat the best lawyer in the world!"

Tyrone smiled at his daughter, who'd rushed home from school, to catch Christopher Reid's trial on TV, and had been talking about it ever since she, Tyrone, and Lisa sat at the dinner table.

"What makes you think that he's the best lawyer in the world?" He asked her.

"Because the news people said that he's never lost a trial, until today," she answered.

"So, what does that make me?"

"The best prosecutor in the world!"

Tyrone furrowed his eyebrows. "I thought that I was already the best prosecutor in the world."

"So, that makes you the best prosecutor in the whole wide universe!"

Tyrone laughed, "Sounds good to me."

"I don't think that other prosecutor was a bad person," Ebony let on.

"You don't?"

"He didn't look like a bad person."

"You can't judge a book by its cover, sweetheart," he said, shifting his gaze to Lisa, whose mind seemed to be elsewhere, as she mechanically tended to her meal. "We all have a dark side within us."

As if she could sense that he was watching her, Lisa lifted her head. "Huh?"

"How was your day?" He asked.

"The same, as usual," she said. "Can you take Ebony to school, on your way to work, in the morning?"

"I don't mind," he said, "but why?"

"The bus drivers are on strike, again."

***

The following day, in his office, Tyrone was seated behind his desk, drawing up a court order, when someone knocked on the door. Ruminating the hardness of their knock, he pretty much had an idea of who was on the other side of the door.

"Come in!"

The door swung open, and just as he thought, Avery Stewart marched in, slamming the door behind him.

"I want my money, and I want it now!" Avery necessitated, now standing directly in front of the desk, looking down on Tyrone.

"Have you been drinking?" Tyrone asked, remaining reticent.

"Don't give me that!" Avery shot back. "How could you send my nephew to prison?"

Tyrone placed his ink pen on the desk, then leaned back in his leather chair. "I was doing my job," he said.

"That's not what we agreed to!"

"It doesn't matter what we agreed to. Your nephew is a rapist, and the jury saw it. They found him guilty, and the judge sentenced him. Everybody did their jobs. Case closed."

"I want my money back!" Avery repeated.

"No refunds."

"You'll pay for this!" The head District Attorney threatened. "I'll see to it!"

With that, Avery Stewart turned, and stormed out of the office, again, slamming the door behind him.

***

Later that day, at Ellen's place, she and Sara were sitting at the kitchen table, which is where Sara was waiting when Ellen returned home from work.

"I appreciate you for letting me stay," Sara was saying, "but I can't hide forever. I don't even know what I'm hiding from."

"You better go and get your car out of impound, before they auction it off for five dollars!" Ellen jested.

"Yeah. I need my baby," Sara said, standing. "Well, I'm out of your hair."

"Don't say it like that!" Said Ellen, who was now on her feet. "You make it seem as if I'm kicking you out. You know I would never do that."

"I know."

"Call me?"

"Of course," Sara replied, hugging her friend.

"You be careful out there!" Ellen told her. "If you need anything, you know where I am."

"Okay."

Ellen watched Sara, as she let herself out. Then, she grabbed the cordless phone off the counter, dialed a phone number, and listened until the recipient picked up.

"It's me," she said into the device.

***

In the gray Ford Mustang that she'd rented, Sara pulled into the lot of her apartments and parked. After shutting off the engine, she opened the glove compartment, and retrieved the .38 caliber pistol that she scored from the pawn shop, Saturday. Although she bought a box of bullets, and loaded the gun on the same day, she still checked it to make sure that it was still loaded.

As she got out, and made for her apartment, Sara thought about Danny, and his 'sudden' death, which made her suspicious, being that the doctors confirmed that, although Danny was badly injured, none of it was life-threatening. Sara had already inferred that

Tyrone was responsible for the accident, because clearly, Danny, after taking on Christopher Reid's case, had become a threat to Tyrone's chance of getting the D.A.'s position. She just wished that she knew what happened to that tape.

Getting to her apartment door, with one hand inside of her pocketbook, clutching the gun, Sara looked around once more, before unlocking the door, and pushing it open. On instinct, as she crossed the threshold, she pulled the gun from her pocketbook. As soon as she began to close the door back, Bull, who was standing behind the door, struck her on the back of her head with the butt of his handgun, rendering her unconscious. As she toppled to the floor, the .38 caliber landed beside her.

"You got to teach me how to do that!" Rick said, emerging from the back. "And she was carrying!"

***

Entering the dim-lit warehouse, Tyrone came upon Bull and Rick. They were standing around Sara, who was bound to a chair, blindfolded and gagged. Rick held out a ski mask to him, but he waved it off, telling them to put theirs back on. Then, he told Bull to remove the blindfold and gag, in which he complied.

Tyrone was standing directly in front of Sara, when she was finally able to see. There was no mistaking the apprehension in her eyes.

"Hello stranger!" He said. "Why haven't you called me? She didn't respond.

"Oh! The silent treatment, huh?" Tyrone pressed. "You must be high? Are you still using heroin? Is that why you can't talk?"

"I'm not a drug addict!" She contended, through clenched teeth. "I've never used drugs a day in my life!"

"Sure, you have. Remember?" He pulled out a small tape recorder akin to the one Sara owned, and pressed play.

"All white people didn't grow up in the suburbs, with silver spoons in their mouths. And I'm not as innocent as I appear. I've done things."

"Like what?"

"I used to date a drug dealer, years back. I've done and wit-nessed horrible things I can't really speak on. He's the one who'd come up with the bright idea of sending me to law school. First, I had to wing myself away from heroin."

"I don't think I need to play it any further," Tyrone said, stop-ping the tape. "You have a board meeting in two weeks. I wonder if I should send this self-incriminating tape to Mr. Boyd."

"Why are you doing this to me!" Sara yelled out, as tears cas-caded down her face. "What have I done to you!"

"You tried to set me up," he told her, placing the recorder back into his pocket. "You should be lying at the bottom of the ocean, right now!"

"I'm sorry!" She blubbered. "I swear I am!"

"'Sorry' won't get it this time, Sara! You owe me!"

***

Seated inside the Ford Mustang, Sara could not bring herself to stop crying, as she absently fondled the .38 caliber in her lap. Peri-odically, she would look out at the Victorian house that she was parked in front of, wondering if she could even muster up enough courage to attempt such an act that's required of her. But, consider-ing the circumstances, she knew that it had to be done.

It took several minutes, but Sara managed to get a hold of her-self. After double-checking herself in the rear-view mirror, she tossed the gun into her pocketbook, got out, and walked the stone walkway up to the front door of the house, thankful that it was still nighttime, and hoping that no one drives past the house within the next five minutes.

Approaching the door, she didn't hesitate to press the doorbell, which seemed to chime a melody throughout the large house. Mo-ments later, Avery Stewart peered through the transom, before dis-arming the locks, and pulling the door open.

"For you to show up at my house like this," the District Attor-ney said, "Something has to be wrong."

"It is," she said, tears forming.

"What is it?"

"I have to do this."

Avery furrowed his eyebrows. "Do what, Sara?"

Her hand had already disappeared inside her pocketbook, taking hold of the gun, in which she slowly brandished, and aimed at his forehead.

"Sara!" Avery cried out.

That was all he could get out, before Sara pulled the trigger. As if everything was in slow-motion, she saw the hole open in the center of his forehead, as his body collapsed onto the tiled floor. With her eyes transfixed on Avery's cadaver, she was oblivious to the fact that she was taking steps back, until she stumbled off one step, landing on her back. That's when realization kicked in, and trepidation rushed at her unabated.

With the gun still clutched in her hand, Sara clambered to her feet, and scurried toward the car, not knowing that, from across the street, someone had seen the whole thing through the lens of a camcorder.

Chapter 34

The following day, in his office, Tyrone was sitting at his desk, talking on the office phone, when someone knocked on the door. He covered the mouthpiece of the receiver.

"Come in!"

Ellen Martinez entered, closing the door. She was carrying a small paper bag, in which she placed atop the desk. Telling the person on the phone that he'd call them back, Tyrone hung up the phone, grabbed the paper bag, and looked inside of it. There was a similar bag in his drawer. He handed it to Ellen. Without a word, she received the bag, turned on her heels, and made for the door.

"Hey!" Tyrone called out, stopping Ellen in her tracks. She turned to face him. "What about the other thing?" He asked.

"It's done," she said, then made her exit.

***

When Sara finally made it home, last night, she didn't bother with taking off any item of clothing, as she collapsed on top of her unmade bed, and cried herself to sleep.

Now, she was awakened by the sound of her apartment door being kicked in. Before she could sit up, a troupe of FBI Task Force agents, in full gear, and carrying assault rifles, stormed her bedroom, circling the bed, with their guns trained on her.

***

Later that night, at home, in his bedroom, Tyrone was sitting on the edge of his bed, watching the evening news. They were showing footage of Sara Jennings, being taken from her apartment, by the FBI Task Force, as a male's voice reported.

Reporter: "FBI agents claims that a video tape of the murder was taped to the front door of the Federal building, when they arrived for work, this morning. After viewing the video, they were able to identify Ms. Sara Jennings. This is the same Sara Jennings that was found in her car, overdosed on heroin, a couple of weeks ago, in the parking garage of the Linkton County Courthouse, where she practiced law as a public defender. Right now, we're still trying to obtain the video of the murder of fifty-one-year-old Avery

Stewart, who was the lead District Attorney of Linkton County Superior court."

Tyrone set his TV to video, grabbed the paper bag that Ellen had given him, off the bed, and extracted a small video tape from it. Getting off the bed, he placed the tape inside the camcorder atop the TV.

"By the time they get the tape, she'll be on death row," he said, pressing play, then flopping down on the bed.

The video showed Sara pulling up to Avery Stewart's house, in the Mustang, where she sat for a while, crying. Regaining her composure. She got out and, to Tyrone's surprise, walked dutifully up to the front door, ringing the doorbell.

Moments later, the door opened. Tyrone couldn't see Avery, for Sara standing in the way. Suddenly, there was a flash of light. That's when he saw the body of Avery Stewart, fall to the floor, and Sara fall backwards onto the stone walkway. Scrambling to her feet, she hurried to the car, and sped off. The screen went blank.

"Good girl, gone bad!" He expressed, with a mischievous grin on his face.

***

"I thought the first incident was spooky," Judge Lathan conveyed across his desk, to Tyrone, who was seated in one of the visitor's chairs. "This one takes the cake! Does heroin have that kind of effect on people?"

"It makes you think that everyone's after you," Tyrone offered. "It has different effects on different people."

"She almost had me thinking that someone had set her up," Lathan said, shaking his head. "I was going to speak on her behalf, at the court hearing. Now, she goes out and murders the District attorney. Could've been me!"

"Could have," Tyrone replied, suppressing a smile.

"I'm stepping down!" The judge voiced. "There's too much going on around here! I mean, who's next?"

***

In a secluded cell of the Linkton County Jail, Sara was sitting atop her bed, curled up, with her arms around her legs, and her chin rested on her knees. She rocked back and forth, staring at the wall in front of her. All she could think about was what she'd done, as her mind incessantly tortured her with the image of Avery Stewart's body falling to the floor, and the blood that exuded from the gunshot wound in his forehead. When she'd committed the act, she knew that her life was over. It was confirmed when the FBI agents that stormed her apartment, advised her of her rights, and slapped the manacle on her wrists.

At that time, someone wrapped on the steel door. Sara looked up to see an older white male's face through the small bars that acted as a window.

"Ms. Jennings," he spoke. "I'm Dr. Wilcox, the psychiatrist, care to talk?"

"Do you think I'm crazy?" Sara asked, not leaving the bed.

"Of course, not."

"I was set up."

"I know," he said, softly, as if speaking to a small child.

"Liar!" Sara yelled out, lunging from the bed, and approaching the door. "You do think I'm crazy!"

"I don't think—"

"Save it!" She cut him off. "I've heard enough lies. What I need now is a cigarette. Can I have a cigarette?"

"I can't give you a cigarette," he told her, writing something down on his clipboard.

"Please, doctor!" She begged. "My nerves are shot to hell! I'm having a nervous breakdown!"

"I can only prescribe you medication. That's it."

"Take that medication and shove it!" She bellowed, then returned to the bed, reclaiming her same position.

Seconds after the doctor left, Sara got off the bed, snatching the sheet off of it. Standing on top of the bed, she began tying one end of the sheet around a water pipe.

***

"I don't know if she can receive visits at this time," the female officer at the front desk told Ellen, who was trying to see Sara.

"I'm her attorney," Ellen lied. "I just need to ask her a few questions."

The officer looked as if she was considering this, then said, "I'll let you up for fifteen minutes, considering you're her lawyer, but someone will have to escort you."

"That's fine."

"If you'll have a seat, someone will be with you shortly."

"Thanks!"

Ellen Martinez took a seat in the waiting area. She still couldn't believe how everything had played out. She betrayed her friend, but it was something that she had to do. Tyrone had left her with no favorable choices.

***

"What would you recommend?" Dr. Bry, a white female, who was now walking with Dr. Wilcox, asked.

"Therazine," he answered. "Right now, for her to be placed in the psychiatric ward, for observation. At least, for forty-eight hours."

"Did she say anything about harming herself?" She asked.

"No. I just have a bad vibe about her."

They made it to Sara's cell, and Dr. Bry peered in to see Sara stationarily hanging from a sheet that was tied around her neck, and the other end around the water pipe overhead.

"Well, you had the right vibe," Bry said, stepping aside for Wilcox to see.

"Damn!" Wilcox exclaimed, hating the fact that he didn't act immediately.

Chapter 35

It was Monday, and the Linkton County Schools bus drivers were still on strike, complaining of being underpaid, which, once again, had Tyrone chauffeuring his daughter to school.

"Thank you, very much!" Ebony replied, smiling as Tyrone held his hand out. "That's eight fifty."

"You're charging me?" She asked, smiling.

"Of course. Gas is not free."

"I should be charging you for how slow you were driving!" Tyrone laughed.

"It's probably lunchtime, already," she added.

"That's what you should be," Tyrone told his daughter, "a comedian!"

"I'm not that funny," she admitted. "Besides, they don't make as much money as a prosecutor."

"You just insist on being a prosecutor, huh?" He said, regarding his daughter, who had that no-nonsense look on her face that she'd inherited from him.

"It's all I dream about," she told him. "You told me that I should always follow my dreams."

Tyrone nodded. "I did. You know what? If that's what you want, I'm behind you, one hundred percent.

"Really!" She beamed smiling.

"Of course," he said, grabbing her book bag off the backseat, and placing it in her lap. "Now, get in there, and make it happen!"

"Okay." Unbuckling her safety-belt, Ebony kissed him on the jaw. "Love you, daddy!"

"Love you too, sweetheart!"

With a smile on his face, he watched as his little girl cavorted toward the school's entrance.

***

In the courtroom, Tyrone and Michelle Johnson were seated at the State's table. Being that this was the motion for new trial hearing for Carlos West, Tonya and Bobby were present, sitting on the third row, amongst other people. At that moment, attorney Kyle Johnson entered, nodding to Bobby, who nodded back. He stopped by the State's table.

"Mr. Tyrone Davis!" Kyle extended his hand.

"Mr. Kyle Johnson!" Tyrone shook his hand.

"How's it going?"

"I can't complain," Tyrone answered.

"And you shouldn't," Kyle said, grinning. "I saw how you beat Greg Bush last week. That was phenomenal!"

"Who'd you bet on?" Tyrone wanted to know.

"To be honest, I had my money on him."

Now, Tyrone was grinning. "Too bad!"

"I know," Kyle replied, shaking his head. "So, what happened this morning?"

"What'd you mean?"

"Why was the hearing pushed from nine to two?"

"The judge had to leave for a while," Tyrone told him.

"Oh! Well, let me get over here and set up." Tyrone nodded.

Getting to the defense table, Kyle sat his briefcase on top of it and began pulling out documents. Finished, he placed the briefcase on the floor, took a seat, and looked back at Bobby.

"Have you been here all day?" He asked.

"We left around ten-thirty," Bobby told him. "Just got back, like, fifteen minutes ago."

Kyle nodded, turning back around in his seat.

"You know him?" Tonya asked Bobby.

He smiled. "Ever since I was eight years old."

"Remain seated!" Judge Lathan bided, upon entering the courtroom, taking his seat. "Sorry for the delay, everyone! Without further ado, we'll go ahead and begin. State, where were we?"

"Carlos West," Tyrone answered.

"Is that the new trial hearing?" He asked, then looked over to the defense table. "Sure, it is! I didn't notice Mr. Johnson sitting over there. How are you?

"I'm hanging in there," Kyle replied, nodding.

"That's good!" Lathan offered. "It's good to see you, again!"

"Likewise."

The judge looked to his officer. "Bailiff, bring in Mr. West!"

"Are you okay?" Bobby asked Tonya, once the bailiff left the room.

"Yeah," she answered, knowing that it was a lie, before it escaped her tongue.

Bobby put an arm over her shoulder. Seconds later, Carlos, in an orange jumpstart, and cuffed to the front, was escorted in. He spotted Tonya, who was staring at him. Then, as the bailiff was removing the cuffs, he shifted his gaze over to Tyrone, who wasn't paying him any attention.

"Are you ready?" Kyle asked, when Carlos had taken a seat beside him.

Carlos nodded.

"In Carlos West versus the State," Judge Lathan began, "petitioner has filed a motion for new trial, by, and through his attorney, Mr. Kyle Johnson. Mr. Johnson, why should this motion be granted?"

"Your Honor," Kyle said, getting to his feet, "this motion should be granted, because, for one, this is my client's first offense. Two, my client was convicted of burglary, when, in fact, the victim testified to letting him into her apartment on the day of the incident. And third, the prosecutor claimed that my client could not be charged with domestic violence, because a weapon was involved. That law has yet to be passed. Therefore, petitioner prays that the court considers these grounds, and grants him relief." Kyle genuflected, then took his seat.

Lathan looked to Tyrone. "State? Your reason why the motion should not be granted?"

Tyrone stood, clearing his throat. "Your Honor, it doesn't matter that this is Mr. West's first offense. The burglary doesn't matter. Aggravated assault. Domestic violence. Same thing! As if Tonya Smith wasn't enough, Mr. West goes to prison and catches another assault, during a riot that he incited. Despite the inmate that he stabbed multiple times with a sharp metal object, another inmate was found dead from a stab wound to the neck. Therefore, the state prays that the court will consider these acts of terror, and deny said motion. "Tyrone re-took his seat.

"Does the defendant wish to speak?"

Kyle looked to Carlos, who shook his head. "No, Your Honor," the attorney answered.

Lathan nodded. "Okay. After hearing from both sides, I have to make my ruling, which is my very own decision. I decide to rule in favor of the State and deny motion for a new trial. Prisoner may be taken into custody."

Carlos grabbed Kyle's metal ink pen off the table, as he stood, looking back at Tonya, who was watching him. Once the bailiff approached with the handcuffs, Carlos jammed the pen in the side of his neck. As the officer stumbled back, gagging, Carlos relieved him of his .9mm Beretta, just before he went down.

Before Carlos could turn around, people, including Lathan, Kyle, Michelle, Tonya, and Bobby, got to the floor, with some screaming. Tyrone tried to make a break for the exit, but Carlos fired three shots, hitting him in the torso.

When Tyrone hit the floor, Carlos quick stepped over to him, gun aimed. Slowly, Tyrone rolled over onto his back, with blood oozing from his mouth, as he clutched his side, where one of the bullets entered.

"Well, I'd be damned!" Tyrone said, in a gruff voice, looking up at Carlos. "I guess thirty years ain't enough. You want the gas chamber. You're better off shooting yourself in the head. It's less painful."

"Carlos! Don't! Tonya had gotten to her feet. "You'll only make it worse."

"I know what happened," he told her. "It's not your fault. He scared you into it. Didn't he?"

She didn't speak.

"Answer me, Tonya!" Carlos yelled, causing her to wince. "Didn't he?"

Before she could answer, a white, male court official burst through the entrance, with his gun drawn. He stopped about five feet away from Tyrone's head.

"Now, that's what I'm talking about!" Tyrone voiced, looking over his head at the officer. "Shoot him!"

"Sir, put the gun down!" The officer tried to reason.

"Damn that!" Tyrone spat. "Shoot him!"

"I'm gonna ask you one more time –"

"Officer!" Tyrone cut him off. "Do you not see that this is an armed criminal? Take him down!"

"Carlos!" Tonya called out. "Please, don't make it worse."

"It's too late," he told her.

Carlos shot Tyrone in the head, killing him, then raised the gun on the officer. The officer fired, first, squeezing off four shots, knocking Carlos backwards, to the floor, where he breathed his last breath.

Playa Ray

Chapter 36

School was letting out for the day, and Ebony exited the building amongst a mass of other children, all in search of the vehicle of whoever was designated to pick them up. Whenever the bus drivers were on strike, it was total chaos with the throng of vehicles sitting in front of the school, as if they'd come to a gridlock. It made it hard for Ebony to spot the gray Mercedes belonging to her mother, who'd always picked her up from school, when this occurred. But, her mother would always be one of the first parents to arrive, parking right in front of the building. Today, she was nowhere to be found.

***

"Why do I always have to break the news?" Detective Patrick, a black male, asked his partner, as he drove the gray Ford Crown Victoria through a residential street.

"Because," Detective Harris replied, "you know the right way to go about it. Me? I would do it over the phone. I'd call and be like, look, we just found so-and-so dead. Sorry! Then, I'm done."

Patrick shook his head. "You don't have any compassion."

"With a job like this, it's best not to."

"At least, she's home," Patrick said, pulling into the driveway of Tyrone Davis's house, parking behind the gray Mercedes.

Getting out, they both approached the front door, which was ajar. Noticing the damaged locks, they immediately drew their guns, and looked at each other. Once they both nodded that they were ready, Patrick nudged the door open, and they entered, with their guns up.

Harris cut through the kitchen, and Patrick made for the living room, where he stopped dead in his tracks. Lisa Davis, the wife of Tyrone Davis, was lying on the sofa, with a gunshot wound to the side of her temple.

"Damn!" he let out.

***

The schoolyard, and parking lot, was empty, except for a few students, and teachers, who were leaving the building. Plus, Ebony, who was still standing in the same spot, staring at the entrance of the parking lot, where her mother's car should be entering at any minute, now.

"Ebony?"

"Ebony turned around to see the assistant principal, Ms. Palmer, approaching

"Who was supposed to pick you up?" She asked.

"My momma," Ebony answered.

"Has she ever been late?"

"No."

"Come on inside," the woman told her. "We'll call and see why she's late."

***

After calling in, and reporting Lisa's homicide, the two detectives remained outside, where they were now leaning against the Ford.

"Should we start questioning neighbors?" Harris asked.

"Let the locals do it," answered Patrick. "As soon as the coroners get here, I'm going home."

"That sounds like a good idea."

At that time, they heard the house phone ring. Patrick knew that he shouldn't touch anything, until the crime scene techs got there, but as the phone was into its second ring, he was nearing the entrance, with his partner at his heels. Entering the living room, he grabbed the cordless off the coffee table.

"Hello?" He answered. Then, looking over at Lisa's body he said, "um, she's unable to come to the phone, right now. May I ask who's calling? Okay. She is? Keep her right there! I'm on my way."

***

Detective Patrick entered the school's main office, where the only two present, were Ebony Davis, who was seated in the waiting area, with her bookbag in a chair beside her, and the assistant principal, Ms. Palmer, who was seated behind the long, wooden counter. She stood, when he approached.

Ms. Palmer had informed Ebony that a man answered their phone and said that he was on the way. She figured that it was her father, who may have come home early, which was highly atypical. Now, when this swarthy man in a suit and tie entered the office, she knew that her father was not coming. She just hoped that this guy wasn't the man that her mother had left her father for, like she couldn't see what happened between them. She was not going anywhere with him, unless her mother was present.

She watched Ms. Palmer and the man talk. Whatever the man told her made Ms. Palmer's eyes bulge, her mouth to fly open, and her hand to clutch her chest, as if she was about to recite the Pledge of Allegiance. Now, they were headed in her direction.

"Ebony, this is Detective Patrick," Ms. Palmer spoke, her voice cracking. "He's going to take you home, okay?"

"Okay."

Ebony grabbed her bookbag, threw it over her back, and marched out of the office, as if she had other means of getting home. Exiting the building, she made it halfway up the walkway, then stopped, and turned to face the detective who was following behind her.

"What's wrong?" He asked, stopping as well. "Did you leave something?"

"Where's my momma?" She demanded.

"Are you hungry?"

"Nope."

"Well, can you, at least, get in the car?" He asked. "I'll explain everything, then."

"No!" Ebony stood her ground. "You'll explain everything, now. Then, I'll get in the car. Deal, or no deal?"

To Be Continued …
Crime Boss 2:
Coming Soon

About The Author

Playa Ray was born Norris Ray McCoy, November 23, 1979. He was raised in Atlanta, Georgia. As promised, the genius behind the *Kingz of the Game* series is back with another phenomenal story. You can also check out his hot single "Magician" on YouTube or Spotify under the name Playa Ray The Author, and powered by Tripp James and Distro Kid.
Facebook: Author Playa Ray
IG: Playa Ray The Author

Lock Down Publications and Ca$h Presents assisted
publishing packages.

BASIC PACKAGE $499
Editing
Cover Design
Formatting

UPGRADED PACKAGE $800
Typing
Editing
Cover Design
Formatting

ADVANCE PACKAGE $1,200
Typing
Editing
Cover Design
Formatting
Copyright registration
Proofreading
Upload book to Amazon

LDP SUPREME PACKAGE $1,500
Typing
Editing
Cover Design
Formatting
Copyright registration
Proofreading
Set up Amazon account
Upload book to Amazon
Advertise on LDP Amazon and Facebook page

***Other services available upon request. Additional charges may apply
Lock Down Publications
P.O. Box 944
Stockbridge, GA 30281-9998
Phone # 470 303-9761

Submission Guideline

Submit the first three chapters of your completed manuscript to ldpsubmissions@gmail.com, subject line: Your book's title. The manuscript must be in a .doc file and sent as an attachment. Document should be in Times New Roman, double spaced and in size 12 font. Also, provide your synopsis and full contact information. If sending multiple submissions, they must each be in a separate email.

Have a story but no way to send it electronically? You can still submit to LDP/Ca$h Presents. Send in the first three chapters, written or typed, of your completed manuscript to:

LDP: Submissions Dept
Po Box 944
Stockbridge, Ga 30281

DO NOT send original manuscript. Must be a duplicate.

Provide your synopsis and a cover letter containing your full contact information.

Thanks for considering LDP and Ca$h Presents.

<u>NEW RELEASES</u>

THE COCAINE PRINCESS 5 by KING RIO

FOR THE LOVE OF BLOOD 2 by JAMEL MITCHELL

RICH $AVAGE 3 by MARTELL "TROUBLESOME"
BOLDEN

CRIME BO$$ by PLAYA RAY

Crime Bo$$

Coming Soon from Lock Down Publications/Ca$h Presents

BLOOD OF A BOSS **VI**

SHADOWS OF THE GAME II

TRAP BASTARD II

By **Askari**

LOYAL TO THE GAME **IV**

By **T.J. & Jelissa**

TRUE SAVAGE **VIII**

MIDNIGHT CARTEL IV

DOPE BOY MAGIC IV

CITY OF KINGZ III

NIGHTMARE ON SILENT AVE II

THE PLUG OF LIL MEXICO II

CLASSIC CITY II

By **Chris Green**

BLAST FOR ME **III**

A SAVAGE DOPEBOY III

CUTTHROAT MAFIA III

DUFFLE BAG CARTEL VII

HEARTLESS GOON VI

By **Ghost**

A HUSTLER'S DECEIT III

KILL ZONE II

BAE BELONGS TO ME III

TIL DEATH II

By **Aryanna**

KING OF THE TRAP III

By **T.J. Edwards**

GORILLAZ IN THE BAY V

3X KRAZY III

STRAIGHT BEAST MODE III

De'Kari

KINGPIN KILLAZ IV

STREET KINGS III

PAID IN BLOOD III

CARTEL KILLAZ IV

DOPE GODS III

Hood Rich

SINS OF A HUSTLA II

ASAD

YAYO V

Bred In The Game 2

S. Allen

THE STREETS WILL TALK II

By Yolanda Moore

SON OF A DOPE FIEND III

HEAVEN GOT A GHETTO II

SKI MASK MONEY II

By Renta

LOYALTY AIN'T PROMISED III

By Keith Williams

I'M NOTHING WITHOUT HIS LOVE II

SINS OF A THUG II

TO THE THUG I LOVED BEFORE II

IN A HUSTLER I TRUST II

By Monet Dragun

QUIET MONEY IV

EXTENDED CLIP III

THUG LIFE IV

By **Trai'Quan**

Crime Bo$$

THE STREETS MADE ME IV

By **Larry D. Wright**

IF YOU CROSS ME ONCE II

ANGEL V

By **Anthony Fields**

THE STREETS WILL NEVER CLOSE IV

By **K'ajji**

HARD AND RUTHLESS III

KILLA KOUNTY IV

By **Khufu**

MONEY GAME III

By **Smoove Dolla**

JACK BOYS VS DOPE BOYS IV

A GANGSTA'S QUR'AN V

COKE GIRLZ II

COKE BOYS II

LIFE OF A SAVAGE V

CHI'RAQ GANGSTAS V

By **Romell Tukes**

MURDA WAS THE CASE III

Elijah R. Freeman

THE STREETS NEVER LET GO III

By **Robert Baptiste**

AN UNFORESEEN LOVE IV

BABY, I'M WINTERTIME COLD II

By **Meesha**

MONEY MAFIA II

By **Jibril Williams**

QUEEN OF THE ZOO III

Playa Ray

By **Black Migo**
VICIOUS LOYALTY III

By **Kingpen**
A GANGSTA'S PAIN III

By **J-Blunt**
CONFESSIONS OF A JACKBOY III

By **Nicholas Lock**
GRIMEY WAYS III

By **Ray Vinci**
KING KILLA II

By **Vincent "Vitto" Holloway**
BETRAYAL OF A THUG III

By **Fre$h**
THE MURDER QUEENS III

By **Michael Gallon**
THE BIRTH OF A GANGSTER III

By **Delmont Player**
TREAL LOVE II

By **Le'Monica Jackson**
FOR THE LOVE OF BLOOD III

By **Jamel Mitchell**
RAN OFF ON DA PLUG II

By **Paper Boi Rari**
HOOD CONSIGLIERE III

By **Keese**
PRETTY GIRLS DO NASTY THINGS II

By **Nicole Goosby**
PROTÉGÉ OF A LEGEND II

By **Corey Robinson**
IT'S JUST ME AND YOU II

Crime Bo$$

By Ah'Million

BORN IN THE GRAVE II

By Self Made Tay

FOREVER GANGSTA III

By Adrian Dulan

GORILLAZ IN THE TRENCHES II

By SayNoMore

THE COCAINE PRINCESS VI

By King Rio

CRIME BOSS II

Playa Ray

Available Now

RESTRAINING ORDER **I & II**

By **CA$H & Coffee**

LOVE KNOWS NO BOUNDARIES **I II & III**

By **Coffee**

RAISED AS A GOON I, II, III & IV

BRED BY THE SLUMS I, II, III

BLAST FOR ME I & II

ROTTEN TO THE CORE I II III

A BRONX TALE I, II, III

DUFFLE BAG CARTEL I II III IV V VI

HEARTLESS GOON I II III IV V

A SAVAGE DOPEBOY I II

DRUG LORDS I II III

Playa Ray

CUTTHROAT MAFIA I II

KING OF THE TRENCHES

By **Ghost**

LAY IT DOWN **I & II**

LAST OF A DYING BREED I II

BLOOD STAINS OF A SHOTTA I & II III

By **Jamaica**

LOYAL TO THE GAME I II III

LIFE OF SIN I, II III

By **TJ & Jelissa**

BLOODY COMMAS I & II

SKI MASK CARTEL I II & III

KING OF NEW YORK I II,III IV V

RISE TO POWER I II III

COKE KINGS I II III IV V

BORN HEARTLESS I II III IV

KING OF THE TRAP I II

By **T.J. Edwards**

IF LOVING HIM IS WRONG…I & II

LOVE ME EVEN WHEN IT HURTS I II III

By **Jelissa**

WHEN THE STREETS CLAP BACK I & II III

THE HEART OF A SAVAGE I II III IV

MONEY MAFIA

LOYAL TO THE SOIL I II III

By **Jibril Williams**

A DISTINGUISHED THUG STOLE MY HEART I II & III

LOVE SHOULDN'T HURT I II III IV

RENEGADE BOYS I II III IV

PAID IN KARMA I II III

312

Crime Bo$$

SAVAGE STORMS I II III

AN UNFORESEEN LOVE I II III

BABY, I'M WINTERTIME COLD

By **Meesha**

A GANGSTER'S CODE I &, II III

A GANGSTER'S SYN I II III

THE SAVAGE LIFE I II III

CHAINED TO THE STREETS I II III

BLOOD ON THE MONEY I II III

A GANGSTA'S PAIN I II

By J-Blunt

PUSH IT TO THE LIMIT

By **Bre' Hayes**

BLOOD OF A BOSS **I, II, III, IV, V**

SHADOWS OF THE GAME

TRAP BASTARD

By **Askari**

THE STREETS BLEED MURDER **I, II & III**

THE HEART OF A GANGSTA I II& III

By **Jerry Jackson**

CUM FOR ME I II III IV V VI VII VIII

An **LDP Erotica Collaboration**

BRIDE OF A HUSTLA **I II & II**

THE FETTI GIRLS **I, II& III**

CORRUPTED BY A GANGSTA I, II III, IV

BLINDED BY HIS LOVE

THE PRICE YOU PAY FOR LOVE I, II ,III

DOPE GIRL MAGIC I II III

By **Destiny Skai**

WHEN A GOOD GIRL GOES BAD

Playa Ray

By **Adrienne**
THE COST OF LOYALTY I II III
By Kweli
A GANGSTER'S REVENGE **I II III & IV**
THE BOSS MAN'S DAUGHTERS I II III IV V
A SAVAGE LOVE **I & II**
BAE BELONGS TO ME I II
A HUSTLER'S DECEIT I, II, III
WHAT BAD BITCHES DO I, II, III
SOUL OF A MONSTER I II III
KILL ZONE
A DOPE BOY'S QUEEN I II III
TIL DEATH
By **Aryanna**
A KINGPIN'S AMBITON
A KINGPIN'S AMBITION **II**
I MURDER FOR THE DOUGH
By **Ambitious**
TRUE SAVAGE I II III IV V VI VII
DOPE BOY MAGIC I, II, III
MIDNIGHT CARTEL I II III
CITY OF KINGZ I II
NIGHTMARE ON SILENT AVE
THE PLUG OF LIL MEXICO II
CLASSIC CITY
By **Chris Green**
A DOPEBOY'S PRAYER
By **Eddie "Wolf" Lee**
THE KING CARTEL **I, II & III**
By **Frank Gresham**

Crime Bo$$

THESE NIGGAS AIN'T LOYAL **I, II & III**

By **Nikki Tee**

GANGSTA SHYT **I II &III**

By **CATO**

THE ULTIMATE BETRAYAL

By **Phoenix**

BOSS'N UP **I , II & III**

By **Royal Nicole**

I LOVE YOU TO DEATH

By **Destiny J**

I RIDE FOR MY HITTA

I STILL RIDE FOR MY HITTA

By **Misty Holt**

LOVE & CHASIN' PAPER

By **Qay Crockett**

TO DIE IN VAIN

SINS OF A HUSTLA

By **ASAD**

BROOKLYN HUSTLAZ

By **Boogsy Morina**

BROOKLYN ON LOCK I & II

By **Sonovia**

GANGSTA CITY

By **Teddy Duke**

A DRUG KING AND HIS DIAMOND I & II III

A DOPEMAN'S RICHES

HER MAN, MINE'S TOO I, II

CASH MONEY HO'S

THE WIFEY I USED TO BE I II

PRETTY GIRLS DO NASTY THINGS

Playa Ray

Crime Bo$$

FEAR MY GANGSTA I, II, III IV, V

THESE STREETS DON'T LOVE NOBODY I, II

BURY ME A G I, II, III, IV, V

A GANGSTA'S EMPIRE I, II, III, IV

THE DOPEMAN'S BODYGAURD I II

THE REALEST KILLAZ I II III

THE LAST OF THE OGS I II III

Tranay Adams

THE STREETS ARE CALLING

Duquie Wilson

MARRIED TO A BOSS I II III

By Destiny Skai & Chris Green

KINGZ OF THE GAME I II III IV V VI

CRIME BO$$

Playa Ray

SLAUGHTER GANG I II III

RUTHLESS HEART I II III

By Willie Slaughter

FUK SHYT

By Blakk Diamond

DON'T F#CK WITH MY HEART I II

By Linnea

ADDICTED TO THE DRAMA I II III

IN THE ARM OF HIS BOSS II

By Jamila

YAYO I II III IV

A SHOOTER'S AMBITION I II

BRED IN THE GAME

By S. Allen

TRAP GOD I II III

Playa Ray

RICH $AVAGE I II III

MONEY IN THE GRAVE I II III

By Martell Troublesome Bolden

FOREVER GANGSTA I II

GLOCKS ON SATIN SHEETS I II

By Adrian Dulan

TOE TAGZ I II III IV

LEVELS TO THIS SHYT I II

IT'S JUST ME AND YOU

By Ah'Million

KINGPIN DREAMS I II III

RAN OFF ON DA PLUG

By Paper Boi Rari

CONFESSIONS OF A GANGSTA I II III IV

CONFESSIONS OF A JACKBOY I II

By Nicholas Lock

I'M NOTHING WITHOUT HIS LOVE

SINS OF A THUG

TO THE THUG I LOVED BEFORE

A GANGSTA SAVED XMAS

IN A HUSTLER I TRUST

By Monet Dragun

CAUGHT UP IN THE LIFE I II III

THE STREETS NEVER LET GO I II

By Robert Baptiste

NEW TO THE GAME I II III

MONEY, MURDER & MEMORIES I II III

By **Malik D. Rice**

LIFE OF A SAVAGE I II III IV

A GANGSTA'S QUR'AN I II III IV

Crime Bo$$

MURDA SEASON I II III

GANGLAND CARTEL I II III

CHI'RAQ GANGSTAS I II III IV

KILLERS ON ELM STREET I II III

JACK BOYZ N DA BRONX I II III

A DOPEBOY'S DREAM I II III

JACK BOYS VS DOPE BOYS I II III

COKE GIRLZ

COKE BOYS

By Romell Tukes

LOYALTY AIN'T PROMISED I II

By Keith Williams

QUIET MONEY I II III

THUG LIFE I II III

EXTENDED CLIP I II

A GANGSTA'S PARADISE

By **Trai'Quan**

THE STREETS MADE ME I II III

By **Larry D. Wright**

THE ULTIMATE SACRIFICE I, II, III, IV, V, VI

KHADIFI

IF YOU CROSS ME ONCE

ANGEL I II III IV

IN THE BLINK OF AN EYE

By **Anthony Fields**

THE LIFE OF A HOOD STAR

By Ca$h & Rashia Wilson

THE STREETS WILL NEVER CLOSE I II III

By K'ajji

CREAM I II III

Playa Ray

THE STREETS WILL TALK
By Yolanda Moore
NIGHTMARES OF A HUSTLA I II III
By King Dream
CONCRETE KILLA I II III
VICIOUS LOYALTY I II
By Kingpen
HARD AND RUTHLESS I II
MOB TOWN 251
THE BILLIONAIRE BENTLEYS I II III
By Von Diesel
GHOST MOB
Stilloan Robinson
MOB TIES I II III IV V VI
SOUL OF A HUSTLER, HEART OF A KILLER
GORILLAZ IN THE TRENCHES
By SayNoMore
BODYMORE MURDERLAND I II III
THE BIRTH OF A GANGSTER I II
By Delmont Player
FOR THE LOVE OF A BOSS
By C. D. Blue
MOBBED UP I II III IV
THE BRICK MAN I II III IV
THE COCAINE PRINCESS I II III IV V
By King Rio
KILLA KOUNTY I II III IV
By Khufu
MONEY GAME I II
By Smoove Dolla

320

Crime Bo$$

A GANGSTA'S KARMA I II
By FLAME
KING OF THE TRENCHES I II III
by **GHOST & TRANAY ADAMS**
QUEEN OF THE ZOO I II
By **Black Migo**
GRIMEY WAYS I II
By Ray Vinci
XMAS WITH AN ATL SHOOTER
By Ca$h & Destiny Skai
KING KILLA
By Vincent "Vitto" Holloway
BETRAYAL OF A THUG I II
By Fre$h
THE MURDER QUEENS I II
By Michael Gallon
TREAL LOVE
By Le'Monica Jackson
FOR THE LOVE OF BLOOD I II
By Jamel Mitchell
HOOD CONSIGLIERE I II
By Keese
PROTÉGÉ OF A LEGEND
By Corey Robinson
BORN IN THE GRAVE
By Self Made Tay
MOAN IN MY MOUTH
By XTASY
TORN BETWEEN A GANGSTER AND A GENTLEMAN
By J-BLUNT & Miss Kim

BOOKS BY LDP'S CEO, CA$H

TRUST IN NO MAN

TRUST IN NO MAN 2

TRUST IN NO MAN 3

BONDED BY BLOOD

SHORTY GOT A THUG

THUGS CRY

THUGS CRY 2

THUGS CRY 3

TRUST NO BITCH

TRUST NO BITCH 2

TRUST NO BITCH 3

TIL MY CASKET DROPS

RESTRAINING ORDER

RESTRAINING ORDER 2

IN LOVE WITH A CONVICT

LIFE OF A HOOD STAR

XMAS WITH AN ATL SHOOTER